The Royal Life Guard

Alexandre Dumas

Black & Gold House of Books

First Black & Gold House of Books printing, April 2022

Black & Gold House of Books and the B&G logo are copyrighted © by Todd Kirby

All rights reserved. This publication may not be reproduced, stored in a retrieval system or transmitted in any form or by any means, electronic, mechanical, photocopying, recording or otherwise, without the prior permission of the publishers.

Cover image: "Captain John Walter Roberts" by Unknown (1792-1845)

Contents

About the Author..iii
Other Works...v
A New Lease on Life..1
The Federation of France..6
Where the Bastille Stood..12
The Lodge of the Invisibles..19
The Conspirator's Account...25
Women and Flowers...31
The King's Messenger..42
The Husband's Promise..48
Off and Away..52
On the Highway..60
The Queen's Hairdresser...66
Mischance...70
Stop, King!..75
The Capture..83
Poor Catherine..94
The Man of the People...100
The Feud...108
On the Back Track..117
The Dolorous Way..123
Mirabeau's Successor...133
Another Dupe...139
The Center of Catastrophes..147
The Bitter Cup..152
At Last They Are Happy!...158
Correcting the Petition...164
Cagliostro's Counsel..172
The Squeezed Lemon...177
The Field of Blood...182
In the Hospital..187
The Mother's Blessing...193
Fortier Executes His Threat...198

About the Author

Alexandre Dumas was born in France on July 24, 1802. His birth name was "Dumas Davy de la Pailleterie". His parents were Thomas-Alexandre Dumas, the mixed-race son of a Haitian slave woman and a French Marquis, and Marie-Louise Élisabeth Labouret, the daughter of a French innkeeper.

When he became an adult, Dumas began writing newspaper articles and plays. His first play, *Henry III and His Courts*, was produced in 1829. It was met with almost universal acclaim, and the following year, his second play, *Christine*, was equally popular. The success of these first two plays provided enough income for Dumas to begin writing full-time.

The tumultuous political environment of revolutionary France provided a historic background for much of Dumas' writing. After several years of writing successful plays, he began writing novels. Like many of his contemporaries, Dumas began his foray into novels by writing serials in the newspaper. His first story was *La Comtesse de Salisbury; Édouard III* in the summer of 1836. In 1838, Dumas wrote another serial called *Le Capitaine Paul*, which was actually a rewrite of one of his plays.

His novels became so popular, that they were translated into several languages, and Dumas earned a great deal of money for them. However, he was still usually poor, because he spent the money faster than he could make it. He had, by some accounts, over 40 mistresses, and by 1846 had built a huge chateau outside of Paris with a writing studio. Dumas was known to entertain extravagantly, and to be taken advantage of mercilessly. By 1848 he had to sell the property to cover his ever-increasing debts.

Dumas was not universally admired. After his book *The Fencing Master*, which included stories about the Decembrist revolt in Russia, both Dumas and his novel were banned from that country by Czar Nicholas I. And after Napoléon Bonaparte was elected to power in France, Dumas was so despised by the president that he had to flee to Brussels, Belgium. Of course, that flight may have also had to do with creditors.

In March 1861, Dumas traveled to Italy, where he befriended Giuseppe Garibaldi. Dumas would share several commonalities with Garibaldi, including liberal republican principles and membership within Freemasonry. Garibaldi would become the subject of Dumas' book *Joseph Balsamo*.

As stated earlier, Dumas was of mixed-race heritage, and was sometimes discriminated against because of it. At one time he responded to a particular critic in what is now a famous quote: "My father was a mulatto, my grandfather was a Negro, and my great-grandfather a monkey. You see, Sir, my family starts where yours ends."

Dumas died of natural causes on December 5, 1870 (he was 68 years old). He was buried in the same area where he was born—in Aisne, France. In 2002, for the bicentenary of Dumas' birth, French President Jacques Chirac held a ceremony to honor the author. He had Dumas' ashes re-interred at the mausoleum of the Panthéon of Paris.

Other Works

Louis XV Series
The Conspirators (1843)
The Regent's Daughter (1845)

The D'Artagnan Romances
The Three Musketeers (1844)
Twenty Years After (1845)
The Vicomte de Bragelonne (1847)
Louise de la Valliere (1847)
The Man in the Iron Mask (1847)

The Marie Antoinette Romances
Joseph Balsamo (or Balsamo the Magician) (1846)
Andrea de Taverney (or The Mesmerist's Victim) (1846)
The Queen's Necklace (1849)
Taking the Bastille (1846)
The Hero of the People (1846)
The Royal Life Guard (or The Flight of the Royal Family) (1846)
The Countess de Charny (1853)
*** *Related to the Marie Antoinette Romances***
The Knight of Maison-Rouge (1845)

The Sainte-Hermine Trilogy
The Companions of Jehu (1857)
The Whites and the Blues (1867)
The Knight of Sainte-Hermine (or The Last Cavalier) (1869)

The Valois Romances
La Reine Margot (or Marguerite de Valois) (1845)
La Dame de Monsoreau (or Chico the Jester) (1846)
The Forty-Five Guardsmen (1847)
*** *Related to the Valois Romances***
Ascanio, Vol. I (1843)
Ascanio, Vol. 2 (1843)
The Two Dianas (1846)
The Page of the Duke of Savoy (1854)
The Horoscope: a romance of the reign of Francois II (1858)

Standalone Novels
Captain Paul (1838)
Captain Pamphile (1839)
The Fencing Master (1840)
Castle Eppstein (1843)
Georges (1843)
The Women's War / The War of Women (1844)
The Nutcracker (1844)
The Corsican Brothers (1844)
The Count of Monte Cristo (1845)
Horror At Fontenay (1849)
The Black Tulip (1850)
Olympe de Clèves (1852)
The Mohicans of Paris (1854)
The Wolf-Leader (1857)
Robin Hood: The Outlaw (1863)

CHAPTER I

A New Lease on Life

France had been changed to a limited monarchy from an absolute one, and King Louis XVI had solemnly sworn to defend the new Constitution. But it had been remarked by shrewd observers, that he had not attended the Te Deum[1] at the Paris Cathedral with the members of the National Assembly. That is, he would tell a lie but not commit perjury. The people were therefore on their guard against him—while they felt that his Queen, Marie Antoinette, the daughter of Austria, was ever their foe.

But the murders by the rabble had frightened all property holders. And when the court brought Mirabeau over to its cause by paying his debts and a monthly salary, the majority of the better classes thought the Royal Family would yet regain their own. In point of fact, Mirabeau had obtained from the House of Representatives that the King should have the right to rule the army and direct it and propose war. He would have obtained more in the reaction after the Taking of the Bastille, except that an unknown hand had distributed full particulars of his purchase by the royalists in a pamphlet, given away by thousands in the streets.

Hence he retired from the senate, broken by his victory, though carrying himself proudly. In face of danger, the strong athlete thought of the antagonist, not of his powers. On going home, he flung himself on the floor, rolling on flowers. He had two passionate loves: for the fair sex, because he was an ugly though robust man, and for flowers.

This time he felt so exhausted that he resisted his attendant feebly, who wanted to send for a doctor, when "Dr. Gilbert" was announced. A man still young, though with a grave expression like one tried in the furnace of personal and political heats, entered the room. He was clothed in the wholly black suit which he introduced from America, where it was popular among Republicans. He was a friend of Washington and Lafayette, who like him, had returned to make a sister Republic of France to that of the Thirteen United States.

---

1   A Latin Christian hymn

Dr. Gilbert was a friend of Mirabeau, for he wished to preserve the King at the head of the State even though he knew it was but the gilded figurehead. Without which, if knocked off in the tempest, the Ship rights itself and lives through all without feeling the loss.

Nevertheless, Gilbert, who was one of the Invisibles, had been warned by its Chief that the Queen cajoled him and that royalty was doomed. The Invisibles were that Secret Society which worked for years to bring about the downfall of monarchy in Europe. The Grand Copt of which was Cagliostro, alias Balsamo the Mesmerist, alias Baron Zannone—newly renamed since he had escaped from the Papal dungeons under cover of his being supposedly dead and buried there.

"I have come to congratulate you, my dear count," said the doctor to the orator. "You promised us a victory, and you have borne away a triumph."

"A Pyrrhic one—another such and we are lost. I am very ill of it. Oh doctor, tell me of something—not to keep me alive, but to give me force while I do live."

"How can I advise for a constitution like yours," said the physician, after feeling the nobleman's pulse. "You do not heed my advice. I told you not to have flowers in the room as they spoil the air, and you are smothered in them. As for the ladies, I bade you beware, and you answer that you would rather die than be rid of their society."

"Never mind that. I suffer too much to think of aught but myself. I sometimes think that as I am slandered, so that the Queen hesitated to trust me, so have I been physically done to death. Do you believe in the famous poisons which slay without anyone knowing they are used until too late?"

"Yes; I believe." Gilbert frowned as he remembered that his secret brotherhood was allowed to use the Aqua Tofana[2] where an enemy could not be otherwise reached. "But in your case, it is the sword wearing out its sheath. The electric spark will explode the crystal chamber in which it is confined. Still I can help you."

---

2   A strong poison created in Sicily around 1630 that was reputedly widely used in Naples, Perugia, and Rome

He drew from his pocket a phial holding about a couple of thimblefuls of a green liquid.

"One of my friends—whom I wish were yours—deeply versed in natural and occult sciences, gave me the recipe of this brew as a sovereign elixir of life. I have often taken it to cure what the English call the 'blue devils'. And I am bound to say that the effect was instant and salutary. Will you taste it?"

"I will take anything from your hand, my dear doctor."

A servant was rung up, who brought a spoon and a little brandy in a glass.

"Brandy to mollify it," said Mirabeau. "It must be liquid fire, then!"

Gilbert added the same quantity of his elixir to the half-dozen drops of *eau-de-vie*[3], and the two fluids mixed to the color of wormwood bitters, which the exhausted man drank off. Immediately he was invigorated and sprang up, saying: "Doctor, I will pay a diamond a drop for that liquor, for it would make me feel invincible."

"Count, promise me that you will take it only each three days, and I will leave you a phial every week."

"Give it, and I promise everything."

"Now, I have come for another matter. I want you to come out of town for carriage exercise, and at the same time to select a residence there."

"It chances that I was looking for one, and my man found a nice house at Argenteuil. It was recommended by a fellow countryman of his, one Fritz, whose master, a foreign banker, had lived in it. It is delightful, and being vacant, could be moved into at once. My father had a house out there, whence he drove me with his cane."

"Let us go to Argenteuil, then," said Gilbert. "Your health is so valuable that we must study everything bearing upon it."

Mirabeau had no establishment, and a hack had to be called for the gentlemen. In this they proceeded to the village where, a hundred paces on the Besons Road, they saw a house

---

3 A clear, colorless fruit brandy that is produced by means of fermentation and double distillation

buried in the trees. It was called the Marsh House. On the right of the road was a humble cottage, in front of which sat a woman on a stool. She was holding a child in her arms, who seemed devoured with fever.

"Doctor," said the orator, fixing his eyes on the sad sight, "I am as superstitious as an ancient. If that child dies, I would not live in this house. Just see what you think of the case."

Gilbert got down while the carriage went on. A gardener was keeping the house, which he showed to the inquirer. It belonged to St. Denis Abbey, and was for sale under the decree of confiscating Church property. Over against the gardener's lodge was another, a summerhouse simply overgrown with flowers. Mirabeau's passion for them made this sufficient lure—for this alone he would have taken the house.

"Is this little cottage, this Temple of Flora, on the property?" he asked.

"Yes, sir. It belongs to the big house, but it is at present occupied by a lady with her child. A pretty lady, but of course she will have to go if the house and estate are bought."

"A lovely neighbor does no harm," said the count. "Let me see the interior of the house."

The rooms were lofty and elegant, the furniture fine and stylish. In the main room, Mirabeau opened a window to look out, and it commanded a view of the summerhouse. What was more, he had a view of a lady, sewing, half reclining, while a child of five or six played on the lawn among flowering shrubs. It was the lady tenant.

It was not only such a pretty woman as one might imagine a Queen among the roses, but it was the living likeness of Queen Marie Antoinette. And to accentuate the resemblance, the boy was about the age of the Prince Royal.

Suddenly, the beautiful stranger perceived that she was under observation. She uttered a faint scream of surprise, rose, called her son, and drew him inside by the hand. But not without looking back two or three times.

At this same moment, Mirabeau started, for a hand was laid on his shoulder. It was the doctor, who reported that the peasant's child had caught swamp fever from being set down beside a stagnant pool while the mother reaped the grass. The disease was deadly but the doctor hoped to save the sufferer by Jesuit's Bark, as quinine was still styled at this date. But he warned his friend against this House in the Marsh, where the air might be as fatal to him as that of the senate house. The bad ventilation there made the atmosphere mephitic[4].

"I am sorry the air is not good, for the house suits me wonderfully."

"What an eternal enemy you are to yourself? If you mean to obey the orders of the Faculty, begin by renouncing the idea of taking this residence. You will find fifty around Paris better placed."

Perhaps Mirabeau, yielding to Reason's voice, would have promised. But suddenly, in the first shades of evening, behind a screen of flowers, appeared the head of a woman in white and pink flounces. He fancied that she smiled on him. He had no time to assure himself, as Gilbert dragged him away, suspecting something was going on.

"My dear doctor," said the orator, "remember that I said to the Queen when she gave me her hand to kiss on our interview for reconciliation, 'By this token, the Monarchy is saved.' I took a heavy engagement that time, especially if they whom I defend plot against me. But I shall hold to it, though suicide may be the only way for me to get honorably out of it."

Within a day, Mirabeau bought the Marsh House.

---

4   Poisonous or noxious

CHAPTER II

The Federation of France

All the realm had bound itself together in the girdle of Federation, one which preceded the United Europe of later utopists. Mirabeau had favored the movement, thinking that the King would gain by the country people coming to Paris, where they might overpower the citizens. He deluded himself into the belief that the sight of royalty would result in an alliance which no plot could break. Men of genius sometimes have these sublime but foolish ideas, at which the tyros in politics may well laugh.

There was a great stir in the Congress when the proposition was brought forward for this Federation ceremony at Paris, which the provinces demanded. It was disapproved by the two parties dividing the House, the Jacobins (So called from the old Monastery of Jacobins where they met) and the royalists. The former dreaded the union more than their foes, from not knowing the effect Louis XVI might have on the masses. The King's-men feared that a great riot would destroy the royal family as one had destroyed the Bastille.

But there was no means to oppose the movement which had not its like since the Crusades. The Assembly did its utmost to impede it, particularly by resolving that the delegates must come at their own expense; this was aimed at the distant provinces. But the politicians had no conception of the extent of the desire. All doors opened along the roads for these pilgrims of liberty. And the guides of the long procession were all the discontented soldiers and under-officers who had been kept down, that aristocrats should have all the high offices. Seamen who had won the Indies and were left poor, whom the storms had left stranded. They found the strength of their youth to lead their friends to the capitol. And hope marched before them.

All the pilgrims sang the same song: "It must go on!" (that is, the Revolution). The Angel of Renovation had taught it to all as it hovered over the country.

To receive the five hundred thousand of the city and country, a gigantic area was required. The field of Mars did for that, while the surrounding hills would hold the spectators. But as it was flat, it had to be excavated. Fifteen thousand regular workmen—that is, of the kind who loudly complain that they have no work to do and under their breath thank heaven when they do not find it—started in on the task converting the flat into the pit of an amphitheatre. At the rate they worked, they would be three months at it. It was promised for the Fourteenth of July, the Anniversary of the Taking of the Bastille.

Thereupon a miracle occurred, by which one may judge the enthusiasm of the masses. Paris volunteered to work at night after the regular excavators had gone off. Each brought his own tools. Some rolled casks of refreshing drink, others food. They included all ages and both sexes; in all conditions, from the scholar to the carter. Children carried torches; musicians played all kinds of instruments to cheer the multitude, and from one hundred thousand workers sounded the song "It shall go on!"

Among the most fevered toilers, might be remarked two who had been among the first to arrive. They were in National Guards uniforms. One was a gloomy-faced man of forty, with robust and thickset frame; the other a youth of twenty. The former did not sing and spoke seldom. The latter had blue eyes in a frank and open countenance, with white teeth and light hair. He stood solidly on long legs and large feet. With his full-sized hands, he lifted heavy weights, rolled dirt carts and pulled hurdles without rest. He was always singing, while watching his comrade out of the corner of the eye. He said joking words, to which the other did not reply. He brought his fellow a glass of wine, which he refused. Returning to his place with sorrow, he fell to work again like ten men, and singing like twenty.

These two men were newly elected Representatives by the Aisne District, ten miles from Paris. Having heard that hands were wanted, they ran in hot haste to offer one his silent co-operation, the other his merry and noisy assistance. Their names were François Billet and Ange Pitou. The first was a wealthy farmer, whose land was owned by Dr. Gilbert, and the second a boy of the district, who had been the schoolmate of Gilbert's son Sebastian. Thanks to their help, with that of others as energetic and patriotically inspired, the enormous works were finished on the Thirteenth of July 1790.

To make sure of having places the next day, many workers slept on the battlefield. Billet and Pitou were to officiate in the ceremonies, and they went to join their companions on the main street. Hotel-keepers had lowered their prices, and many houses were open to their brothers from the country. If any distinction was made, the farther they came, the more kindly they were treated.

On its part, the Assembly had received a portion of the shock. A few days before, it had abolished hereditary nobility, on the motion of Marquis Lafayette. Contrarily, the influence of Mirabeau was felt daily. A place was assigned in the Federation to him as Orator. Thanks to so mighty a champion, the court won partisans in the opposition ranks. The Assembly had voted liberal sums to the King for his civil list, and for the Queen, so that they lost nothing by pensioning Mirabeau.

The fact was, he seemed quite right in appealing to the rustics. The Federalists, whom the King welcomed, seemed to bring love for royalty along with enthusiasm for the National Assembly. Unhappily the King, dull and neither poetical nor chivalric, met the cheers coolly. Unfortunately also, the Queen, too much of a Lorrainer[5] to love the French and too proud to greet common people, did not properly value these outbursts of the heart.

Besides, poor woman, she had a spot on her sun: one of those gloomy fits which clouded her mind. She had long loved Count Charny, lieutenant of the Royal Lifeguards. But his loyalty to the King, who had treated him like a brother in times of danger, had rendered him invulnerable to the woman's wiles. Marie Antoinette was no longer a young woman, and sorrow had touched her head with her wing. This was making threads of silver appear in the blonde tresses—but she was fair enough to bewitch a Mirabeau, and might have enthralled George Charny.

But Charny had been married to a lady of the court to save the Queen's reputation. And contrary to the Queens wishes, he was starting to fall in love with his wife, Andrea de Taverney, who had loved him at first sight. This new love of Charny's naturally fortified his tacit pledge never to wrong his sovereign.

---

5   Lorraine was an independent duchy until annexed by France in 1766

Hence the Queen was miserable. And all the more as Charny had departed on some errand for the King, of which he had not told her the nature. Probably this was why she had played the flirt with Mirabeau. The genius had flattered her by kneeling at her feet, but she too soon compared the bloated, heavy, leonine man with Charny.

George Charny was elegance itself. He was a noble and a courtier, and yet more a seaman. Charny had saved a war-ship by nailing the colors to the mast and bidding the crew fight on. In his brilliant uniform, he looked like a prince of battles. While Mirabeau, in his black suit, resembled a canon of the church.

The fourteenth of July came impassibly. It was draped in clouds and promising rain and a gale, when it ought to have illumined a splendid day. But the French laugh even on a rainy day. Though drenched with rain and dying of hunger, the country delegates and National Guards made merry and sang. But the population, while unable to keep the wet off them, were not going to let them starve. Food and drink were lowered by ropes out of the windows. Similar offerings were made in all the thoroughfares they passed through.

During their march, a hundred and fifty thousand people took places on the edges of the Field of Mars, and as many stood behind them. It was not possible to estimate the number on the surrounding hills. Never had such a sight struck the eye of man. The Field was changed into a pit in short order, with the auditorium holding three hundred thousand. In the midst was the Altar of the Country, to which led four staircases, corresponding with the faces of the obelisk which over-towered it.

At each corner smoked incense dishes—incense being decreed henceforth to be used only in offerings to God. Inscriptions heralded that the French People were free, and invited all nations to the feast of Freedom. One grand stand was reserved for the Queen, the court and the Assembly. It was draped with the Red, White and Blue which she abhorred, since she had seen them flaunted above her own Austrian black.

For this day only, the King was appointed Commander-in-chief. But he had transferred his command to Lafayette, who ruled six millions of armed men in the National Guards of France. The tricolor surmounted everything—even to the distinctive banners of each body of delegates. At the same time as the President of the Assembly took his seat, the King and the Queen took theirs.

Alas, poor Queen! Her court was meager, for her best friends had fled in fright. Perhaps some would have returned if they knew what money Mirabeau had obtained for her. But they were ignorant.

She knew that Charny, whom she vainly looked for, would not be attracted by the power or by gold. She looked for his younger brother, Isidore, wondering why all the Queen's defenders seemed absent from their post. Nobody knew where he was. At this hour, he was conducting his sweetheart, Catherine (daughter of the gloomy farmer Billet), to a house in Bellevue, Paris. It was required for refuge from the contempt of her sisters in the village, and the wrath of her father.

Who knows, though, but that the heiress to the throne of the Caesars would have consented to be an obscure peasant girl. To be loved by George again, as Isidore loved the farmer's daughter. She was no doubt revolving such ideas, when Mirabeau saw her. She held glances half thunderous weather, half sunshine, and Mirabeau could not help exclaiming: "Of what is the royal enchantress thinking?"

She was brooding over the absence of Charny, and his love having died out.

The mass was said by Talleyrand, the French "Vicar of Bray," who swore allegiance to all manner of Constitutions himself. It must have been of evil augury. The storm redoubled as though protesting against the false priest who burlesqued the service.

Here followed the ceremony of taking the oath. Lafayette was the first, binding the National Guards. The Assembly Speaker swore for France; and the King in his own name. After the vows were made in deep silence, a hundred pieces of artillery burst into flame at once, and bellowed the signal to the surrounding country. From every fortified place, an immense flame issued, followed by the menacing thunder invented by man. So the circle enlarged until the warning reached the frontier and surpassed it. When the

King rose to declare his purpose, the clouds parted and the sun peered out like the Eye of God.

"I, King of the French," he said, "swear to employ all the power delegated to me by the Constitutional Law of the State to maintain the Constitution."

Why had he not eluded the solemn pledge as before? For his next step, flight from the kingdom, was to be the key to the enigma set that day. But, true or false, the cannon-fire none the less roared the oath to the confines. It took the warning to the monarchs: "Take heed! France is afoot, wishing to be free. And she is ready like the Roman envoy, to shake peace or war, as you like it, from the folds of her dress."

CHAPTER III

Where the Bastille Stood

Night came. The morning festival had been on the great parade ground; the night rejoicing was to be on the site where the Bastille had stood. Eighty-three trees, one for each department of France, were stuck up to show the space occupied by the infamous states-prison, on whose foundation these trees of liberty were planted. Strings of lamps ran from tree to tree. In the midst rose a large pole, with a flag lettered: "Freedom!"

Near the moats, in a grave left open on purpose, were flung the old chains, fetters and instruments of torture found in it. The dungeons were left open and lighted ghastly, where so many tears and groans had been vainly expanded. Lastly, in the inmost courtyard, a ballroom had been set up. And as the music pealed, the couples could be seen promenading. The prediction of Cagliostro was fulfilled, that the Bastille should be a public strolling-ground.

At one of the thousand tables set up around the Bastille, under the shadow of the trees outlining the site of the old fortress, two men were repairing their strength. They were exhausted by the day's marching, and other military manœuvres. Before them was a huge sausage—a four-pound loaf—and two bottles of wine.

"By all that is blue," said the younger, who wore the National Guards captain's uniform, "it is a fine thing to eat when you are hungry and drink when a-thirst." He paused. "But you do not seem to be hungry or thirsty, Father Billet."

"I have had all I want, and only thirst for one thing—"

"What is that?"

"I will tell you Pitou, when the time for me to sit at my feast shall come."

Pitou did not see the drift of the reply. Pitou was a lover of Catherine Billet, but he self-acknowledged that he could have no chance against the young nobleman who had captivated the rustic maid. When her father tried to shoot the gallant, Pitou had—while not shielding her or her lover, helped her to conceal herself from Billet.

It was not he, however, but Isidore who had brought the girl to Paris, after she had given birth to a boy. This occurred in the absence of Billet and Pitou, both of whom were ignorant of the removal. Pitou had housed her in a quiet corner, and he went to Paris without anything arising to cause him sadness. He had found Dr. Gilbert, to whom he had to report that with money he had given, Captain Pitou had equipped his Guards at Haramont in uniform, which was the admiration of the county. The doctor gave him five-and-twenty more gold pieces to be applied to maintaining the company at its present state of efficiency.

"While I am talking with Billet," said Gilbert, "who has much to tell me, would you not like to see Sebastian?"

"I should think I do," answered the peasant, "but I did not like to ask your permission."

After meditating a few instants, Gilbert wrote several words on a paper, which he folded up like a letter and addressed to his son.

"Take a hack and go find him," said Gilbert. "Probably from what I have written, he will want to pay a visit. Take him thither and wait at the door. He may keep you an hour or so, but I know how obliging you are. You will not find the time hanging heavy when you know you are doing me a kindness."

"Do not bother about that," responded the honest fellow; "I never feel dull. Besides, I will get in a supply of something to feed on, and I will kill time by eating."

"A good method," laughed Gilbert. "Only you must not eat dry bread as a matter of health, but wash it down with good wine."

"I will get a bottle, and some head cheese, too," replied Pitou.

"Bravo!" exclaimed the physician.

Pitou found Sebastian in the Louis-the-Great College, in the gardens. He was a winsome young man of eighteen or less, with handsome chestnut curls framing his melancholy and thoughtful face. And he had blue eyes darting juvenile glances like a Spring sun.

In him were combined the lofty aspirations of two aristocracies. That of the intellect, as embodied in his father, and of race, personified in his mother, the Countess of Charny. She had become his mother while unconscious in a mesmeric sleep.

The sleep was induced by Cogliostro, but it was Gilbert who profited passionately by the trance.

It was to the countess's that Gilbert had suggested his son should go. On the way, Pitou readied the provisions to bide time, should he have to wait any great while for the youth to come out of his mother's. As the countess was at home, the janitor made no opposition to a well-dressed young gentleman entering. Five minutes after, while Pitou was slicing up his loaf and sausage, and taking a pull at his wine, a footman came out to say: "Her ladyship, the countess of Charny, prays Captain Pitou to do her the honor to step inside, instead of awaiting Master Sebastian in a hired conveyance."

The Assembly had abolished titles but the servants of the titled had not yet obeyed.

Pitou had to wipe his mouth, pack up the uneaten comestibles with a sigh, and follow the man in a maze. His astonishment doubled when he saw a lovely lady, who held Sebastian in her arms and said, "Captain Pitou, you give me such great and unhoped-for joy in bringing Sebastian to me, that I wanted to thank you myself."

Pitou stared and stammered, but let the hand remain untaken.

"Take and kiss the lady's hand," prompted Sebastian. "It is my mother."

"Your mother? Oh, Gemini!" exclaimed the peasant, while the other young man nodded.

"Yes, his mother," said Andrea with her glance beaming with delight. "You bring him to me after nine months' parting, and then I had only seen him once before. In the hope you will again bring him, I wish to have no secrets from you, though it would be my ruin if revealed."

Every time the heart and trust of our rural friend was appealed to, one might be sure that he would lose his hesitation and dismay.

"Oh my lady, be you easy, your secret is here," he responded. He grasped her hand and kissed it, before laying his own, with some dignity, on his heart.

"My son tells me, Captain Pitou, that you have not breakfasted," went on the countess. "Pray step into the dining-room, and you can make up for lost time while I speak with my boy."

Soon on the board were arrayed two cutlets, a cold fowl and a pot of preserves. Nearby was a bottle of Bordeaux, a fine Venice glass and a pile of china plates. But for all the elegance of the set out edibles, Pitou rather deplored the head cheese, bread and common wine in the cab.

As he was attacking the chicken after having put away the cutlets, the door opened and a young gentleman appeared. But as Pitou lifted his head, they both recognized each other, and uttered a simultaneous cry:

"Viscount Charny!"

"Ange Pitou!"

The peasant sprang up, his heart violently throbbing. The sight of the patrician aroused his most painful memories. Not only was this his rival, but his successful rival. The man who had wronged Catherine Billet, causing her to lose her father's respect and her place at her mother's side in the farmhouse. Isidore only knew that Catherine was under obligations to this country lad; he had no idea of the latter's profound love for his mistress. Love out of which Pitou drew his devoutness. Consequently, he walked right up to the other, in whom he saw only the poacher and farm boy of Haramont—despite the uniform,

"Oh, you here, Pitou?" said he. "Delighted to meet you, to thank you for all the services you have done us."

"My lord viscount, I did all for Miss Catherine alone," returned the young man, in a firm voice though all his frame thrilled.

"That was all well up to your knowing that I loved her. Then, I was bound to take my share in the gratitude. And as you must have gone to some outlay, say for the letters transmitted to her—"

He clapped his hand to his pocket to prick Pitou's conscience. But the other stopped him, saying with the dignity sometimes astonishing to appear in him: "My lord, I do services when I can, but not for pay. Besides, I repeat, these were for Miss

Catherine solely. She is my friend. If she believes she is in any way indebted to me, she will regulate the account. But you, my lord, owe me nothing. For I did all for her, and not a stroke for you. So you have to offer me nothing."

These words, but especially the tone, struck the hearer. Perhaps it was only then that he noticed that the speaker was dressed as a captain in the new army.

"Excuse me, Captain Pitou," said Isidore, slightly bowing. "I do owe you something, and that is my thanks. And I offer you my hand. I hope you will do me the pleasure of accepting one, and the honor of accepting the other."

There was such grandeur in the speech and the gesture in company with it, that Pitou held out his hand. And with the fingers' ends, touched Isidore's.

At this juncture Countess Charny appeared on the threshold.

"You asked for me, my lord," she said; "I am here."

Isidore saluted the peasant and walked into the next room. He swung the door closed behind him, but the countess caught it and checked it so that it remained ajar. Pitou understood that he was allowed, nay, invited to hear what was spoken. He remarked that on the other side of the sitting room was another door, leading into a bedroom. If Sebastian was there, he could hear on that side as well as the captain on this other.

"My lady," began Isidore, "I had news yesterday from my brother George. As in his other letters, he begs me to ask you to remember him. He does not yet know when he is to return, and will be happy to have news from you either by letter or by your charging me."

"I could not answer the letter he sent me from want of an address. But I will profit by your inter-mediation to have the duty of a submissive and respectful wife presented him. If you will take charge of a letter for my lord, one shall be ready on the morrow."

"Have it ready," said Isidore, "but I cannot call for it till some five or six days, as I have a mission to carry out. A journey of necessity, and unknown duration. But I will come here at once on my return and take your message."

As he passed through the dining-room, he saw that Pitou was spooning deeply into the preserves. He had finished when the countess came in, with Sebastian. It was difficult to recognize the grave Countess Charny in this radiant young mother, whom two hours of chat with her son had transformed. The hand which she gave to Pitou seemed to be of marble still, but mollified and warmed.

Sebastian embraced his mother with the ardor he infused in all he did, and Pitou took leave without putting a question. He was silent on the way to the college, absorbing the rest of his head cheese, bread and wine. There was nothing in this incident to spoil his appetite. But he was chilled on his arrival to see how gloomy Farmer Billet was. He resolved to dissipate this sadness.

"I say, Father Billet," he resumed, after preparing his stock of words as a sharpshooter makes a provision of cartridges, "who the devil could have guessed, in a year and two days, that since Miss Catherine received me on the farm, so many events should have taken place."

"Nobody," rejoined Billet, whose terrible glance at the mention of Catherine had not been remarked.

"The idea of the pair of us taking the Bastille," continued he, like the sharpshooter having reloaded his gun.

"Nobody," replied the farmer mechanically.

"*Plague on it, he has made up his mind not to talk,*" thought the younger man. "Who would think that I should become a captain and you a Federalist? And we both be taking supper under an arbor in the very spot where the old prison stood?"

"Nobody," said Billet for the third time, with a more sombre look than before.

The younger man saw that there was no inducing the other to speak, but he found comfort in the thought that this ought not to alienate his right. So he continued, leaving Billet the right to speak if he chose.

"I suppose, like the Bastille, all whom we knew have become dust, as the Scriptures foretold. To think that we stormed the Bastille on your saying so, as if it were a chicken-house. And that here we sit—where it used to be—drinking merrily! Oh, the racket we kicked up that day. Talking of racket," he interrupted himself, "what is this rumpus all about?"

The uproar was caused by the passing of a man who had the rare privilege of creating noise wherever he walked. It was Mirabeau, who, with a lady on his arm, was visiting the Bastille site. Anyone other than he would have shrank from the cheers, in which were mingled some sullen murmurs. But he was the bird of the storm. He smiled amid the thunderous tempest, while supporting the woman, who shivered under her veil at such dreadful popularity.

Pitou jumped upon a chair, and waved his cocked hat on the tip of his sword as he shouted: "Long live Mirabeau!"

Billet let escape no token of feelings either way. He folded his arms on his burly chest and muttered in a hollow voice: "It is said he betrays the people."

"Pooh, that has been said of all great men, from antiquity down," replied his friend.

In his excitement, he only now noticed that a third chair, drawn up to their table, was occupied by a stranger who seemed about to accost them. To be sure, it was a day of fraternity, and familiarity was allowable among fellow-citizens. But Pitou, who had not finished his repast, thought it going too far. The stranger did not apologize, but eyed the pair with a jeering manner, apparently habitual to him.

Billet was in no mood to support being "quizzed," as the current word ran, for he turned on the new-comer. But the latter made a sign before he was addressed, which drew another from Billet. The two did not know each other, but they were brothers. Like Billet, he was clad like one of the delegates to the Federation. But his particulars reminded Billet of the party of Anacharsis Clootz, the German anarchist.

CHAPTER IV

The Lodge of the Invisibles

"You do not know me, brothers," said the stranger, when Billet had nodded and Pitou smiled condescendingly, "but I know you both. You are Captain Pitou, and you, Farmer Billet. Why are you so gloomy? Because, though you were the first to enter the Bastille, they have forgotten to hang at your buttonhole the medal for the Conquerors of the Bastille? And to do you the honors accorded to others this day?"

"Did you really know me, brother," replied the farmer with scorn, "you would know that such trifles do not affect a heart like mine."

"Is it because you found your fields unproductive when you returned home in October?"

"I am rich—a harvest lost little worries me."

"Then, it must be," said the stranger, looking him hard in the face, "that something has happened to your daughter Catherine—"

"Silence," said the farmer, clutching the speaker's arm. "Let us not speak of that matter."

"Why not, if I speak in order that you may be revenged?"

"Then that is another thing—speak of it," said the other, turning pale but smiling at the same time.

Pitou thought no more of eating or drinking, but stared at their new acquaintance as at a wizard.

"But what do you understand by revenge?" went on the stranger with a smile. "Tell me. In a paltry manner, by killing an individual as you tried to do?"

Billet blanched like a corpse, and Pitou shuddered all over.

"Or by pursuing a whole class?"

"By hunting down a whole caste," said Billet, "for of such are the crimes of all his ilk. When I mourned before my friend Dr. Gilbert, he said: 'Poor Billet, what has befallen you has already happened to a hundred thousand fathers. What would the young noblemen have in the way of pastime if they did not steal away the poor man's daughter—and the old ones steal away the King's money?'"

"Oh, Gilbert said that, did he?"

"Do you know him?"

"I know all men," replied the stranger, smiling. "As I know you two, and Viscount Charny, Isidore, Lord of Boursonnes... as I know Catherine, the prettiest girl of the county."

"I bade you not speak her name, for she is no more—she is dead."

"Why, no, Father Billet," broke in Pitou, "for she—"

He was no doubt going to say that he saw her daily, but the farmer repeated in a voice admitting of no reply,

"She is dead."

Pitou hung his head for he understood.

"Ha, ha," said the stranger. "If I were my friend Diogenes, I should put out my lantern, for I believe I have found an honest man." Rising, he offered his arms to Billet, saying, "Brother, come and take a stroll with me, while this good fellow finishes the eatables."

"Willingly," returned Billet, "for I begin to understand to what feast you invite me. Wait for me here," he added to his friend; "I shall return."

The stranger seemed to know the gastronomical taste of Pitou, for he sent by the waiter some more delicacies. The likes of which he was still discussing, while wondering, when Billet reappeared. His brow was illumined with something like pleasure.

"Anything new, Father Billet?" asked the captain.

"Only that you will start for home to-morrow, while I remain."

This is what Billet remained for. A week after, he might have been seen in the dress of a well-to-do farmer in Plastriere Street. Two thirds up the thoroughfare was blocked by a crowd around a ballad singer. He had a fiddler to accompany him, who was singing a lampoon at the characters of the day. Billet paused only an instant to listen to the strain. In it, the attributes of horses were given to the characters, such as "the Roarer," to Mirabeau, etc.

Slipping in at an alleyway at the back of the throng, Billet came to a low doorway. Over it was scrawled in red chalk—"L. P. D." This was the way down into a subterranean passage. Billet could not read, but he may have understood that these letters were a token. He took the underground road with boldness.

At its end, a pale light glimmered. By it was seated a man who was reading, or pretending to read, a newspaper. Such was the custom of the Paris janitor in the evening. At the sound of steps he got up, and with a finger touching his breast, waited. Billet presented his forefinger bent, and laid it like the ring of a padlock on his lips. This was probably the sign of recognition expected by the door-guard, for he opened a door on his right, which was wholly invisible when shut. He pointed out to the adventurer, a narrow and steep flight of steps going down into the earth.

When Billet entered, the door shut behind him swiftly and silently. He counted seventeen steps, and though he was not talkative, he could not help saying, "Good, I am going right."

Before a door floated a tapestry. He went straight to it, lifted it, and was within a large circular hall where some fifty persons were gathered. The walls were hung with red and white cloth, on which were traced the Square, the Compass and the Level. A single lamp hung from the center of the ceiling, and cast a wan light insufficient to define those who preferred to stand out of its direct beams. A rostrum up which four steps led, awaited orators or new members. And on this platform, next the wall, a desk and chair stood for the chairman.

In a few minutes, the hall filled so completely that there was no moving about. The men were of all conditions and sorts, from the peasant to the prince. They arrived like Billet, solitarily and standing wherever they liked, without knowing or being known to each other. Each wore under his overcoat either the masonic apron, if only a mason, or the scarf of the Illuminati, if affiliated to the Grand Mystery. Only three restricted themselves to the masonic apron. One was Billet, the second was a young man, and the third a man of forty-two who appeared by his bearing to belong to the highest upper class.

Some seconds after he had arrived, though no more noticed than the meanest, a second panel opened. The chairman appeared, wearing the insignia of the Grand Orient and the Grand Copt. Billet uttered faintly his astonishment, for the Master was the man who had accosted him at the Bastille.

He mounted the dais, and turning to the assembly, said: "Brothers, we have two pieces of business to do this day. I have to receive three new candidates; and I have to render account of how the Work has gone on. For as it grows harder and harder, it is meet that you should know if I am ever worthy of your trust, and that I should know if I still deserve it. It is only by receiving light from you, and imparting it, that I can walk in the dark way. Let the chiefs alone stay in the lodge to receive or reject the applicants. Once they are dealt with, all are to return into session, from the first to the last. For it is in the presence of all, and not only within the Supreme Circle, that I wish to lay bare my conduct. To receive censure, or ask for recompense."

At these words, a door flew open opposite the one that he had come in by. Vast vaulted depths were beheld, as the crypt of an ancient basilica. The arcades were feebly lighted by brass lamps, hung so as to make darkness visible.

Only three remained: the novices. Chance fixed it that they should be standing up by the wall at nearly regular distances, and they looked at each other with astonishment. Only thus and now did they learn that they were the heroes of the occasion. At this instant, the door by which the chairman had come opened to admit six masked men. They came to place themselves beside the Master, three on each hand.

"Let Numbers Two and Three disappear for the time," said the Master. "None but the supreme chiefs must know the secrets of the reception or refusal of a would-be mason in the Order of the Illuminated."

The young man and the high-born one retired through the lobby by which they had come, leaving Billet alone.

"Draw nearer," said the chairman. "What is your name among the profane?" he demanded.

"François Billet, and it is Strength among the elect."

"Where did you first see the Light?"

"In the lodge of the Soissons Friends of Truth."

"How old are you?"

"Seven years," replied Billet, making the sign to show what rank he had attained in the order.

"Why do you want to rise a step and be received among us?"

"Because I am told that it is a step nearer the Universal Light."

"Have you supporters?"

"I have no one to speak for me, save him who came to me and offered to have me welcomed." He looked fixedly at the chairman.

"With what feelings would you walk in the way which we may open unto you?"

"With hate of the powerful and love for equality."

"What answers for these feelings?"

"The pledge of a man who has never broken his word."

"What inspired your wish for equality?"

"The inferior condition in which I was born."

"What the hatred of those above you?"

"That is my secret, yet it is known to you. Why do you want me to say aloud what I hesitate to say in a whisper to myself?"

"Will you walk in the way to Equality, and lead all those whom you can control?"

"Yes."

"As far as your will and strength can go, will you overthrow all obstacles opposing the freedom of France, and the emancipation of the world?"

"I will."

"Are you free from any anterior engagement? Or if made, will you break it if contrary to this new pledge?"

"I am ready."

Turning to the chiefs, the Master said: "Brothers, this man speaks the truth. I invited him to be one of ours. A great grief binds him to our cause by the ties of hatred. He has already done much for the Revolution, and may do more. I propose him, and answer for him in the past, the present and the future."

"Receive him," said all the six.

The presiding officer raised his hand and said in a slow and solemn voice: "In the name of the Architect of the Universe, swear to break all carnal bonds still binding you to parents, sister, brother, wife, kinsmen, mistress, kings, benefactors, and to whomsoever you have promised faith, obedience, service or gratitude."

Billet repeated in a voice as firm as the speaker's.

"Good! Henceforth you are freed from the so-called oath of allegiance made to the country and the laws. Swear therefore to reveal to your new chief what you see and do, hear or learn, read or divine. And moreover, to seek out and find that which is not offered to the sight."

"I swear," said Billet.

"Swear to honor and respect steel, fire and poison. They are the sure and prompt means necessary to purge the world by the death of those who try to lessen truth—or snatch it from our hands.

"Swear to avoid Naples, Rome, Spain and all accursed places, and to shun the temptation of revealing anything seen and heard in our meetings. For the lightning is not swifter to strike than our invisible and inevitable knife, wherever you may hide. And now, live in the Name of the Three!"

A brother hidden in the crypt opened the door where the inferior members were strolling till the initiation was over. The Master waved Billet to go there. And bowing, he went to join those whom the dreadful words he had uttered made his associates.

The second candidate was the famous St. Just, the Revolutionist whom Robespierre sent to the guillotine. He was initiated in the same terms as Billet, and similarly joined the band.

The third candidate was Louis Philippe, Duke of Orleans, whom hatred of his relatives had induced to take this step. He did so in order to have the aid of powerful partners in his attempt to seize the throne. He was already at the degree of Rose-Croix. He took the oath, which was administered in a different order from before, in order to test him at the outset. Instead of saying 'Yes', he repeated the very words of the section binding him to break all ties of affection, or allegiance to royalty. When he darted into the crypt he exclaimed: "At last I shall have my revenge!"

CHAPTER V

The Conspirator's Account

On being left together, the six masked men and the chairman whispered among themselves.

"Let all come in," said Cagliostro, for he was the Master. "I am ready to make the report I promised."

The door was instantly opened, and the members of the league walked in to crowd the hall once more. Hardly was the door closed behind the last, before the Master spoke. Holding up his hand quickly, like one who knew the value of time and wished not to lose a second, he said, "Brothers, there may be some here who were present at a meeting held just twenty years ago. It was a couple of miles from Danenfels, in a cavern of Thunder Mountain, five miles from the Rhine. If so, let the venerable upholders of the Great Cause which we have embraced, signify the same by holding up the hand, saying: 'I was there!'"

Five or six hands were held above the throng, and as many voices cried: "I was there."

"So far, so good," continued the speaker. "The others are in the Temple above, or scattered over the earth. They are working at the common and holy work, for it is that of all mankind. Twenty years ago, this work which we have pursued in its different periods was scarce commenced. The light was at its dawning, and the steadiest eyes beheld the future only through the cloud, which none but the eyes of the chosen could pierce. At that meeting, I explained by what miracle death did not exist for me, it being merely for man forgetfulness of the past. Or rather how, during twenty centuries, I had dwelt in succeeding bodies for my immortal soul. Slowly, I saw people pass from slavery to serfdom, from serfdom to the state of those aspirations for freedom which precede it. Like the stars of the night hinting what a sun can be, we have seen the republics try their rules, at Genoa, Venice, and Switzerland—but this is not what we needed.

"A great country was wanted to give the impetus. A wheel in which would be cogged all the others; a planet which should illumine the world."

A cheering murmur ran through the audience, and Cagliostro proceeded with an inspired air. "Heaven indicated to me that it would be France. Indeed, having tried all systems, she appeared likely to suit our purpose, and we decided on her being first freed. But look back on France twenty years ago, and grant that it was great boldness—or rather sublime faith—to undertake such a task. In Louis XV's weak hands, it was still the realm of Louis XIV. An aristocratic kingdom, where the nobles had all the rights, and the rich all the privileges. At the head was a man who represented at once the lowest and the loftiest, the grandest and the paltriest, heaven and the masses. With a word, he could make you wealthy or a beggar, happy or miserable, free or captive—keep you living or send you to death.

"He had three grandsons, young princes who were called to succeed him. Chance had it that he whom nature designated was also the choice of the people, if the people had any choice at the epoch. He was accounted kind, just, honest, learned, and a lover of wisdom. In order to quench the wars which the fatal succession of Charles II kindled, the daughter of Maria Theresa was chosen for his wife. The two nations were to be indissolubly united, which are the counterbalances west and east of Europe: France and Austria. So calculated Maria Theresa, the foremost politician of Europe.

"It was at this period when France—supported by Austria, Spain and Italy—was to enter on a new and desired reign that we determined. Not that she should be the chief of kingdoms, but that the French should be the first people freed.

"It was asked who would be the new Theseus to rush into the den of this Minotaur. To thread the innumerable turnings of the maze, while guided by the light of Truth, and to face the royal monster. I replied that it should be me. Some eager spirits, uneasy characters, wanted to know how long a time it would take to accomplish the first period of my enterprise. I divided it into three portions, and said that I required twenty years. They cried out against that. Can you understand this? Man had been serf or slave for twenty centuries, and he mocked me because I wanted twenty years to make him free!"

He looked upon the meeting, where his last words had provoked ironical smiles.

"In short, I obtained the twenty years. I gave my brothers the famous device: 'Lilia Pedibus Destrue—the Lilies shall be trodden underfoot!' and I set to work, urging all to do likewise. I entered France under arches of triumph. The rose and the laurel made the road from Strasburg to Paris like a trellis garlanded with flowers. Everybody was shouting: 'Long live the Dauphiness! Our future Queen!' Now, far from me to take credit myself for the initiative or the merit of events. The Builder had planned all this, and He laid each stone well and truly. He allowed this humble mason, who officiates in this fane[6], to see the Hand divinely wielding the Line and the Level. Praise unto Him! I have done some leveling. The rocks have been removed off the way, the bridge has been thrown over the flood, and the gulfs have been filled up so that the cart has rolled smoothly. Listen brothers, to what has been performed in a score of years.

"Parliaments broken up. Louis XV, once called the Well-Beloved, dies amid general scorn! The Queen, after seven years of unfruitful wedlock, gives birth to children whose paternity is contested. She is defamed as mother of the Crown Prince, and dishonored as a woman in the case of the Diamond Necklace.

"The new King, consecrated under the name of Louis the Desired, is impotent in politics as in love. He tries one utopia after another, until he reaches national bankruptcy, and has all kinds of ministers down to a Calonne. The Assembly of Worthies decrees the States General Congress, which was appointed by universal suffrage, and declares itself the National Assembly. The clergy and nobility are overcome by the other classes. The Bastille is stormed, and the foreign troops driven out of the capital. The night of August 4th, 1789, shows the aristocracy that they are reduced to nothing. On the 5th and 6th October, the King and Queen are shown that royalty is nothing. On the 14th of July, 1790, the unity of France is shown to the world.

"The princes are deprived of popularity by their absconding. The King's brother loses his hold by the Favras conspiracy, showing that he casts off his friends to save his neck. Lastly, the Constitution is sworn unto, on the Altar of the Country.

---

6   Temple

The Speaker of the House of Representatives sits on a chair on the level with the King's. It is the Law and the Nation sitting side by side. Attentive Europe leans towards us, silently watching—all who do not applaud are trembling. Now, is not France the cornerstone on which Free Europe shall be laid? The wheel which turns all the machine, the sun which shall illuminate the Old World?"

"Yea, yea, yea!" shouted all voices.

"But, brothers," continued the magician, "do you believe the work is so far advanced that we may leave it to get on by itself? Although the Constitution has been sworn to, can we trust to the royal vow?"

"Nay, nay, nay," cried every voice.

"Then we begin the second stage of the revolutionary work," pursued Cagliostro. "As your eyes see, I perceive with delight that the Federation of 1790 is not the goal, but a halting-place. After the repose, the court will recommence the task of counter-revolution. Let us also gird up our loins and start afresh. No doubt, for timid hearts there will be hours of weakening and of distrust. Often the beam from the All-seeing Eye will seem to be eclipsed—the Hand that beckons us will cease to be seen. More than once during the second period, the cause will appear injured, even lost, by some unforeseen and fortuitous accident. All will seem to show that we are wrong; circumstances will look as if unfavorable; our enemies will have some triumph; and our fellow-citizens will be ungrateful. After many real fatigues and apparent uselessness, many will ask themselves if they have not gone astray on the bad path.

"No, brothers, no. I tell you at this hour, for the words to ring everlastingly in your ears. In victory as a blast of trumpets, in defeat as the rallying cry—No! Leading races have their providential mission which must be unerringly accomplished. The Arch-Designer laid down the road, and found it true and straight. His mysterious goal cannot be revealed until it is attained in its full splendor. The cloud may obscure it and we think it gone, and an idea may recoil. But like the old-time knights, it is only to set the lance and rush forward to slay the dragon.

"Brothers, brothers, our goal is the bonfire on the high mount, believed extinct because the ridge concealed it as we sank in the vale. Then the weaklings muttered as they halted and whined, 'We have no beacon—we are blundering in the dark. Let us stay where we are; what is the good of getting lost?' But the strong hearts continue smiling confidently, and soon the light will reappear on the heights. Albeit it may disappear again, but each time it is brighter and clearer because it is more near!

"Thus will it be with the chosen band. Through struggling, pressing on, persevering, and above all believing in the Republic to be, they will arrive at the foot of the lighthouse. The lighthouse whose radiance will join the one that was cast across the Atlantic by the other Republic which we have helped throw off the tyrant's yoke. Let us swear brothers, for ourselves and our descendants, never to stop until we establish on this temple of the Architect, the holy device of which we have conquered one portion: 'Liberty, Equality and Fraternity.'"

The speech was hailed with uproarious approbation.

"But do not confine it to France solely. Inscribe it on the banner of mankind, as the whole world's motto. And now brothers, go out upon your task, which is great. So great, that through whatever vale of tears and of the shadow of death you must pass, your descendants will envy the holy errand you shall have accomplished. And like the crusaders, who became more numerous and eager as their foregoers were slain, they march over the road whitened by the bones of their fathers. Be of good cheer, apostles. Courage, pilgrims of freedom—courage, soldiers, Apostles, converts! Pilgrims, march on! Soldiers, fight!"

Cagliostro stopped, but that would have happened from the applause. Three times the cheering rose and was extinguished in the gloomy vaults like an earthquake's rumbling. Then the six masked men bowed to him one after another, kissed his hand and retired. Each of the brothers preached the renewal of the political crusade by repeating the motto: "We shall Trample the Lilies under."

As the last went forth, the lamps were extinguished. The Arch-Revolutionist remained alone, buried in the bowels of the earth. He was lost in silence and darkness, like those divinities of the Indies, whose mysteries he asserted himself to have been initiated into two thousand years before.

CHAPTER VI

Women and Flowers

Some months after the previously recorded events, about the end of March, 1791, Dr. Gilbert was hurriedly called to his friend Mirabeau by the latter's faithful servant Deutsch, who had been alarmed. Mirabeau had spoken in the House on the question of Mines, the interests of owners, and of the State not being very clearly defined. To celebrate his victory, he gave a supper to some friends and was prostrated by internal pains. Gilbert was too skillful a physician not to see how grave the invalid was. He bled him, and the black blood relieved the sufferer.

"You are a downright great man," said he.

"And you a great blockhead to risk a life so precious to your friends for a few hours of fictitious pleasure," retorted his deliverer.

The orator smiled almost ironically, in melancholy.

"I think you exaggerate, and that my friends and France do not hold me so dear."

"Upon my honor," replied Gilbert laughing, "great men complain of ingratitude, and they are really the ungrateful ones. If it were a most serious malady of yours, all Paris would flock under your window. Were you to die, all France would come to your obsequies."

"What you say is very consoling, let me tell you," said the other, merrily.

"It is just because you can see one without risking the other that I say it. And indeed, you need a great public demonstration to restore your morale. Let me take you to Paris within a couple of hours, my dear count. Let me tell the first man on the street corner that you are ailing, and you will see the excitement."

"I would go if you put off the departure till this evening, and let me meet you at my house in Paris at eleven."

Gilbert looked at his patient, and the latter saw that he was seen through.

"My dear count, I noticed flowers on the Dining-room table," said he. "It was not merely a supper to friends."

"You know that I cannot do without flowers; they are my craze."

"But they were not alone."

"If they are a necessity, I must suffer from the consequences they entail."

"Count, the consequences will kill you."

"Confess doctor, that it will be a delightful kind of suicide."

"I will not leave you this day."

"Doctor, I have pledged my word, and you would not make me fail in that."

"I shall see you this night, though?"

"Yes, really, I feel better."

"You mean to drive me away?"

"The idea of such a thing."

"I shall be in town; I am on duty at the palace."

"Then you will see the Queen," said Mirabeau, becoming gloomy once more.

"Probably. Have you any message for her?"

Mirabeau smiled bitterly.

"I should not take such a liberty, doctor; do not even say that you have seen me. For she will ask if I have saved the monarchy, as I promised, and you will be obliged to answer 'No'! It is true," he added with a nervous laugh, "that the fault is as much hers as mine."

"You do not want me to tell her that your excess of exertions in the tribune is killing you."

"Nay, you may tell her that," he replied after brief meditation. "You may make me out as worse than I am, to test her feelings."

"I promise you that, and to repeat her own words."

"It is well. I thank you, doctor. What are you prescribing?"

"Warm drinks, soothing, strict diet and—no nurse-woman less than fifty—"

"Rather than infringe the regulation, I would take two of twenty-five!"

At the door, Gilbert met Deutsch, who was in tears.

"All this through a woman—just because she looks like the Queen," said the man. "How stupid of a genius, as they say he is."

He let out Gilbert who stepped into his carriage, muttering, "What does he mean by a woman like the Queen?" He thought of asking Deutsch, but it was the count's secret, and he ordered his coachman to drive to town. On the way, he met Camille Desmoulins—the living newspaper of the day—to whom he told the truth of the illness, because it was the truth. When he announced the news to the King, the latter inquired if the count had lost his appetite.

"Yes, Sire," was the doctor's reply.

"Then it is a bad case," sighed the monarch, shifting the subject.

When the same words were repeated to the daughter of Maria Theresa, her forehead darkened.

"Why was he not so stricken on the day of his panegyric on the tricolor flag?" she sneered. "Never mind," she went on, as if repenting the expression of her hatred before a Frenchman. "It would be very unfortunate for France if this malady makes progress. Doctor, I rely on your keeping me informed about it."

At the appointed hour, Gilbert called on his patient at his town house. His eyes caught sight of a lady's scarf on a chair.

"Glad to see you," said Mirabeau quickly, as though to divert his attention from it. "I have learned that you kept half your promise. Deutsch has been busy answering friendly inquiries from our arrival. Are you true to the second part? Have you been to the palace and seen the King and Queen?"

"Yes; and told them you were unwell. The King sincerely condoled when he heard that you had lost your appetite. The Queen was sorry and bade me keep her informed."

"But I want the words she used."

"Well, she said that it was a pity you were not ill when you praised the new flag of the country."

Mirabeau wished to judge of the Queen's influence over the orator. He started on the easy chair, as if receiving the discharge of a galvanic battery.

"Ingratitude of monarchs," he muttered. "That speech of mine blotted out remembrance of the rich Civil List and the dower I obtained for her. This Queen must be ignorant that I was compelled to regain the popularity I lost for her sake. But she no more remembers it than my proposing the adjournment of the annexation of Avignon to France, in order to please the King's religious scruples. But these, and other faults of mine, I have dearly paid for," continued Mirabeau. "Not that these faults will ruin them, but there are times when ruin must come, whether faults help them forward or not. The Queen does not wish to be saved, but to be revenged. Hence, she relishes no reasonable ideas.

"I have tried to save liberty and royalty at the same time. However, I am not fighting against men, or tigers—but an element. It is submerging me like the sea. Yesterday up to the knee, today up to the waist, to-morrow I shall be struggling with it up to my neck. I must be open with you, doctor; I felt chagrin first, then disgust. I dreamed of being the arbiter between the Revolution and the monarchy. I believed I should have an ascendancy over the Queen as a man. And some day, when she was going under the flood, I meant to leap in and rescue her. But, no! They would not honestly take me. They try to destroy my popularity; ruin me, annihilate me, and make me powerless to do either good or evil. So now that I have done my best, I tell you doctor, that the best thing I can do is die in the nick of time. To fall artistically like the Dying Gladiator, and offer my throat to be cut with gracefulness. To yield up the ghost with decency."

He sank back on the reclining chair and bit the pillow savagely. Gilbert knew what he sought, on what Mirabeau's life depended.

"What will you say if the King or the Queen should send to inquire after your health?" he asked.

"The Queen will not do it—she will not stoop so low."

"I do not believe, but I suppose... I presume..."

"I will wait till to-morrow night."

"And then?"

"If she sends a confidential man, I will say that you are right and I am wrong. But if on the contrary none come, then it will be the other way around."

"Keep tranquil till then. But this scarf?"

"I shall not see her, on my honor," he said, smiling.

"Good. Try to get a good quiet night, and I will answer for you," said Gilbert, going out.

"Your master is better, my honest Deutsch," said he to the attendant at the door.

The old valet shook his head sadly.

"Do you doubt my word?"

"I doubt everything since his bad angel will be beside him."

He sighed as he left the doctor on the gloomy stairs. At the landing corner, Gilbert saw a veiled shadow, which seemed waiting. On perceiving him, it uttered a low scream, and disappeared so quickly by a partly opened door that it resembled a flight.

"Who is that woman?" questioned the doctor.

"The one who looks like the Queen," responded Deutsch.

For the second time, Gilbert was struck by the same idea on hearing this phrase. He took a couple of steps, as though to chase the phantom. But he checked himself, saying, "It cannot be."

He continued his way, leaving the old domestic in despair that this learned man could not conjure away the demon whom he believed to be the agent of the Inferno.

The next day, all Paris called to inquire after the invalid orator. The crowd in the street would not believe Deutsch's encouraging report, but forced all vehicles to turn into the side streets, so that their idol should not be disturbed by their noise. Mirabeau got up and went to the window to wave a greeting to these worshipers, who shouted their wishes for his long life. But he was thinking of the haughty woman who did not trouble her head about him, and his eyes wandered over the mob to see if any servants in the royal blue livery were trying to make their way through the mass. By evening, his impatience changed into gloomy bitterness. Still he waited for the almost promised token of interest, and still it did not come.

At eleven, Gilbert came. He had written his best wishes during the day. He came in smiling, but he was daunted by the expression on Mirabeau's face—faithful mirror of his soul's perturbations.

"Nobody has come," said he. "Will you tell me what you have done this day?"

"Why, the same as usual—"

"No, doctor. I saw what happened, and I will tell you the same as though present. You called on the Queen and told her how ill I was. She said she would send to ask the latest news, and you went away, happy and satisfied, relying on the royal word. She was left laughing, bitter and haughty, ignorant that a royal word must not be broken—mocking at your credulity."

"Truly, had you been there, you could not have seen and heard more clearly," said Gilbert.

"What numb-skulls they are," exclaimed Mirabeau. "I told you they never did a thing at the right time. Men in the royal livery coming to my door would have wrung shouts of 'Long live the King!' from the multitude, and given them popularity for a year."

He shook his head with grief.

"What is the matter, count?" asked Gilbert.

"Nothing."

"Have you had anything to eat?"

"Not since two o'clock."

"Then take a bath and have a meal."

"A capital idea!"

Mirabeau listened in the bath, until he heard the street door close after the doctor, then he rang for his servant. Not Deutsch, but another—to have the table in his room decked with flowers, and "Madam Oliva" invited to sup with him. He closed all the doors of the supper-room, except that to the rooms of the strange woman whom the old German called his bad angel.

At about four in the morning, Deutsch sat up when he heard a violent ring of the room bell. He and another servant rushed to the supper-room, but all the doors were fastened so that they had to go round by the strange lady's rooms. There they found her in the arms of their master, who had tried to prevent her giving the alarm. She had rung the table-bell from inability to get at the bell pull.

She was screaming as much for her own relief as her lover's, as he was suffocating her in his convulsive embrace. It seemed to be Death trying to drag her into the grave. Jean ran to rouse Dr. Gilbert, while Deutsch got his master to a couch. In ten minutes the doctor drove up.

"What is it now?" he asked of Deutsch, in the hall.

"That woman again, and the cursed flowers! Come and see."

At this moment something like a sob was heard. Gilbert ran up the stairs, at the top step of which a door opened. A woman in a white wrapper ran out suddenly and fell at the doctor's feet.

"Oh, Gilbert," she screamed, "save him!"

"Nicole Legay," cried the doctor. "Was it you, wretch, who have killed him?" A dreadful thought overwhelmed him. "I saw her bully Beausire selling broadsides against Mirabeau, and she became his mistress. He is undoubtedly lost, for Cagliostro set himself against him."

He turned back into his patient's room, fully aware that no time was to be lost. Indeed, he was too versed in secrets of his craft still to hope, far less to preserve any doubt. In the body before his eyes, it was impossible to see the living Mirabeau. From that time, his face assumed the solemn cast of great men dying.

Meanwhile the news had spread that there was a relapse, and that the doom impended. Then could it be judged what a gigantic place one man may fill among his fellows. The entire city was stirred as on great calamities. The door was besieged by persons of all opinions, as though everybody knew they had something to lose by his loss. Mirabeau caused the window to be opened, that he might be soothed by the hum of the multitude beneath.

"Oh, good people," Mirabeau murmured: "slandered, despised and insulted like me. It is right that those Royals should forget me, and the Plebes bear me in mind."

Night drew near.

"My dear doctor," Mirabeau said to Gilbert, who would not leave him. "This is my dying day. At this point, nothing is to be done but embalm my corpse and strew flowers roundabout."

Scarcely had Jean said he wanted flowers for his master, than all the windows opened, and flowers were offered from conservatories and gardens of the rarest sorts. By nine in the morning, the room was transformed into a bower of bloom.

"My dear doctor, I beg a quarter of an hour to say goodbye to a person who ought to quit the house before I go. I ask you to protect her in case they hoot her."

"I leave you alone," said Gilbert, understanding.

"Before going, kindly hand me the little casket in the secretary."

Gilbert did as requested. The money-box was heavy enough to be full of gold.

At the end of half an hour, spent by Gilbert in giving news to the inquirers, Jean ushered a veiled lady out to a hackney-carriage at the door. Gilbert ran to his patient.

"Put the casket back," said he in a faint voice. "Odd, is it not?" he continued, seeing how astonished the doctor looked at its being as heavy as before. "But where the deuce will disinterestedness next have a nest?"

Near the bed, Gilbert picked up a lace handkerchief wet with tears.

"Ah, she would take nothing away—but she left something," remarked Mirabeau.

Feeling it was damp he pressed it to his forehead.

"Tears? Is she the only one who has a heart?" he murmured.

Mirabeau fell back on the bed, with closed eyes. He might have been believed dead or swooning, but for the death-rattle in his breast. How came it that this man of athletic, herculean build should die? Was it not because he had held out his hand to stay the tumbling throne from toppling over? Was it not because he had offered his arm to that woman of misfortune known as Marie Antoinette? Had not Cagliostro predicted some such fate to Gilbert for Mirabeau? And the two strange creatures—Beausire, blasting the reputation, and Nicole, blasting the health of the great orator who had become the supporter of the monarchy. Were they not for him, Gilbert, a proof that all things which were obstacles to this man—or rather the idea he stood for—must go down before him as the Bastille had done?

Nevertheless he was going to try upon him the elixir of life which he owed to Cagliostro. It was irony to save his victim with his own remedy. The patient had opened his eyes.

"Nay," said he, "a few drops will be vain. You must give me the whole phial. I had the stuff analyzed, and found it was Indian hemp. I had some compounded for myself, and I have been taking it copiously. Not to live, but to dream."

"Unhappy man that I am," sighed Gilbert. "He has led to my dealing out poison to my friend."

"A sweet poison, by which I have lengthened out the last moments of my life a hundredfold. In my dream, I have enjoyed what has really escaped me: riches, power, and love. I do not know whether I ought to thank God for my life, but I thank you, doctor, for your drug. Fill up the glass and let me have it."

Gilbert presented the extract which the patient absorbed with gusto.

"Ah, doctor," he said after a short pause, as if the veil of the future were raised at the approach of eternity. "Blessed are those who die in this year, 1791! For they will have seen the sunny side of the Revolution. Never has a great one cost so little bloodshed up to now, because it is the mind that was conquered. But on the morrow, the war will be upon facts and in things. Perhaps you believe that the tenants of the Tuileries will mourn for me? Not at all. My death rids them of an engagement. With me, they had to rule in a certain way; I was less support than hindrance. She excused herself to her brother, for leaning on me. *Mirabeau believes that he is advising me—I am only amusing myself with him.*' That is why I wished that woman, her likeness, to be my mistress, and not my Queen.

"What a fine part he shall play in History who undertook to sustain the young nation with one hand, and the old monarchy in the other. Forcing them to tread the same goal—the happiness of the governed and the respect of the governors. It might have been possible, and might be but a dream, but I am convinced that I alone could have realized the dream. My sorrow is not in dying, but in dying with work unfinished. Who will glorify my idea, which is left mangled? The part of me that will be remembered will be the part that should be buried in oblivion—my wild, reckless, rakish life, and my obscene writings.

"I shall be blamed for having made a bond with the court, out of which comes gain for no man. I shall be judged, dying at forty-two, like one who lived man's full age. They will take me to task, as if instead of trying to walk on the waters in a storm, I had trodden a broad way paved with laws, statutes, and regulations. To whom shall I league my memory, to be cleansed and be an honor to my country?

"But I could do nothing without her, and she would not take my helping hand. I pledged myself like a fool, while she remained unfettered. But it is so—all is for the best. And if you will promise one thing, no regret will trouble my last breath."

"Good God, what would I not promise?"

"If my passing from life is tedious, make it easy. I ask the aid not only of the doctor, but of the man and the philosopher—promise to aid me. I do not wish to die dead, but living. And the last step will not be hard to take."

The doctor bent his head towards the speaker.

"I promised not to leave you, my friend. If heaven hath condemned you—though I hope we have not come to that point—leave to my affection, at the supreme instant, the care of accomplishing what I ought to do. If death comes, I shall be at hand also."

"Thanks," said the dying one, as if this were all he awaited.

The abundant dose of *cannabis indicus*[7] had restored speech to the doomed one, but this vitality of the mind vanished. And for three hours, the cold hand remained in the doctor's without a throb. Suddenly he felt a start—the awakening had come.

"*It will be a dreadful struggle,*" he thought.

Such was the agony in which the strong frame wrestled, that Gilbert forgot that he had promised to aid death, not to oppose it. Reminded of his pledge, he seized the pen to write a

---

7   Indian hemp

prescription for an opiate. Scarcely had he written the last words than Mirabeau rose on the pillow and asked for the pen. With his hand clenched by death he scrawled: "Flee, flee, flee!" He tried to sign but could only trace four letters of his name.

"For her," he gasped, holding out his convulsed arm towards his companion. He fell back without breath, movement or look—he was dead.

Gilbert turned to the spectators of this scene and said: "Mirabeau is no more." Taking the paper, whose destination he alone might divine, he rapidly departed from the death chamber.

Some seconds after the doctor's going, a great clamor arose in the street and was prolonged throughout Paris. The grief was intense and wide. The Assembly voted a public funeral, and the Pantheon, formerly Church of St. Genevieve, was selected for the great man's resting-place. Three years subsequently, the Convention sent the coffin to the Clamart Cemetery to be bundled among the corpses of the publicly executed. Petion claimed to have discovered a contra-revolutionary plot written in the hand of Mirabeau, and Congress reversed its previous judgment. They declared that genius could not condone corruption.

CHAPTER VII

The King's Messenger

On the morning of the second of April, an hour before Mirabeau yielded up his last breath, a man entered the Tuileries Palace like one to whom the ways were familiar, and took the private stairs to the King's apartments. One could tell he was a superior officer of the navy, because he was wearing the full dress uniform of a captain. There, by the study, a valet saw him and uttered a cry of surprise.

"Hue," he said, laying a finger on his lips, "can the King receive me?"

"His Majesty gave word that you were to be shown in whenever you arrived."

Hue opened a door, and as a proof that the King was alone, he called out: "The Count of Charny!"

"Let him enter," said the King. "I have been expecting him since yesterday."

Charny entered quickly, and said with respectful eagerness, "Sire, I am a few hours behindhand, but I hope to be forgiven when your Majesty hears the reasons for the delay."

"Come, come, my lord. I awaited you with impatience, it is true, but I was of your opinion beforehand that an important cause alone could delay your journey. You have come, and you are welcome."

He held out his hand which the courier kissed with reverence.

"Sire, I received your order early the day before yesterday, and I started at three A. M. yesterday from Montmedy by the post."

"That explains the few hours delay," observed the sovereign, smiling.

"Sire," went on the count, "I might have dashed on and made better speed, but I wanted to study the road, to remark the posting-houses where the work is well or ill done. I wished to jot the time down by the minute. I have noted everything, and am consequently in a position to answer on any point."

"Bravo, my lord," cried the King. "You are a first-rate servitor. But let me begin by showing how we stand here, you can give me the news of the position out there afterwards."

"Things are going badly, if I may guess by what I have heard," observed Charny.

"To such a degree that I am a prisoner in the place, my dear count. I was just saying to General Lafayette that I would rather be King at Metz than over France. But never mind, you have returned. You know my aunts have taken to flight? It is very plain why. You know the Assembly will allow no priests to officiate at the altar unless they take oaths to the country. The poor souls became frightened as Easter came near, thinking they risked damnation by confessing to a priest who had sworn to the Constitution. And I must confess, it was on my advice that they went to Rome.

"No law opposes their journey, and no one can think two poor women will much strengthen the party of the fugitive nobility. They charged Narbonne with getting them off, but I do not know how the movement was guessed. A visit of the same nature as we experienced at Versailles in October was projected upon them, but they happily got out by one door while the mob rushed in by another. Just think of the crosses! Not a vehicle was at hand, though three had been ordered to be ready. They had to go to Meudon from Bellevue on foot.

"They found carriages there and made the start. Three hours afterwards, there was a tremendous uproar in Paris. Those who went to stop the flight found the nest warm, but empty. Next day, the press fairly howled. Marat said that they were carrying away millions; Desmoulins, that they were taking the Dauphin. They were doing nothing of the sort. The two poor ladies had a few hundred thousand francs in their purses, and had enough to take care of without burdening themselves with a boy who might bring about their recognition. The proof was that they were recognized, without him. First at a place where they were let go through, and then at Arnay, where they were arrested. I had to write to the Assembly to get them passed, and in spite of my letter, the Assembly debated all day. However, they were authorized to continue their journey, on condition that the committee of the House should present a bill against quitting the kingdom."

"Yes," said Charny, "but I understood that, in spite of a magnificent speech from Mirabeau, the Assembly rejected the proposition."

"True, it was thrown out. But beside this slight triumph was a great humiliation for me. When the excitement was noticed over the departure of the two ladies, a few devoted friends—more than you may believe being left to me—some hundreds of noblemen hastened to the Tuileries and offered me their lives. The report was immediately spread that a conspiracy was discovered to spirit me away. Lafayette, who had been gulled into going to the Bastille under a story that an attempt to rebuild it was under way, came back here furious at the hoax. He entered with sword and bayonet! My poor friends were seized and disarmed. Pistols were found on some, stilettos on others, each having snatched up at home any weapon handy. But the day is written down in history as that of the Knights of the Dagger!"

"Oh Sire, in what dreadful times do we live," said Charny, shaking his head.

"Yes, and Mirabeau perhaps dying, maybe dead at present speaking."

"The more reason to hasten out of this cauldron."

"Just what we have decided on. Have you arranged with Bouille? I hope he is strong enough now. The opportunity was presented and I reinforced him."

"Yes, Sire. But the War Minister has crossed your orders. The Saxon Hussars have withdrawn from him, and the Swiss regiments refused. He had trouble to keep the Bouillon Foot at Montmedy Fort."

"Does he doubt now?"

"No Sire, but there are so many chances less. What does it matter? In these dashes, one must reckon on luck, and we still have a ninety percent chance. The question is if your Majesty holds to the Chalons Route, although the posting at Varennes is doubtful?"

"Bouille already knows my reasons for the preference."

"That is why I have minutely mapped out the route."

"The route-chart is a marvel of clearness, my dear count. I know the road as though I had myself traveled it."

"I have the following directions to add—"

"Let me look at them by the map." And he unfolded on the table a map drawn by hand with every natural feature laid in. It was a work of eight months. The two stooped over the paper.

"Sire, the real danger begins at St. Menehould and ceases at Stenay. On those eighteen leagues must be stationed the soldiers."

"Could they not be brought nearer Paris—say, up to Chalons?"

"It is difficult," was the response. "Chalons is too strong a place for even a hundred men to do anything efficacious to your safety if menaced. Besides, Bouille does not answer for anything beyond St. Menehould. All he can do is set his first troops at Sommevelle Bridge. That is the first post beyond Chalons."

"How much time will it take?"

"The King can go from Paris to Montmedy in thirty-six hours."

"What have you decided about the relay of horses at Varennes? We must be certain not to want for them; it is most important."

"I have investigated the spot and decided to place the horses on the other side of the little town. It will be better to dash through, coming full speed from Clermont, and change horses five hundred paces from the bridge. We can be guarded and defended if signaled by three or four men."

Charny gave the King a paper. It was Bouille's arrangement of the troop stations along the road for the royal escape. The cover would be that the soldiers were waiting to convoy some money sent by the War Minister.

"Everything has been foreseen," said the King delightedly. "But talking of money, do you know whether Bouille has received the million I sent him?"

"Yes, but as assigns are below par, he would lose twenty percent on the gross amount. He was able to get a faithful subject of your Majesty to cash, as if gold, a hundred thousand crowns' worth."

"And the rest?" inquired the King, eyeing the speaker.

"Count Bouille got his banker to take it; so that there will be no lack of the sinews of war."

"I thank you, my lord count," said the sovereign. "I should like to know the name of the faithful servitor who perhaps lessened his cash by giving the sum to Bouille."

"He is rich, and consequently there was no merit in what he did. The only condition he put in doing the act was to have his name kept back."

"Still you know him?"

"Yes, I know who it is."

"Then, Lord Charny," said the monarch with the hearty dignity which he sometimes showed, as he took a ring off his finger, "here is a jewel very dear to me. I took it off the finger of my dying father when his hand was chill in death. Its value is therefore that which I attach to it; it has no other. But for a soul which understands me, it will be more precious than the finest diamond. Repeat to the faithful servitor what I say, my lord, and give him this gem from me."

Charny's bosom heaved as he dropped on one knee to receive the ring from the royal hand. At this juncture the door opened. The King turned sharply, for a door to open thus was worse than infraction of etiquette; it was an insult only to be excused by great necessity. It was the Queen, pale and holding a paper. She let it drop with a cry of astonishment at seeing Count Charny at the feet of her consort.

The noble rose and saluted the lady, who faltered: "Charny here, in the King's rooms, in the Tuileries!" And she said to herself: "Without my knowing it!"

There was such sorrow in the tone, that Charny guessed the reason and took two steps towards her.

"I have just arrived and I was going to crave the King's permission for me to pay my respects to your Majesty," he said.

The blood reappeared on her cheeks. She had not heard that voice for a long while, and the sweet tone charmed her ears. She held out both hands towards him, but brought back one upon her heart from its beating too violently. Charny noticed all this in the short space required for the King to pick up the paper, which the draft from the door had floated to the side of the room. The King read without understanding.

"What is the meaning of the word 'Flee' three times written, and the fragment of a signature?" inquired he.

"Sire, it seems that Mirabeau died ten minutes ago, and that is the advice he sends you."

"It is good advice," returned the King, "and this time the instant to put it into execution has come."

The Queen looked at them both, and said to the count: "Follow me, my lord."

CHAPTER VIII

The Husband's Promise

The Queen sank upon a divan when she had arrived within her own apartments, making a sign for Charny to close the door. Scarcely was she seated before her heart overflowed, and she burst into sobs. They were so sincere and forcible that they went down into the depths of Charny's heart, and sought for his former love. Such passions burning in a man never completely die out, unless from one of those dreadful shocks which turn love to loathing.

He was in that strange dilemma which they will appreciate who have stood in the same: between old love and the new. He loved his wife with all the pity in his bosom, and he pitied the Queen with all his soul. He could not help feeling regret and giving words of consolation. But he saw that reproach pierced through this sobbing. That recrimination came to light among the tears, reminding him of the exaction of this love, the absolute will, the regal despotism mingled with the expressions of tenderness and proofs of passion. He steeled himself against the exaction and took up arms against the despotism, entering into the strife against the will.

He compared all this with Andrea's sweet, unalterable countenance. Charny preferred the statue of Andrea, though he believed it to be of snow, to this glowing bronze of Marie Antoinette, heated from the furnace. The Queen seemed ever ready to dart from its eyes the lightnings of love, pride and jealousy.

This time the Queen wept without saying anything. It was more than eight months since she had seen him. Before this, for two or three years she had believed that they could not separate without their hearts breaking. Her only consolation had been that he was working for her sake in doing some deed for the King. But it was a weak consolation.

She wept for the sake of relief, for her pent-up tears would have choked her if she had not poured them forth. Was it joy or pain that held her silent? Both, perhaps, for many mighty emotions dissolve in tears.

With more love even than respect, Charny went up to her, took one of her hands away from her face, and said as he applied his lips to it: "Madam, I am proud and happy to say that not an hour has been without toil for you since I went hence."

"Oh, Charny," retorted the Queen, "there was a time when you might have been less busy on my account, but you would have thought the more of me."

"I was charged by the King with grave responsibility, which imposed the more strict silence until the business was accomplished. It is done at present. I can see and speak with you now, but I might not write a letter up to this period."

"It is a fine sample of loyalty, and I regret that it should be performed at the expense of another sentiment, George," she said with melancholy.

She pressed his hand tenderly. Meanwhile, she was eyeing him with that gaze for which once he would have flung away the life still at her service. She noticed that he was not the courier dusty and bloody from spurring, but the courtier, spic and span according to the rules of the Royal Household. This complete attire visibly fretted the woman, while it must have satisfied the exacting Queen.

"Where do you come from?" she asked.

"Montmedy, in post-chaise."

"Half across the kingdom. And you are spruce, brushed and dandified like one of Lafayette's aid-de-camps. Were the news you brought so unimportant as to let you dally at the toilet table?"

"Very important; but I feared that if I stepped out of the mud be-splattered post-chaise in the palace yard, all disordered with travel, suspicion would be roused. The King had told me that you are closely guarded, and that made me congratulate myself on walking in, clad in my naval uniform like an officer coming to present his devoirs[8] after a week or two on leave."

She squeezed his hand convulsively. The Queen had a question to put to him, but it appeared so far from important.

"I forgot that you had a Paris house. Of course you dropped in at Coq-Heron Street, where the countess is keeping house?"

---

8   An act or expression of respect or courtesy

Charny was ready to spring away like a high-mettled steed spurred in the raw. But there was so much hesitation and pain in her words that he had to pity one so haughty for suffering so much, and for showing her feelings though she was so strong-minded.

"Madam," he replied, with profound sadness not wholly caused by her pain. "I thought I had stated before my departure that the Countess of Charny's residence is not mine. I stopped at my brother Isidore's to change my dress."

The Queen uttered a cry of joy and slid down on her knees, carrying his hand to her lips, but he caught her up in both arms and exclaimed: "Oh, what are you doing?"

"I thank you—ask me not for what! Do you ask me for what? For the only moment of thorough delight I have felt since your departure. God knows this is folly, and foolish jealousy, but it is most worthy of pity. You were jealous once, though you forget it. Oh, you men are happy when you are jealous, because you can fight with your rivals and kill or be slain. But we women can only weep, though we perceive that our tears are useless, if not dangerous. For our tears part us from our beloved, rather than wash us nearer. Our grief is the vertigo of love—it hurls us towards the abyss which we see without avail. I thank you again, George; you see that I am happy anew and weep no more."

She tried to laugh, but in her repining she had forgotten how to be merry. And the tone was so sad and doleful that the count shuddered.

"Be blessed, O God!" she said, "for he would not have the power to love me from the day when he pities me."

Charny felt he was dragged down a steep hill, where in time he would realize the impossibility of checking himself. He made an effort to stop, like those skaters who lean back on their heels at the risk of breaking through the ice.

"Will you not permit me to offer the fruit of my long absence by explaining what I have been happy to do for your sake?" he said.

"Oh Charny, I like better to have things as I said just now. But you are right: the woman must not too long forget she is a

Queen. Speak, ambassador, the woman has obtained all she had a right to claim—the Queen listens."

The count related how he had surveyed the way for the flight of the Royal Family, and how all was ready. She listened with deep attention and fervent gratitude. It seemed to her that mere devotion could not go so far. That it must be ardent and unquiet love to foresee such obstacles, and invent the means to cope with and overcome them.

"So you are quite happy to save me?" she asked at the end, regarding him with supreme affection.

"Oh, can you ask me that? It is the dream of my ambition, and it will be the glory of my life if I attain it."

"I would rather it were simply the reward of your love," replied Marie Antoinette with melancholy. "But let that pass! You ardently desire this great deed of the rescue of the Royal Family to be performed by you?"

"I await but your consent to set aside my life to it."

"I understand it, my dear one," said the sovereign. "Your dedication ought to be free from all alien sentiment and material affection. My husband and our children should not doubt that your hand would be stretched out towards them if they slipped on the road we are to travel in company. I place their lives and mine in your custody, as to a brother. But you will feel some pity for me?"

"Pity?"

"You cannot wonder that all should fail because I had not your promise that you loved me? One needs courage, patience and coolness—for in the night one may see the specters which would not frighten in the day."

"Lady," interrupted Charny, "above all I aim at your Majesty's bliss, and the glory of achieving the task I have begun. And I confess that I am sorry the sacrifice I make is so slight; but I swear not to see the Countess of Charny without your Majesty's permission."

Coldly and respectfully saluting the monarch's consort, he retired without her trying to detain him, so chilled was she by his tone. Hardly had he shut the door after him, than she wrung her hands and ruefully moaned: "Oh, rather that he made the vow not to see me, but loved me as he loves her!"

CHAPTER IX

Off and Away

In spite of all precautions, or perhaps because they necessitated changes in the usual order of things, suspicion was engendered in Paris by the plot at the palace. Lafayette went straight to the King, who mocked at his half-accusations. Bailly sent a denunciatory letter to the Queen, having become quite courteous, not to say a courtier.

About nine in the night of the 20th of June, two persons were conversing in the sitting-room of the Countess of Charny, in Coq-Heron Street. She was apparently calm but was deeply moved, as she spoke with Isidore, who wore a courier's dress. It was composed of a buff leather riding jacket, tight breeches of buckskin and top-boots, and he carried a hunting-sword. His round laced hat was held in his hand.

"But in short, viscount, since your brother has been two months and a half in town, why has he not come here?" she persisted.

"He has sent me very often for news of your health."

"I know that, and I am grateful to both of you. But it seems to me that he ought to come to say good-bye if he is going on another journey."

"Of course, my lady, but it is impossible. So he has charged me to do that."

"Is the journey to be a long one?"

"I am ignorant."

"I said 'yours' because it looks from your equipment that you are going too."

"I shall probably leave town this midnight."

"Do you accompany your brother or go by another route?"

"I believe we take the same."

"Will you tell him you have seen me?"

"Yes, my lady. For he would not forgive me omitting to perform the errand of asking after you, judging by the solicitude he put in charging me, and the reiterated instructions he gave me."

She ran her hands over her eyes, sighed, and said after short meditation: "Viscount, as a nobleman, you will comprehend the reach of the question I am putting. Answer as you would were

I really your sister; as you would to heaven. In the journey he undertakes, does my Lord Charny run any serious danger?"

"Who can tell where no danger is or is not in these times?" evasively responded young Charny. "On the morning of the day when my brother Valence was struck down, he would have surely answered No, if he had been asked if he stood in peril. Yet he was laid low in death by the morrow. At present, danger leaps up from the ground, and we face death without knowing whence it came, and without calling it."

Andrea turned pale and said, "There is danger of death, then? You think so if you do not say it."

"I think, lady, that if you have something important to tell my brother, the enterprise we are committed to is serious enough to make you charge me by word of mouth, or writing with your wish be transmitted to him."

"It is well: viscount, I ask five minutes," said the countess, rising.

With the mechanical, slow step habitual to her, she went into her room and shut the door. The young gentleman looked at his watch with uneasiness.

"A quarter past nine, and the King expects me at half after," he muttered: "luckily it is but a step to the palace."

But the countess did not take the time she had stated. In a few seconds, she returned with a sealed letter, and said with solemnity, "Viscount, I entrust this to your honor."

Isidore stretched out his hand to take it.

"Stay, and clearly understand what I am telling you," said Andrea. "If your brother count fulfills the undertaking, there is nothing to be said to him beyond what I stated—sympathy for his loyalty, respect for his devotion and admiration for his character. If he be wounded"—here her voice faltered—"badly hurt, you will ask the favor for me to join him, whereupon you will send a messenger who can conduct me straight to him for I shall start directly. If he be mortally injured—" here emotion checked her voice: "Hand him this note; if he cannot read it, read it to him, for I want him to know this before he dies. Your pledge as a nobleman to do this, my lord?"

"On my honor," replied Isidore, as much affected as the speaker.

He kissed her hand and went out. When she was sure he was gone, Andrea cried to herself, "Oh, if he should die, I must have him know that I love him!"

At the same time as he quitted his sister-in-law's and thrust the letter in his breast, beside another of which he had read the address by the light of a street lamp, two men, dressed just like himself, were ushered into the Queen's boudoir, but by different ways. These two did not know each other, but judging that the same business thus arrayed them, they bowed to one another.

Immediately another door opened, and in walked Viscount Charny. He was as unknown to the other two, Royal Lifeguardsmen Malden and Valory, as they were to each other. Isidore alone knew the aim of their being brought together, and the common design. No doubt he would have replied to the inquiries they were going to put, but the door opened and Louis XVI appeared.

"Gentlemen," said he to Malden and Valory, "excuse me disposing of you without your permission, but you belonged to my guards and I hold you to be faithful servitors of the crown. So I suggested your going to a certain tailor's and trying one courier's costume, which you would find there, and be at the palace at half-past nine this evening. Your presence proves that you accept the errand with which I have to charge you."

The two guardsmen bowed.

"Sire," said Valory, "your Majesty was fully aware that he had no need to consult his gentlemen about laying down their lives on his behalf."

"Sire, my brother-soldier answers for me in answering for himself, and I presume for our third companion," said Malden.

"Your third companion, gentlemen, is an acquaintance good to form, being Viscount Charny, whose brother was slain defending the Queen's door at Versailles. We are habituated to the devotion of members of his family, so that we do not thank them for it."

"According to this," went on Valory, "my Lord of Charny would know the motive of our gathering, while we are ignorant and eager to learn."

"Gentlemen," said the King, "you know that I am a prisoner to the National Guard, the Assembly, the Mayor of Paris, the mob, and to anybody else who is currently the master. I rely on you to help me shake off this humiliation, and recover my liberty. My fate, that of the Queen and of our children, rests in your hands. All is ready for me to make away to-night. Will you undertake to get me out of this place?"

"Give the orders, my lord," said the three young men.

"You will understand that we cannot go forth together. We are to meet at the corner of St. Nicaise Street, where Count Charny awaits us with a hired carriage. You, viscount, will take care of the Queen, and use the name of Melchior. You, Malden, under the name of Jean, escort Lady Elizabeth and the Princess Royal. You, Valory, guard Lady Tourzel and the Dauphin, they will call you François. Do not forget your new names and await further instructions."

He gave his hand all round to them and went out, leaving three men ready to die for him. He went to dress, while the Queen and the others were also attiring themselves plainly, with large hats to conceal their faces. Louis put on a plain grey suit with short breeches, grey stockings and buckled shoes. For the week past, his valet Hue had gone in and out in a similar dress, so as to get the sentinels used to the sight. He went out by the private door of Lord Villequier, who had fled the country six months before.

In provision of this flight, a room of his quarters had been set aside on the eleventh of the month. Here were the Queen and the others assembled. This flat was believed uninhabited, but the King had the keys. The sentries were accustomed to see a number of the servants quit the palace in a flock at about eleven.

Isidore Charny, who had been over the road with his brother, would ride on ahead. He would get the post-boys ready so that no delay would be incurred. Malden and Valory, on the driver's box, were to pay the postilions. They were given extra money, as the carriage for the journey was a specially built one, and very heavy from having to carry so many persons. Count

Charny was to ride inside, ready for all emergencies. He would be well armed, like the three outriders. A pair of pistols for each were to be in the vehicle. At a fair pace, they reckoned to be at Chalons in thirteen hours.

All promised to obey the instructions settled between Charny and the Count of Choiseul. Lights were blown out, and all groped their way at midnight into Villequier's rooms. But the door by which they ought to have passed straightway was locked. The King had to go to his smithy for keys and a pick-lock. When he opened the door, he looked round triumphantly in the light of a little night-lamp.

"I will not say that a locksmith's art is not good sometimes," said the Queen; "but it is also well to be the King at others."

They had to regulate the order of the sallying forth. Lady Elizabeth led, with the Princess Royal. At twenty paces she was followed by Lady Tourzel and the Dauphin. Malden came on behind to run to their succor. The children stepped on tiptoe and trembling, with love before and behind them, to enter the ring of glare from the lamps. A reflector was lighting the palace doors at the courtyard, but they passed before the sentinel without his appearing to trouble about them.

At the Carrousel Gate, the sentinel turned his back and they could easily pass. Had he recognized the illustrious fugitives? They believed so, and sent him a thousand blessings. On the farther side of the wicket they perceived Charny's uneasy face. He was wearing a large blue coat with cape, called a Garrick from the English actor having made it popular, and his head was covered with a tarpaulin hat.

"Thank God, you have got through," he said, "what about the King, and the Queen?"

"They follow us," said Lady Elizabeth.

"Come," said he, leading them to the hack in St. Nicaise Street.

Another was beside theirs, and its driver might be a spy. So Malden jumped into it and ordered the man to drive him to the Opera-house as if he were a servant going to join his master there. Scarcely had he driven off before the others saw a plain sort of fellow in a gray suit, with his hat cocked over his nose and his hands in his pocket, saunter out of the same gate as had given passage to Lady Elizabeth, like a clerk who was strolling home after his work was over. This was the King, attended by Valory.

Charny went up to meet them; for he had recognized Valory, and not the King. He was one of those who always wish to see a king acting king-like. He sighed with pain, almost with shame, as he murmured: "Come, Sire, come. Where is the Queen?" he asked of Valory.

"Coming with your brother."

"Good. Take the shortest road and wait for us at St. Martin's Gate; I will go by the longer way round. We meet at the coach."

Both arrived at the rendezvous and waited half an hour for the Queen. We shall not try to paint the fugitives' anxiety. Charny, on whom the whole responsibility fell, was like a maniac. He wanted to go back and make inquiries, but the King restrained him. The little prince wept and cried for his mother. His sister and the two ladies could not console him. Their terror doubled when they saw Lafayette's carriage dash by, surrounded by soldiers, some bearing torches.

When at the palace gates, Viscount Charny wanted to turn to the left. The Queen, on his arm, stopped him and said that the count was waiting at the waterside gate of the Tuileries. She was so sure of what she asserted that doubt entered his mind.

"Be very careful, lady, for any error may be deadly to us," he said.

"I heard him say by the waterside," she repeated.

So he let her drag him through three courtyards, separated by thick walls and with chains at each opening, which should have been guarded by sentinels. They had to scramble through the gaps and clamber over the chains. Not one of the watchers had the idea of saying anything to them. How could they believe that a buxom woman in such dress as a housemaid would wear, and climbing over the chains on the arm of a strapping young chap in livery, was the Queen of the French? On arriving at the water's edge they found it deserted.

"He must mean the other side of the river," said the crazed Queen.

Isidore wanted to return, but he said as if in a vertigo: "No, no, there it is!"

She drew him upon the Royal Bridge, which they crossed to find the other shore as blank as the nigher one.

"Let us look up this street," said she.

She forced Isidore to go up the Ferry Street a little. At the end of a hundred paces she owned that she was wrong, but she stopped, panting. Her powers almost fled her.

"Now, take me where you will," she said.

"Courage, my lady," said Isidore.

"It is not courage I lack so much as strength. Oh, heaven, will I never get my breath again," she gasped.

Isidore paused, for he knew that the second wind she panted was as necessary to her as to the hunted deer.

"Take breath, madam," he said. "We have time, for my brother would wait till daylight for your sake."

"Then you believe that he loves me?" she exclaimed rashly, while pressing her arm against her breast.

"I believe that his life is yours as mine is, and that the feeling in others which is love and respect, becomes adoration in him."

"Thanks," she said, "that does me good! I breathe again. On, on!"

With a feverish step, she retraced the path they had gone, and they went out by the small gate of the Carousel. The large open space was covered with stalls and prowling cabs till midnight. But it was now deserted and gloomy. Suddenly they heard a great din of carriages and horses. They saw a light: no doubt the flambeaux accompanying the vehicles.

Isidore wanted to keep in the dark, but the Queen pressed forward. He dragged her into the depths of the gateway, but the torchlight flooded this cave with its beams. In the middle of the escort of cavalry, half reclining in a carriage, was Marquis Lafayette. As it whizzed by, Isidore felt an arm, strong with will if not real power, elbow him aside. It was the Queen's left arm, while with a cane in her right hand she struck the carriage wheels.

"A fig for you, Jailer!" she said. "I am out of your prison!"

"What are you doing, and what are you risking?" ejaculated the Viscount.

"I am taking my revenge," said the silly victim of spite, "and one may risk a good deal for that."

Behind the last torch-bearer she bounded along, radiant as a goddess, and gleeful as a child.

CHAPTER X

On the Highway

The Queen had not taken ten paces beyond the gateway before a man in a blue garrick caught her convulsively by the arm. His face was hidden by a tarpaulin hat, and he dragged her to a hackney coach stationed at the St. Nicaise corner. It was Count Charny.

After this half hour of delay, they expected to see the Queen come up dying, downcast and prostrated. But they saw her merry and gladsome. The cut of the cane which she had given a carriage-wheel, and fancied was on the rider, had made her forget her fatigue. Likewise her blunder, her obstinacy, the lost time, and the consequences of the delay.

Charny pointed out a saddled horse, which a servant was holding at a little distance to his brother, who mounted and dashed ahead to pioneer the way. He would have to get the horses ready at Bondy. Seeing him go, the Queen uttered some words of thanks which he did not hear.

"Let us be off, madam; we have not one second to lose," said Charny. He had that firmness of will mixed with respect, which great men use for grand occasions.

The Queen entered the hackney-coach, which held five already: the King, Lady Elizabeth, the Princess Royal, her brother and Lady Tourzel. She had to sit at the back with her son on her lap, with the King beside her. The two ladies and the girl were on the front seat. Fortunately, the hackney carriages were roomy in those days.

Charny got upon the box, and to avert suspicion, turned the horses round and had them driven to the gate circuitously. Their special conveyance was waiting for them there, on the side-road leading to the ditch. This part was lonesome. The traveling carriage had the door open, and Malden and Valory were on the steps. In an instant, the six travelers were out on the road. Charny drove the hack to the ditch before returning to the party.

They royalty were all inside, Malden got up behind, and Valory joined Charny on the box. The four horses went off at a rattling good pace as a quarter past one sounded from the church clock. In an hour they were at Bondy, where Isidore had better teams ready. He saw the royal coach come up.

Charny got down to get inside the coach, as had been settled. But Lady Tourzel, who was to be sent back to town alone, had not been consulted. With all her profound devotion to the Royal Family, she was unalterable on points of court etiquette. She stated that her duty was to look after the royal children, whom she was bound not to quit for a single instant, unless by the King's express order, or the Queen's. But there being no precedent of a Queen having ordered the royal governess away from her charges, she would not go. The Queen quivered with impatience, for she doubly wished Charny in the vehicle. As a lover, who would make it pleasanter, and as a Queen, as he would guard her. Louis did not dare pronounce on the grave question. He tried to get out of the dilemma by a side-issue. Lady Tourzel stood ready to yield to the King's command, but he dared not command her, so strong are the minutest regulations in the courtly-bred.

"Arrange anyway you like, count," said the fretful Queen, "only you must be with us."

"I will follow close to the carriage, like a simple servant," he replied. "I will return to town to get a horse by the one my brother came therefrom. And changing my dress, I will join you at full speed."

"Is there no other means?" said Marie Antoinette in despair.

"I see none," remarked the King.

Lady Tourzel took her seat triumphantly, and the stage-coach started off. The importance of this discussion had made them forget to serve out the firearms, which went back to Paris in the hack. By daybreak, which was three o'clock, they changed horses at Meaux, where the King was hungry. They brought their own provisions in the boot of the coach, cold veal and bread and wine, which Charny had seen to. But there were no knives and forks, and the King had to carve with "Jean," that is, Malden's hunting-knife. During this, the Queen leaned out to see if Charny were returning.

"What are you thinking of, madam?" inquired the King, who had found the two guards would not take refreshment.

"That Lafayette is in a way at this hour," replied the lady.

But nothing showed that their departure had been seen. Valory said that all would go well.

"Cheer up!" he said, as he got upon the box with Malden, and off they rolled again.

At eight o'clock, they reached the foot of a long slope, where the King had everyone get out of the coach to walk up. Scattered over the road, there were pretty children romping and playing. A sister was resting on her brother's arm and smiling. The pensive women looked backward, and all was lit up by the June sun, while the forest flung a transparent shade upon the highway. They seemed a family going home to an old manor to resume a regular and peaceful life, and not a King and Queen of France fleeing from the throne which would be converted into their scaffold.

An accident was soon to stir up the dormant passions in the bosoms of the party. The Queen suddenly stopped, as though her feet had struck root. A horseman appeared a quarter-league away, wrapped in the cloud of dust which his horse's hoofs threw up.

Marie Antoinette dared not say: "It is Count Charny!" but she did exclaim, "News from Paris!"

Everybody turned round except the Dauphin, who was chasing a butterfly. Compared with its capture, the news from the capital little mattered. Being shortsighted, the King drew a small spy-glass from his pocket.

"I believe it is only Lord Charny," he said.

"Yes, it is he," said the Queen.

"Go on," said the other. "He will catch up to us and we have no time to lose."

The Queen dared not suggest that the news might be of value. It was only a few seconds at stake anyhow, for the rider galloped up as fast as his horse could go. He stared as he came up, for he could not understand why the party should be scattered all over the road. He arrived as the huge vehicle stopped at the top of the ridge to take up the passengers.

It was indeed Charny, as the Queen's heart and the King's eyes had told them. He was now wearing a green riding coat with flap collar, a broad brimmed hat with steel buckle, white waistcoat, tight buckskin breeches, and high boots reaching above the knee. His usually dead white complexion was animated by the ride, and sparks of the same flame which reddened his cheeks shot from his eyes.

He looked like a conqueror as he rushed along; the Queen thought she had never seen him look handsomer. She heaved a deep sigh as the horseman leaped off his horse and saluted the King. Turning, he bowed to the Queen. All grouped themselves round him, except two guardsmen who stood aloof in respect.

"Come near, gentlemen," said the King. "What news Count Charny brings concerns us all."

"To begin with, all goes well," said Charny. "At two in the morning, none suspected our flight."

They breathed easier, and the questions were multiplied. He related that he had entered the town and been stopped by a patrol of volunteers, who were convinced that the King was still in the palace. He entered his own room and changed his dress. The aid of Lafayette, who first had a doubt, had become calm and dismissed the extra guards.

Charny had returned on the same horse, from the difficulty of getting a fresh one so early. It almost foundered, poor beast, but he reached Bondy upon it. There he took a fresh one and continued his ride, with nothing alarming along the road. The Queen found that such good news deserved the favor of her extending her hand to the bearer. He kissed it respectfully, and she turned pale. Was it from joy that he had returned, or with sorrow that he did not press it? When the vehicle started off, Charny rode by the side.

At the next relay house, all was ready except a saddle horse for the count, which Isidore had not foreseen the want of. There would be delay for one to be found. The vehicle went off without him, but he overtook it in five minutes. It was settled that he should follow and not escort it. Still he kept close enough for the Queen to see him if she put her head out of the window, and thus he exchanged a few words with the illustrious couple when the pace allowed it.

Charny changed horses at Montmirail, and was dashing on thinking it had a good start of him when he almost ran into it. It had been pulled up from a trace breaking. He dismounted and found a new leather in the boot, filled with repairing stuff. The two guardsmen profited by the halt to ask for their weapons, but the King opposed their having them. On the objection that the vehicle might be stopped, he replied that he would not have blood spilled on his account. They lost half an hour by this mishap, when seconds were priceless, and arrived at Chalons by two o'clock.

"All will go well if we reach Chalons without being stopped," the King had said.

Here the King showed himself for a moment. In the crowd around the huge conveyance, two men watched him with sustained attention. One of them suddenly went away while the other came up.

"Sire, you will wreck all if you show yourself thus," he said. "Make haste, you lazybones," he cried to the post-boys. "This is a pretty way to serve those who pay you handsomely."

He set to work, aiding the hostlers. It was the postmaster. At last the horses were hooked on, and the post-boys in their saddles and boots. The first tried to start his pair, when they went clean off their feet. They got them up and clear again, when the second span went off their feet! This time the post-boy was caught under them. Charny, who was looking on in silence, seized hold of the man and dragged him out of his heavy boots, remaining under the horse.

"What kind of horses have you given us?" demanded he of the posting-house master.

"The best I had in," replied the man.

The horses were so entangled with the traces, that the more they pulled at them the worse the snarl became. Charny flew down to the spot.

"Unbuckle and take off everything," he said, "and harness up afresh. We shall get on quicker so."

The postmaster lent a hand in the work, cursing with desperation. Meanwhile, the other man who had been looking on had run to the mayor, whom he told that the Royal Family were in a coach passing through the town. Luckily the official was far from being a republican, and did not care to take any responsibility on himself. Instead of making the assertion sure, he shilly-shallied so that time was lost, and finally arrived as the coach disappeared round the corner. But more than twenty minutes had been frittered away.

Alarm was in the royal party. The Queen thought that the downfall of the two pair of horses were akin to the four candles going out one after another, which she had taken to portend the death of herself, her husband and their two children. Still, on getting out of the town, she and the King and his sister had all exclaimed: "We are saved!"

But a hundred paces beyond, a man shouted in at the window: "Your measures are badly taken—you will be arrested!"

The Queen screamed but the man jumped into the hedge and was lost to sight. Happily they were but four leagues from Sommevelle Bridge, where Choiseul and forty hussars were to be posted. But it was three in the afternoon and they were nearly four hours late.

CHAPTER XI

The Queen's Hairdresser

On the morning of the twenty-first of June, the Count of Choiseul was told that a messenger from the Queen was at last at his house in Paris. Choiseul had notified the King that he could wait no longer, he must pick up his detachments along the road and fall back towards Bouille.

The messenger was Leonard, the Queen's hairdresser. He was a favorite who enjoyed immense credit at the court, but the duke had wished for a more weighty confidant. Alas, how could the Queen go into exile without the artist who alone could build up her hair into one of those towers which caused her to be the envy of her sex, and the stupefaction of the sterner one?

Leonard was wearing a round hat pulled down to his eyes, and an enormous "wraprascal[9]," which he explained was the property of his brother. The Queen, in confiding to him her jewels, had ordered him to disguise himself. He therefore placed himself under the command of Choiseul. His instructions were not only verbal, but also listed in a note which the duke read and burned. He ordered a cab to be made ready, and when the servant reported it at the door, he said to the hairdresser: "Come, my dear Leonard."

"But where?"

"A little way out of town where your art is required."

"But the diamonds?"

"Bring them along."

"But my brother will come home and see I have taken his best hat and overcoat—he will wonder what has become of me."

"Let him wonder! Did not the Queen bid you obey me as herself?"

"True, but Lady Ange will be expecting me to do up her hair. Nobody can make anything of her scanty wisp but me, and —"

"Lady Ange must wait till her hair grows again."

Without paying farther heed to his lamentations, the lord forced Leonard into his cab, and the horse started off at a fast gait.

---

9   A loose greatcoat worn by people of elegance about 1740, in supposed imitation of the coarse coats of the poorer people

When they stopped to renew the horse, he believed they were going to the world's end, though the duke confessed that their destination was the frontier. At Montmirail they were to pass the balance of the night, and indeed, beds were ready at the inn. Leonard began to feel better, in pride at having been chosen for such an important errand.

At eleven they reached Sommevelle Bridge, where Choiseul got out to put on his uniform. His hussars had not yet arrived. Leonard watched his preparations, particularly his freshening the pistol primings, with sharp disquiet and heaved sighs, which touched the hearer.

"It is time to let you into the truth, Leonard. You are true to your masters, so you may as well know that they will be here in a couple of hours. The King, the Queen, Lady Elizabeth, and the royal children. You know what dangers they were running, and dangers they are running still, but in two hours they will be saved. I am awaiting a hussar detachment to be brought by Lieut. Goguelat. We will have dinner, and take our time over it."

But they heard the bugle, and the hussars arrived. Goguelat brought six blank royal warrants, and the order from Bouille for Choiseul to be obeyed like himself by all military officers, whatever their ranking seniority. The horses were hobbled, wine and eatables were served out to the troopers, and Choiseuil sat at table.

Not that the lieutenant's news was good. He had found ferment everywhere along the road. For more than a year, rumors of the King's flight had circulated in the country as well as in town, and the stationing of the soldiers had aroused talk. In one township, the village church bells had sounded the alarm.

This was calculated to dull even a Choiseuil's appetite. So he got up from the board in an hour, as the clock struck half after twelve, and left Lieut. Boudet to take care of the horses. He went out on a hill by the town entrance which commanded a good view. Every five minutes he pulled out his watch, and each time Leonard groaned: "Oh, my poor masters, they will not come. Something bad has happened them."

His despair added to the duke's disquiet. Three o'clock came without any tidings. It will be remembered that this was the hour when the King left Chalons. While Choiseul was fretting, fate was preparing an event which had much to do with influencing the drama in this performance.

A few days before, some peasants on the Duchess of Elbœuf's estate, near Sommevelle Bridge, had refused payment of some nonredeemable taxes. They were threatened with the sheriff calling in the military. But the Federation business had done its work, and the inhabitants of the neighborhood vowed to make common cause with their brothers of the plow. They came armed to resist the process-servers.

On seeing the hussars ride in, the clowns thought that they were here for this purpose. So they sent runners to the surrounding villages, and at three o'clock, the alarm-bells were booming all over the country. Choiseul went back on hearing this, and found Lieut. Boudet uneasy. Threats were heard against the hussars, who were the most hated corps in the army. The crowd bantered them, and sang a song at them which was made for the occasion: "Than the hussars there is no worse, But we don't care for them a curse!"

Other persons, better informed or keener, began to whisper that the cavalry were here not to execute a writ on the Elbœuf tillers, but to wait for the King and Queen coming through. Meanwhile four o'clock struck without any courier with intelligence. The count put Leonard in his cab with the diamonds, and sent him on to Varennes with order to say all he could to the commanders of each military troop on the road.

To calm the agitation, Choiseul informed the mob that he and his company were there, not to assist the sheriff, but to guard a treasure which the War Minister was sending along. This word "treasure," with its double meaning, confirmed suspicions on one side while allaying irritability on the other. In a short time, he saw that his men were so outnumbered and hedged in, that they could do nothing in such a mass. They would have been powerless to protect the Royal Family if they came then. His orders were to "act so that the King's carriage should pass without hindrance," while his presence was becoming an obstacle instead of protection.

Even if the King came up, Choiseul had better be out of the way. Indeed, his departure would remove the block from the highway. But he needed an excuse for the going. The postmaster was there among half-a-dozen leading citizens whom a word would turn into active foes. He was close to Choiseul who inquired: "My friend, did you hear anything about this military money-chest coming through?"

"This very morning," replied the man, "the stage-coach came along for Metz with a hundred thousand crowns. Two gendarmes rode with it."

"You don't say so?" cried the nobleman, amazed at luck so befriending him.

"It is so true that I was one of the escort," struck in a gendarme.

"Then the Minister preferred that way of transmitting the cash," said Choiseul, turning to his lieutenant, quietly. "And we were sent only as a blind to highwaymen. As we are no longer needed, I think we can be off. Boot and saddle, my men!"

The troop marched out with trumpets sounding, and the count at the head. As the clock struck half-past five, he branched off the road to avoid St. Menehould, where great hubbub was reported to prevail. At this very instant, Isidore Charny, spurring and whipping a horse which had taken two hours to cover four leagues, dashed up to the posthouse to get another. Asking about a squad of hussars, he was told that it had marched slowly out of the place a quarter of an hour before. Leaving orders about the horses for the carriage, he rode off at full speed of the fresh steed, hoping to overtake the count. Choiseul had taken the side road precisely as Isidore arrived at the post, so that the viscount never met him.

CHAPTER XII

Mischance

Ten minutes after young Charny rode out, the King's coach rumbled in. As the duke had foreseen, the crowd had dissolved almost completely. Knowing that a detachment of soldiery was to be at Sommevelle, Charny had thought he need not linger. He had galloped beside the door, urging on the postilions, and keeping them up to the hand-gallop. On arriving and seeing neither Choiseul nor the escort, the King stuck his head out of the window.

"For mercy's sake, do not show yourself," said Charny. "Let me inquire."

In five minutes he returned from the posting house where he had learned all, and he repeated it to the monarch. They understood that the count had withdrawn to leave the road open. No doubt he had fallen back on St. Menehould, where they ought to hasten to find him with the hussars and dragoons.

"What am I to do?" asked Charny, as they were about to proceed again. "Does the Queen order me to go ahead, or ride in the rear?"

"Do not leave me," said the Queen.

He bowed, and rode by the carriage side. During this time, Isidore rode on, gaining on the vehicle. He feared that the people of St. Menehould would also take umbrage at having the soldiers in their town. He was not wrong.

The first thing he perceived was that there was a goodly number of National Guards scattered about the streets. They were the first seen since he left the capital. The whole town seemed in a stir, and on the opposite side, drums were beating. He dashed through the streets without appearing to notice the tumult. Crossing the square, he stopped at the posting house.

On a bench in the square, he noticed a dozen dragoons—not in their helmets, but fatigue in caps, sitting at ease. Up at a ground floor window lounged Marquis Dandoins, with a riding whip in his hand. Isidore passed without seeming to look, presuming that the captain would recognize the royal courier by his uniform and not need any other hint. At the post-house was a young man whose hair was cut short in the Emperor Titus fashion, which the Patriots adopted in the period. He wore his beard all round the lower face from ear to ear. He was in a dressing gown.

"What do you want?" challenged the black-whiskered man, seeing that the new-comer was looking round.

"To speak to the postmaster."

"He is out just now, but I am his son, Jean Baptiste Drouet. If I can replace him, speak."

He had emphasized his name as though he foreknew that it would take a place on the historic page.

"I want six horses for two carriages coming after me."

Drouet nodded to show that he would fulfill the order, and walked into the stable yard, calling out: "Turn out there! Six horses for carriages, and a nag for the courier."

At this nick, Marquis Dandoins hurriedly came up to Isidore.

"You are preceding the King's coach, I suppose?" he questioned.

"Yes, my lord, and I am surprised to see that you and your men are not in the battle array."

"We have not been notified. Besides, very ugly manifestations have been made around us—attempts to make my men mutiny. What am I to do?"

"Why, as the King passes, guard the vehicle, act as circumstances dictate, and start off half an hour after the Royal Family to guard the rear." But he interrupted himself saying: "Hush, we are spied. Perhaps we have been overheard. Get away to your squadron and do all you can to keep your men steadfast."

Indeed, Drouet was at the kitchen door where this dialogue was held. Dandoins walked away. At this period, the cracking of whips was heard. The royal coach rolled up across the square and stopped at the post-house. At the noise it made, the population mustered around the spot with curiosity.

Captain Dandoins, whose heart was sore about the oversight, and wanting to explain why his men were standing at ease instead of being ready for action, darted up to the carriage window. Taking off his cap and bowing, he expressed all kind of respect to excuse himself to the sovereign and the Royal Family.

To answer him, the King put his head out of the window several times.

Isidore, with his foot in the stirrup, was near Drouet who watched the conveyance with profound attention. He had been up to town to the Federation Festival, and he had seen the King, whom he believed he recognized. That morning, he had received a number of the new issue of the paper money of the State, which bore the monarch's head. He pulled one out and compared it with the original. This seemed to cry out to him: "You have the man before you."

Isidore went round the carriage to the other side where his brother was masking the Queen by leaning his elbow on the window.

"The King is recognized," he said. "Hurry off the carriage, and take a good look at that tall dark fellow—the postmaster's son, who has recognized the King. His name is Jean Baptiste Drouet."

"Right," responded George. "I will look to him. You, be off!"

Isidore galloped on to Clermont to have the fresh horses ready there. Scarcely was he through the town before the vehicle started off. Malden and Valory were pressing, due to the promise of extra money. Charny had lost sight of Drouet, who did not budge, but was talking with the groom. The count went up to him.

"Was there no horse ordered for me, sir?" he demanded.

"One was ordered, but we are out of them."

"What do you mean—when here is a saddled horse in the yard."

"That is mine."

"But you can let me have it. I do not mind what I pay."

"Impossible. I have a journey to make, and it cannot be postponed."

To insist was to cause suspicions; to take by force was to ruin all. He thought of a means to smooth over the difficulty. He went over to Captain Dandoins, who was watching the royal carriage going around the corner. He turned on a hand being laid on his shoulder.

"Hush, I am Count Charny," said the Lifeguard. "I cannot get a horse here. Let me have one of your dragoons', as I must follow the King and the Queen. I alone know where the relays set by the Count of Choiseul are, and if I am not at hand, the King will be brought to a standstill at Varennes."

"Count, you must take my charger, not one of my men's."

"I accept. The welfare of the Royal Family depends on the least accident. The better the steed the better the chances."

The two went through the town to the marquis' lodgings. Before departing, Charny charged a quarter-master to watch young Drouet. Unfortunately, the nobleman's rooms were five hundred paces away. When the horses were saddled, a quarter of an hour had gone by. For the marquis had another got ready as he was to take up the rear guard duty over the King.

Suddenly, it seemed to Charny that he heard great clamor, and could distinguish shouts of "The Queen, the Queen!" He sprang from the house, begging Dandoins to have the horse brought to the square. The town was in an uproar. Scarcely had Charny and his brother noble gone, when Drouet shouted out: "That carriage which went by is the King's! In it are the King, the Queen, and the Royals!" He jumped on his horse, but some friends sought to detain him.

"Where are you off to? What do you intend? What is your project?"

"The colonel and the troop are here. We could not stop the King without a riot, which might turn out ill for us. What cannot be done here can be done at Clermont. Keep back the dragoons, that is all I ask."

And away he galloped on the track of the King. Hence the shouting that the King and the Queen had gone through, as Charny heard. Those shouts set the mayor and councilmen afoot. The mayor ordered the soldiers into the barracks, as eight o'clock was striking, and it was the hour when soldiers had no business to be about in arms.

"Horses!" cried Charny as Dandoins joined him.

"They are coming."

"Have you pistols in the holsters?"

"I loaded them myself."

"Good! Now, all hangs on the goodness of your horse. I must catch up with a man who has a quarter-hour's start, and kill him."

"You must kill him?"

"Or, all is lost!"

"Do not wait for the horses, then."

"Never mind me; you get your men out before they are coaxed over. Look at the mayor speechifying to them! You have no time to lose either, make haste!"

At this instant, up came the orderly with the two chargers. Charny took the nearest at hazard, snatching the reins from the man's hands. He leaped astride and drove in both spurs, bursting away on the track of Drouet, without clearly comprehending what the marquis yelled after him. Yet these words were important.

"You have taken my horse and not yours, and the pistols are not loaded!"

CHAPTER XIII

Stop, King!

With Isidore riding before it, the royal conveyance flew over the road between St. Menehould and Clermont. Night was falling as the coach entered Argonne Forest. The Queen had noticed the absence of Charny, but she could not slacken the pace or question the post-boys. She did lean out a dozen times, but she discovered nothing. At half-past nine, they reached Clermont—four leagues covered. Count Damas was waiting outside the place, as he had been warned by Leonard. He stopped Isidore on recognizing his livery.

"You are Charles de Damas? Well, I am preceding the King. Get your dragoons in hand and escort the carriage."

"My lord," replied the count, "such a breath of discontent is blowing that I am alarmed, and must confess that my men cannot be answered for if they recognize the King. All I can promise is that I will fall in behind when he gets by, and bar the road."

"Do your best—here they come!"

He pointed to the carriage rushing through the darkness, and visible by the sparks from the horses' shoes. Isidore's duty was to ride ahead and get the relays ready. In five minutes, he stopped at the post-house door. Almost at the same time, Damas rode up with half-a-dozen dragoons, and the King's coach came next. It had followed Isidore so closely that he had not had time to remount. Without being showy, it was so large and well built that a great crowd gathered to see it. Damas stood by the door to prevent the passengers being studied. But neither the King nor the Queen could master their desire to learn what was going on.

"Is that you, Count Damas?" asked the King. "Why are not your dragoons under arms?"

"Sire, your Majesty is five hours behind time. My troop has been in the saddle since four P. M. I have kept as quiet as possible, but the town is getting fretful; and my men want to know what is the matter. If the excitement comes to a head before your Majesty is off again, the alarm bell will be rung and the road will be blocked. So I have kept only a dozen men ready and sent the others into quarters. But I have the trumpeters in my rooms so as

Alexandre Dumas

to sound the Boot-and-Saddle at the first call. Your Majesty sees that all was for the best, for the road is free."

"Very well. You have acted like a prudent man, my lord," said the King. "When I am gone, get your men together and follow me closely."

"Sire, will you kindly hear what Viscount Charny has to say?" asked the Queen.

"What has he to say?" said the King, fretfully.

"That you were recognized by the St. Menehould postmaster's son, who compared your face with the likeness on the new paper money. His brother the count stayed behind to watch this fellow, and no doubt something serious is happening, as he has not rejoined us."

"If we were recognized, the more reason to hurry. Viscount, urge on the post-boys and ride on before."

Isidore's horse was ready. He dashed on, shouting to the postilions: "The Varennes Road!" and led the vehicle, which rattled off with lightning speed. Damas thought of following with his handful of men, but he had positive orders. And as the town was in commotion—lights appearing at windows and persons running from door to door—he thought only of one thing: to stop the alarm bell. He ran to the church tower and set a guard on the door.

But all seemed to calm down. A messenger arrived from Dandoins to say that he and his dragoons were detained at St. Menehould by the people. Besides, as Damas already knew, Drouet had ridden off to pursue the carriage. Although he had probably failed to catch up with it, as they had not seen him at Clermont. Then came a hussar orderly from Commandant Rohrig at Varennes, with Count Bouille and another. He was a young officer of twenty, who was not in the knowledge of the plot, but was told a treasure was in question. Uneasy at the time going by, they wanted to know what news Damas could give. All was quiet with them, and on the road the hussar had passed the royal carriage.

"All's well," thought Count Damas, going home to bid his bugler sound "Boot and Saddle!"

All was therefore going for the best, except for the St. Menehould incident, by which Dandoins' thirty dragoons were locked up. But Damas could dispense with them from having a hundred and forty. Returning to the King's carriage, it was on the road to Varennes.

This place is composed of an upper and a lower town. The relay of horses was to be ready beyond the town, on the farther side of the bridge and a vaulted passage, where a stoppage would be bad. Count Jules Bouille and Raigecourt were to guard these horses, and Charny was to guide the party through the daedalus[10] of streets. He had spent a fortnight in Varennes, and had studied and jotted down every point. He was familiar with every lane, and knew every boundary post. Unfortunately Charny was not to the fore.

Hence the Queen's anxiety doubled. Something grave must have befallen him to keep him remote, when he knew how much he was wanted. The King grew more distressed too, as he had so reckoned on Charny that he had not brought away the plan of the town. Besides, the night was densely dark—not a star scintillated. It was easy to go wrong in a known place, still more a strange one.

Isidore's orders from his brother were to stop before the town. Here, his brother was to change horses and take the lead. He was as troubled as the Queen herself at this absence. His hope was that Bouille and Raigecourt in their eagerness would come out to meet the Royal party. They must have learned the site during three days, and would do as guides. Consequently on reaching the base of the hill and seeing a few lights sparkling over the town, Isidore pulled up irresolutely. He cast a glance around to try and pierce the murkiness, but he saw nothing.

He ventured to call in a low voice, but no reply came. He heard the rumbling of the stage coming along at a quarter of a league off, like a thunder peal. Perhaps the officers were hiding in the woods, which he explored along the skirts without meeting a soul. He had no alternative but to wait. In five minutes the carriage

---

10 Labyrinth

came up, and the heads of the royal couple were thrust out of the windows.

"Have you seen Count Charny?" both asked simultaneously.

"I have not, Sire," was the response. "And I judge that some hurt has met him in the chase of that confounded Drouet."

The Queen groaned.

"What can be done?" inquired the King, who found that nobody knew the place.

"Sire," said the viscount, "all is silent and appears quiet. Please your Majesty, wait ten minutes. I will go into the town, and try to get news of Count Bouille, or at least of the Choiseul horses."

He darted towards the houses. The nearest had opened at the approach of the vehicles, and light was perceptible through the chink of the door. The Queen got out, leaned on Malden's arm, and walked up to this dwelling—but the door closed at their drawing near. Malden had time to dash up and give it a shove which overpowered the resistance. The man who had attempted to shut it was in his fiftieth year; he wore a night gown and slippers. It was not without astonishment that he was pushed into his own house by a gentleman who had a lady on his arm. He started when he cast a rapid glance at the latter.

"What do you want?" he challenged Malden.

"We are strangers to Varennes, and we beg you to point out the Stenay road."

"But if I give you the information, and it is known, I will be a ruined man."

"Whatever the risk, sir," said the Lifeguardsman, "it will be kindness to a lady who is in a dangerous position—"

"Yes, but this is a great lady—it is the Queen," he whispered to the sham courier.

The Queen pulled Malden back.

"Before going farther, let the King know that I am recognized," she said.

Malden took but a second to run this errand, and he brought word that the King wanted to see this careful man. He kicked off his slippers with a sigh, and went on tiptoe out to the vehicle.

"Your name, sir?" demanded the King.

"I am Major Prefontaine of the cavalry, and Knight of the St. Louis Order."

"In both capacities you have sworn fealty to me. It is doubly your duty therefore, to help me in this quandary."

"Certainly. But will your Majesty please be quick about it, lest I am seen," faltered the major.

"All the better if you are seen," interposed Malden. "You will never have a finer chance to do your duty."

Not appearing to be of this opinion, the major gave a groan. The Queen shook her shoulders with scorn and stamped with impatience. The King waved his hand to appease her and said to the lukewarm royalist: "Sir, did you hear by chance of soldiers waiting for a carriage to come through, and have you seen any hussars lately about?"

"They are on the other side of the town, Sire. The horses are at the Great Monarch inn, and the soldiers probably in the barracks."

"I thank you, sir. Nobody has seen you, and you will probably have nothing happen you."

He gave his hand to the Queen to help her into the vehicle, and issued orders for the start to be made again. But as the couriers shouted "To the Monarch Inn!" a shadowy horseman loomed up in the woods and darted crosswise on the road, shouting: "Post-boys, not a step farther! You are driving the fleeing King. In the name of the Nation, I bid ye stand!"

"The King," muttered the postilions, who had gathered up the reins.

Louis XVI saw that it was a vital instant.

"Who are you, sir, to give orders here?" he demanded.

"A plain citizen, but I represent the law, and I speak in the name of the Nation. Postilions, I order you a second time not to stir. You know me well: I am Jean Baptiste Drouet, son of the postmaster at St. Menehould."

"The scoundrel, it is he," shouted the two Lifeguardsmen, drawing their hunting-swords.

But before they could alight, the other had dashed away into the Lower Town streets.

"Oh, what has become of Charny?" murmured the Queen.

Fate had ridden at the count's knee. Dandoins' horse was a good racer, but Drouet had twenty minute's start. Charny dug in the spurs, and the bounding horse blew steam from his nostrils as it darted off. Without knowing that he was pursued, Drouet tore along. But he rode an ordinary nag, while the other was a thoroughbred. The result was that, at a league's end, the pursuer gained a third. Thereupon the postmaster's son saw that he was chased, and redoubled his efforts to keep beyond the hunter. At the end of the second league, Charny saw that he had gained in the same proportion, while the other turned to watch him with more and more uneasiness.

Drouet had gone off in such haste, that he had forgotten to arm himself. The young patriot did not dread death, but he feared being stopped in his mission of arresting the King, whereupon he would lose the opportunity of making his name famous. He had still two leagues to go before reaching Clermont, but it was evident that he would be overtaken at the end of the first league. That is, the third from his leaving St. Menehould.

As if to stimulate his ardor, he was sure that the royal carriage was in front of him. He laid on the lash, and drove in the spurs more cruelly. It was half after nine and night fell. He was but three quarters of a league from Clermont, but Charny was only two hundred paces away.

Drouet knew Varennes was not a posting station, and he surmised that the King would have to go through Verdun. He began to despair; before he caught up with the King he would be seized. He would have to give up the pursuit, or turn to fight his pursuer, and he was unarmed. Suddenly, when Charny was not fifty paces from him, he met postilions returning with the unharnessed horses. Drouet recognized them as those who had ridden the royal horses.

"They took the Verdun Road, eh?" he called out as he forged past them.

"No, the Varennes Road," they shouted.

He roared with delight. He was saved and the King lost! Instead of the long way, he had a short cut to make. He knew all about Argonne Woods, into which he flung himself. By cutting through, he would gain a quarter of an hour over the King, besides being shielded by the darkness under the trees. Charny, who knew the ground almost as well as the young man, understood that he would escape him, and he howled with rage.

"Stop, stop!" he shouted out to Drouet, as he at the same time urged his horse also on the short level separating the road from the woods.

But Drouet took good care not to reply. He bent down on his horse's neck, inciting him with whip and spur and voice. All he wanted was to reach the thicket—he would be safe there. He could do it, but he had to run the gauntlet of Charny at ten paces. He seized one of the horse-pistols and leveled it.

"Stop!" he called out again, "or you are a dead man."

Drouet only leaned over the more and pressed on. The royalist pulled the trigger but the flint on the hammer only shot sparks from the pan. He furiously flung the weapon at the flier, took out the other of the pair, and plunged into the woods after him. He shot again at the dark form, but once more the hammer fell uselessly; neither pistol was loaded. It was then that he remembered that Dandoins had called out something to him which he had heard imperfectly.

"I made a mistake in the horse," he said, "and no doubt what he shouted was that the pistols were not charged. Never mind. I will catch this villain and strangle him with my own hands, if needs must."

He took up the pursuit of the shadow, which he just descried in the obscurity. But he had hardly gone a hundred paces in the forest, before his horse broke down in the ditch, and he was thrown over its head. Rising, he pulled it up and got into the seat again, but Drouet was out of sight. Thus it was that he escaped Charny, and swept like a phantom over the road to bid the King's conductors to make not another step.

They obeyed, for he had conjured them in the name of the Nation, which was beginning to be more mighty than the King's. Scarcely had he dived into the Lower Town, than he heard the sound of another horse coming nearer. Isidore appeared by the same street as Drouet had taken. His information agreed with that furnished by Major Prefontaine, the horses were beyond the town at the Monarch Hotel, and Lieutenant Rohrig had the hussars at the barracks. But instead of filling them with joy by his news, he found the party plunged into the deepest stupor. Prefontaine was wailing, and the two Lifeguardsmen threatening someone unseen.

"Did not a rider go by you at a gallop?"

"Yes, Sire."

"The man was Drouet," said the King.

"Then my brother is dead," ejaculated Isidore with a deep pang at the heart.

The Queen uttered a shriek and buried her face in her hands.

CHAPTER XIV

The Capture

Inexpressible prostration overpowered the fugitives, who were checked on the highway by a danger they could not measure.

"Sire," said Isidore, the first to shake it off. "Dead or living, let us not think of our brother, but of your Majesty. There is not an instant to lose. These fellows must know the Monarch Hotel. So gallop to the Grand Monarch!"

But the postilions did not stir.

"Did you not hear?" queried the young noble.

"Yes, sir, we heard—"

"Well, why do we not start?"

"Because Master Drouet forbade us."

"What? Drouet forbade you? When the King commands and Drouet forbids, do you obey a Drouet?"

"We obey the Nation."

"Then, gentlemen," went on Isidore, "there are moments when a human life is of no account. Pick out your man; I will settle this one. We will drive ourselves."

He grasped the nearest postilion by the collar and set the point of his short sword to his breast. On seeing the three knives flash, the Queen screamed and cried: "Mercy, gentlemen!" She turned to the post-boys: "Friends, fifty gold pieces to share among you, and a pension of five hundred a-year if you save the King!"

Whether they were frightened by the young nobles' demonstration or snapped at the offer, the three shook up their horses and resumed the road. Prefontaine sneaked into his house all of a tremble and barred himself in. Isidore rode on in front to clear the way through the town and over the bridge to the Monarch House. The vehicle rolled at full speed down the slope. On arriving at a vaulted way leading to the bridge and passing under the Revenue Tower, one of the doors was seen closed. They got it open, but two or three wagons were in the way.

"Lend me a hand, gentlemen," cried Isidore, dismounting.

Just then, they heard the bells boom and a drum beat. Drouet was hard at work!

"The scamp! If ever I lay hold of him—" growled Isidore, grinding his teeth. By an incredible effort, he dragged one of the carts aside while Malden and Valory drew off the other. They tugged at the last as the coach thundered under the vault. Suddenly, through the uprights of the tilt, they saw several musket barrels thrust upon the cart.

"Not a step or you are dead men!" shouted a voice.

"Gentlemen," interposed the King, looking out of the window, "do not try to force your way through—I order you."

The two officers and Isidore fell back a step.

"What do they mean to do?" asked the King.

At the same time, a shriek of fright sounded from within the coach. Besides the men who barred the way, two or three had slipped up to the conveyance and shoved their gun barrels under the windows. One was pointed at the Queen's breast. Isidore saw this and darted up, pushing the gun aside by grasping the barrel.

"Fire, fire," roared several voices.

One of the men obeyed but luckily his gun misfired. Isidore raised his arm to stab him, but the Queen stopped his hand.

"Oh, in heaven's name, let me charge this rabble," said Isidore, enraged.

"No, sheathe your sword, do you hear me?"

He did not obey her by half; instead of sheathing his sword he let it fall on the ground.

"If I only get hold of Drouet," he snarled.

"I leave you him to wreck your vengeance on," said the Queen in an undertone, squeezing his arm with strange force.

"In short, gentlemen," said the King, "what do you want?"

"We want to see your passports," returned several voices.

"So you may," he replied. "Get the town authorities and we will show them."

"You are making too much fuss over it," said the fellow who had misfired with his gun, now leveling it at the King.

But the two Guardsmen leaped upon him, and dragged him down. In the scuffle, the gun went off, and the bullet did no harm in the crowd.

"Who fired?" demanded a voice.

"Help," called out the one whom the officers were beating.

Five or six armed men rushed to his rescue. The two Lifeguardsmen whipped out their short swords and prepared to use them. The King and the Queen made useless efforts to stop both parties. The contest was becoming fierce, terrible and deadly. But two men plunged into the struggle, distinguishable by a tricolored scarf and military uniform. One was Sausse, the County Attorney, and the other National Guard Commandant Hannonet. They brought twenty muskets, which gleamed in the torchlight. The King comprehended that these officials were a guarantee if not assistance.

"Gentlemen," he said, "I am ready to entrust myself and party to you, but put a stop to these rough fellow's brutality."

"Ground your arms," cried Hannonet.

The men obeyed, growling.

"Excuse me, sir," said the attorney, "but the story is that the King is in flight, and it is our duty to make sure if it is a fact."

"Make sure?" retorted Isidore. "If this carriage really conveyed his Majesty, you ought to be at his feet. If it is but a private individual, by what right do you stay him?"

"Sir, I am addressing you," went on Sausse, to the King. "Will you be good enough to answer me?"

"Sire, gain time," whispered Isidore. "Damas and his dragoons are somewhere near, and will doubtless ride up in a trice."

The King thought this right and replied to Sausse, "I suppose you will let us go on if our passes are correct?"

"Of course," was the reply.

"Then, Baroness," said the Monarch to Lady Tourzel, "be good enough to find the passports and give them to the gentleman."

The old lady understood what the speaker meant by saying "find!" so she went to seeking in the pockets where it was not likely to be.

"Nonsense," said one of the crowd, "don't you see that they have not got any passport." The voice was fretful and full of menace too.

"Excuse me, sir," said the Queen, "my lady the baroness has the paper, but not knowing that it would be called for, she does not know where she put it."

The bystanders began to hoot, showing that they were not dupes of the trick.

"There is a plainer way," said Sausse. "Postilions, drive on to my store, where the ladies and gentlemen can go in while the matter is cleared up. Go ahead, boys! Soldiers of the National Guard, escort the carriage."

This invitation was too much like an order to be dallied with. Besides, resistance would probably not have succeeded. For the bells continued to ring and the drum to beat, so that the crowd was considerably augmented as the carriage moved on.

"Oh, Colonel Damas," muttered the King, "if you will only strike in before we are put within this accursed house!"

The Queen said nothing, for she had to stifle her sobs as she thought of Charny, and restrained her tears. Damas? He had managed to break out of Clermont with three officers and twice as many troopers, but the rest had fraternized with the people.

Sausse was a grocer as well as attorney, and his grocery had a parlor behind the store where he meant to lodge the visitors. His wife, half-dressed, came from upstairs as the Queen crossed the sill. The Kin was next, with Lady Elizabeth and Lady Tourzel following. More than a hundred persons guarded the coach, and stopped before the store which was in a little square.

"If the lady has found the pass yet," observed Sausse, who had shown the way in, "I will take it to the Town Council and see if it is correct."

As the passport which Charny had got from Baron Zannone, and given to the Queen, was in order, the King made a sign that Lady Tourzel was to hand it over. She drew the precious paper from her pocket and let Sausse have it. He charged his wife to do the honor of his house while he went to the town-house. It was a lively meeting, for Drouet was there to fan the flames. The silence of curiosity fell as the attorney entered with the document. All knew that he harbored the party. The mayor pronounced the pass perfectly good.

"It must be good for there is the royal signature," he said.

A dozen hands were held out for it, but Drouet snatched it up.

"But has it got the signature of the Assembly?" he demanded.

It was signed by a member of the Committee though not for the president.

"This is not the question," said the young patriot. "These travelers are not Baroness von Korff, a Russian lady, with her steward, her governess and her children, but the King and the Queen, the Prince and the Princess Royal and Lady Elizabeth, a court lady, and their guardsmen—the Royal Family in short. Will you or will you not let the Royal Family go out of the kingdom?"

This question was properly put, but it was too heavy for the town governors of a third-rate town to handle. As their deliberation promised to take up some time, Sausse went home to see how his guests were faring. They had refused to lay aside their wraps or sit down, as this concession seemed to delay their approaching departure, which they took for granted. All their faculties were concentrated on the master of the house, who might be expected to bring the council's decision. When he arrived the King went to meet him.

"Well, what about the passport?" he asked, with anxiety he vainly strove to conceal.

"It causes a grave debate in the council," replied Sausse.

"Why? Is its validity doubted by any chance?" proceeded the King.

"No; but it is doubted that it is really in the hands of Lady Korff, and the rumor spreads that it covers the Royal Family."

Louis hesitated an instant. But then, making up his mind, he said: "Well, yes; I am the King. You see the Queen and the children. I entreat you to deal with them with the respect the French have always shown their sovereigns."

The street door had remained open to the staring multitude, and the words were heard without. Unhappily, though they were uttered with a kind of dignity, the speaker did not carry out the idea in his bob wig, grey coat, and plain stockings and shoes. How could anybody see the ruler of the realm in this travesty? The Queen felt the flush come to her eyes at the poor impression made on the mob.

"Let us accept Madam Sausse's hospitality," she hastened to say, "and go upstairs."

Meanwhile the news was carried to the town house, and the tumult redoubled over the town. How was it this did not attract the soldiers in waiting? At about nine in the evening, Count Jules Bouille and Lieut. Raigecourt were at the Monarch inn door with their hussars, when they heard a carriage coming. But it was the cab containing the Queen's hairdresser. He was very frightened, revealing his personality.

"The King got out of Paris last evening," he said: "but it does not look as if he could keep on. I have warned Colonel Damas, who has called in his outposts. The dragoon regiment mutinied, and at Clermont there was a riot—I have had great trouble to get through. I have the Queen's diamonds and my brother's hat and coat, and you must give me a horse to help me on the road."

"Master Leonard," said Bouille, who wanted to set the hairdresser down a peg, "the horses here are for the King's service, and nobody else can use them."

"But as I tell you that there is little likelihood of the King coming along—"

"But still he may, and he would hold me to task for letting you have them."

"What, do you imagine that the King would blame you for giving me his horses when it is to help me out of a fix?"

The young noble could not help smiling. Leonard was comic in the big hat and misfit coat, and he was glad to get rid of him by begging the landlord to find a horse for the cab. Bouille and his brother-officer went through the town and saw nothing on the farther side. They began to believe that the King, eight or ten hours belated, would never come. It was eleven when they returned to the inn. They had sent out an orderly before this, who had reported to Damas, as we have seen. They threw themselves, dressed, on the bed to wait till midnight.

At half past twelve, they were aroused by the tocsin, the drum and the shouting. Thrusting their heads out of the window, they saw the town in confusion, racing towards the town hall. Many armed men ran in the same direction with all sorts of weapons. The officers went to the stables to get the horses out so that they would be ready for the carriage if it crossed the town. They had their own chargers ready, and kept by the King's relay, on which sat the post-boys.

Soon they learned, amid the shouts and menaces, that the royal party had been stopped. They argued that they had better ride over to Stenay, where the little army corps commanded by Bouille was waiting. They could arrive in two hours. Abandoning the relay, they galloped off, so that one of the main forces foiled the King at the critical moment!

During this time, Choiseul had been pushing on. But he lost three quarters of an hour by threading a wood, the guide going wrong by accident or design. This was the very time when the King was compelled to alight and go into Sausse's. At half after twelve, while the two young officers were riding off by the other road, Choiseul presented himself at the gate, coming by the cross-road.

"Who goes there?" was challenged at the bridge where National guards were posted.

"France—Lauzun Hussars," was the count's reply.

"You cannot pass!" returned the sentry, who called up the guard to arms.

At that instant, the darkness was streaked with torchlight, and the cavalry could see masses of armed men with musket-barrels shining. Not knowing what had happened, Choiseul parleyed and said that he wanted to be put in communication with the officers of the garrison.

But while he was talking, he noticed that trees were felled to make a breastwork, and that two field pieces were trained on his forty men. As the gunner finished his aiming, the hussar's provost-marshal's squad arrived, unhorsed. They had been surprised and disarmed in the barracks, and only knew that the King had been arrested. They were ignorant what had become of their comrades. As they were concluding these thin explanations, Choiseul saw a troop of horses advance in the gloom, and heard the bridge guards challenge: "Who goes there?"

"The Provence Dragoons!"

A national Guard fired off his gun. "It is Damas with his cavalry," whispered the count to an officer. Without waiting for more, he shook off the two soldiers who were clinging to his skirts, and suggesting that his duty was to obey the town authorities and know nothing beyond. He commanded his men to go at the trot, and took the defenders so well by surprise that he cut through, and rushed the streets, swarming with people.

On approaching Sausse's store, Choiseul saw the royal carriage without the horses, and a numerous guard before the mean-looking house in the petty square. Not to have a collision with the townsfolk, the count went straight to the military barracks, which he knew. As he came out, two men stopped him and bade him appear before the town council. Still having his troopers within call, he sent them off, saying that he would pay the council a visit when he found time. He ordered the sentry to allow no one entrance.

Inquiring of the stablemen, Choiseul learned that the hussars, not knowing what had become of their leaders, had scattered about the streets. There, the inhabitants had sympathized with them and treated them to drink. He went back into the barracks to see what he might rely upon. He found forty men, as tired as their horses, which had traveled more than twenty leagues that day. But the situation was not one to trifle with.

Choiseul had the pistols inspected to make sure they were loaded. As the hussars were Germans and did not understand French, he harangued them in their tongue to the effect that they were in Varennes, where the Royal Family had been waylaid. He continued that the royals were detained, and that they must be rescued, or the rescuers should die. Short but sharp, the speech made a fine impression. The men repeated in German: "The King! the Queen!" with amazement.

Leaving them no time to cool down, Choiseul arranged them in fours, and led them with sabres drawn to the house where he suspected the King was held in duress. In the midst of the volunteer guards' invective, he placed two videttes[11] at the door, and alighted to walk in. As he was crossing the threshold, he was

---

11 Mounted sentinels stationed in advance of pickets

touched on the shoulder by Colonel Damas, on whose assistance he had no little depended.

"Are you in force?" he inquired.

"I am all but alone. My regiment refused to follow me, and I have but half-a-dozen men."

"What a misfortune! But never mind—I have forty fellows, and we must see what we can do with them."

The King was receiving a deputation from the town, whose spokesman said, "Since there is no longer any doubt that Varennes has the honor to receive King Louis, we come to have his orders."

"My orders are to have the horses put to my carriage and let me depart," replied the monarch.

The answer to this precise request will never be known, as at this point they heard Choiseul's horsemen gallop up, and saw them form a line on the square with flashing swords. The Queen started with a beam of joy in her eyes.

"We are saved," she whispered to her sister-in-law.

"Heaven grant it," replied the holy woman, who looked to heaven for everything.

The King waited eagerly for the town's delegation. Great riot broke out in the outer room, which was guarded by countrymen with scythes. Words and blows were exchanged, and Choiseul, without his hat and sword in hand, appeared on the sill. Above his shoulder was seen the colonel's pale but resolute face. In the look of both was such a threatening expression, that the deputies stood aside so as to give a clear space to the Royal Family.

"Welcome, Lord Choiseul," cried the Queen going over to the officer.

"Alas, my lady, I arrive very late."

"No matter, since you come in good company."

"Nay, on the contrary, we are almost alone. Dandoins has been held with his cavalry at St. Menehould, and Damas has been abandoned by his troop."

The Queen sadly shook her head.

"But where is Chevalier Bouille, and Lieut. Raigecourt?" he looked inquiringly around.

"I have not so much as seen those officers," said the King, joining in.

"I give you my word, Sire, that I thought they would have died under your carriage-wheels before you had come to this," observed Count Damas.

"What is to be done?" asked the King.

"We must save you," replied Damas. "Give your orders."

"My orders?"

"Sire, I have forty hussars at the door. They are exhausted, but we can get as far as Dun."

"But how can we manage?" inquired the King.

"I will dismount seven of my men, on whose horses you should get, the Dauphin in your arms. We will lay the swords about us and cut our way through as the only chance. But the decision must be instant, for in a quarter of an hour perhaps, my men will be bought over."

The Queen approved of the project, but the King seemed to elude her gaze, and the influence she had over him.

"It is a way," he responded to the proposer, "and I daresay the only one. But can you answer for it, that in the unequal struggle of thirty men with seven or eight hundred, no shot will kill my boy or my daughter, the Queen or my sister?"

"Sire, if such a misfortune befell through my suggestion, I should be killed under your Majesty's eyes."

"Then instead of yielding to such mad propositions," returned the other, "let us reason calmly."

The Queen sighed and retired a few paces. In this regretful movement she met Isidore, who was going over to the window whither a noise in the street attracted him. He hoped it was his brother coming.

"The townsfolk do not refuse to let me pass," said the King, without appearing to notice the two in conversation, "but ask me to wait till daybreak. We have no news of the Count of Charny, who is so deeply devoted to us. I am assured that Bouille and Raigecourt left the town ten minutes before we drove in, to notify Marquis Bouille and bring up his troops, which are surely ready. Were I alone, I should follow your advice and break through. But it is impossible to risk the Queen, my children, my sister and the others, with so small a guard as you offer. Especially as part must be dismounted—for I certainly would not leave my Lifeguards here."

He looked at his watch.

"It will soon be three o'clock. Young Bouille left at half after twelve so that, as his father must have ranged his troops in detachments along the road, he will warn them, and they will successively arrive. At about five or six, Marquis Bouille ought to be here with the main body, the first companies outstripping him. Thereupon, without any danger to my family, and no violence, we can quit Varennes and continue our road."

Choiseul acknowledged the logic in this argument, but he felt that logic must not be listened to on certain occasions. He turned to the Queen to beg other orders from her, or to have her get the King to revoke his, but she shook her head and said: "I do not want to take anything upon myself, It is the King's place to command, and my duty to obey. Besides, I am of his opinion—Bouille will soon be coming."

Choiseul bowed and drew Damas aside, while beckoning the two Lifeguards to join in the council he held.

CHAPTER XV

Poor Catherine

The scene was slightly changed in aspect. The little princess could not resist the weariness, and she was put abed beside her brother, where both slumbered. Lady Elizabeth stood by, leaning her head against the wall. Shivering with anger, the Queen stood near the fireplace, looking alternatively at the King, seated on a bale of goods, and on the four officers deliberating near the door. An old woman knelt by the children and prayed. It was the attorney's grandmother, who was struck by the beauty of the children, and the Queen's imposing air.

Sausse and his colleagues had gone out, promising that the horses should be harnessed to the carriage. But the Queen's bearing showed that she attached little faith to the pledge, which caused Choiseul to say to his party: "Gentlemen, do not trust to the feigned tranquility of our masters. The position is not hopeless, and we must look it in the face. The probability is that at present, Marquis Bouille has been informed, and will be arriving here about six, as he ought to be at hand with some of the royal Germans. His vanguard may be only half an hour before him; for in such a scrape, all that is possible ought to be performed. But we must not deceive ourselves about the four or five thousand men surrounding us. The moment they see the troops, there will be dreadful excitement and imminent danger.

"They will try to drag the King back from Varennes, put him on a horse, and carry him to Clermont. They might threaten and have a try at his life perhaps—but this will only be a temporary danger," added Choiseul. "As soon as the barricades are stormed and our cavalry inside the town, the route will be complete. Therefore we ten men must hold out as many minutes. As the land lays, we may hope to lose but a man a minute, so that we have time enough."

The audience nodded. This devotion to death's point, thus plainly set down, was accepted with the same simplicity.

"This is what we must do," continued the count. "At the first shot we hear and shout without, we rush into the outer room, where we kill everybody in it. We take possession of the outlets: three windows, where three of us defend. The seven others stand on the stairs, which the winding will facilitate our defending as one may face a score. The bodies of the slain will serve as rampart. It is a hundred to one that the troops will be masters of the town before we are killed to the last man. And though that happens, we will fill a glorious page in history, as recompense for our sacrifice."

The chosen ones shook hands on this pledge like Spartans, and selected their stations during the action. The two Lifeguards and Isidore, whose place was kept though he was absent, were at the three casements on the street. Choiseul was at the staircase foot; and next him Damas, and the rest of the soldiers. As they settled their arrangements, bustle was heard in the street.

In came a second deputation headed by Sausse, the National Guards commander Hannonet, and three or four town officers. Thinking they came to say the horses were put to the coach, the King ordered their admittance. The officers, who were trying to read every token, believed that Sausse betrayed hesitation, but that Hannonet had a settled will which was of evil omen. At the same time, Isidore ran up and whispered a few words to the Queen before he went out again. She went to the children looking pale, and leaned on the bed.

As the deputation bowed without speaking, the King pretended to infer what they came upon. He said: "Gentlemen, the French have merely gone astray, and their attachment to their monarch is genuine. Weary of the excesses daily felt in my capital, I have decided to go down into the country where the sacred flame of devotion ever burns. I am assured of finding the ancient devotion of the people here, and I am ready to give my loyal subjects the proof of my trust. So I will form an escort, part troops of the line and part National Guards, to accompany me to Montmedy, where I have determined to retire. Consequently commander, I ask you to select the men to escort me from your own force, and to have my carriage ready."

During the silence, Sausse and Hannonet looked at each other for one to speak. At last the latter bowed and said,

"Sire, I should feel great pleasure in obeying your Majesty, but an article of the Constitution forbids the King leaving the kingdom, and good Frenchmen from aiding a flight."

This made the hearer start.

"Consequently," proceeded the volunteer soldier, lifting his hand to hush the King, "the Varennes Council decided that a courier must take the word to Paris, and return with the advice of the Assembly, before allowing the departure."

The King felt the perspiration damp his brow, while the Queen bit her pale lips fretfully, and Lady Elizabeth raised her eyes and hands to heaven.

"Soho, gentlemen," exclaimed the sovereign with the dignity returning to him when driven to the wall. "Am I no longer the master to go my own way? In that case I am more of a slave than the meanest of my subjects."

"Sire," replied the National Guardsman, "you are always the ruler. But all men, King or citizens, are bound by their oath. You swore to obey the law, and ought to set the example—it is also a noble duty to fulfill."

Meanwhile Choiseul had consulted with the Queen by glances and on her mute assent he had gone downstairs. The King was aware that he was lost if he yielded without resistance to this rebellion of the villages, for it was rebellion from his point of view.

"Gentlemen," he said, "this is violence. But I am not so lonely as you imagine. At the door are forty determined men and ten thousand soldiers are around Varennes. I order you to have my horses harnessed to the coach—do you hear, I order!"

"Well said, Sire," whispered the Queen, stepping up. "Let us risk life, but not injure our honor and dignity."

"What will result if we refuse your Majesty?" asked the National Guards officer.

"I shall appeal to force, and you will be responsible for the blood spilled, which will be shed by you."

"Have it so then," replied Hannonet, "call in your hussars —I will let my men loose on them!"

He left the room. The King and the Queen looked at one another, daunted. They would perhaps have given way, had it not been for an incident. Pushing aside her grandmother, who continued to pray by the bedside, Madam Sausse walked up to the

Queen and said with the bluntness and plain speech of the common people, "So you are the Queen, it appears?"

Marie Antoinette turned, stung at being accosted thus.

"At least I thought so an hour ago," she replied.

"Well, if you are the Queen, and get twenty odd millions to keep your place, why do you not hold to it, being so well paid?"

The Queen uttered an outcry of pain and said to the King: "Oh, anything, everything but such insults!"

She took up the sleeping prince off the couch in her arms, and running to open the window, she cried: "My lord, let us show ourselves to the people, and learn whether they are entirely corrupted. In that case, appeal to the soldiers, and encourage them with voice and gesture. It is little enough for those who are going to die for us!"

The King mechanically followed her, and appeared on the balcony. The whole square on which their gaze fell presented a scene of lively agitation. Half of Choiseul's hussars were on horseback. The others, separated from their chargers, were carried away by the mob, having been won over. The mounted men seemed submissive yet to Choiseul, who was talking to them in German, but they seemed to point to their lost comrades. Isidore Charny, with his knife in hand, seemed to be waylaying for some prey like a hunter.

"The King!" was the shout from five hundred voices.

Had the Sixteenth Louis been regally arrayed, or even militarily, with sword or sceptre in his hand, and spoken in the strong, imposing voice seeming still to the masses that of God, he might have swayed the concourse. But in the grey dawn, that wan light which spoils beauty itself, he was not the personage his friends—or even his enemies—expected to behold. He was clad like a waiting-gentleman, in plain attire, with a powderless curly wig. He was pale and flabby, and his beard had bristled out. His thick lip and dull eye expressed no idea of tyranny or the family man. He stammered over and over again: "Gentlemen, my children!"

However, the Count of Choiseul cried "Long live the King!" Isidore Charny imitated him, and such was the magic of royalty that, in spite of his not looking to be head of the great realm, a few voices uttered a feeble "God save the King!"

But one cheer responded, set up by the National Guards commander, and most generally repeated, with a mighty echo—it was: "The Nation forever!" It was rebellion at such a time, and the King and the Queen could see that part of their German hussars had joined in with it. She uttered a scream of rage. And hugging her son to her, who was ignorant of the grandeur of the passing events, she hung over the rail. She hurled at the multitude these words: "You beasts!"

Some heard this and replied by similar language, the whole place being in immense uproar. Choiseul, in despair, was only wishful to get killed.

"Hussars," he shouted, "in the name of honor, save the King!"

But at the head of twenty men, well armed, a fresh actor came on the stage. It was Drouet, come from the council which he had constrained to stay the King from going.

"Ha," he cried, stepping up to the count, "you want to take away the King, do ye? I tell you it will not be unless dead."

Choiseul started towards him with his sword up.

"Stand, or I will have you shot," interrupted the National Guards commander.

Just then a man leaped out of the crowd, who could not stop him. It was Isidore Charny who was watching for Drouet.

"Back, back," he yelled to the bystanders, crushing them away from before the breast of his horse, "this wretch belongs to me."

But as he was striking at Drouet with his short sword, two shots went off together: a pistol and a gun. The bullet of the first flattened on his collarbone, the other went through his chest. They were fired so close to him that the unfortunate young noble was literally wrapped in flame and smoke. Through the fiery cloud, he was seen to throw up his arms as he gasped: "Poor Catherine!" Letting his weapon drop, he bent back in the saddle and slipped from the crupper to the ground.

The Queen uttered a terrible shriek. She nearly let the prince fall, and in her own falling back, she did not see the horseman riding at the top of his pace from Dun, and plunging into the wake Isidore had furrowed in the crowd. The King closed the window behind the Queen. It was no longer most, but all voices that roared "The Nation forever!" The twenty hussars who had been the last reliance of royalty in distress, added their voices to the cheer.

The Queen sank upon an armchair, hiding her face in her hands. For she still saw Isidore falling in her defense, as his brother had been slain at her door at Versailles. Suddenly there was a loud disturbance at the door, which forced her to lift her eyes. We renounce describing what passed in an instant in her heart of Queen and loving woman. It was George Charny, pale and bloody from the last embrace of his brother, who stood on the threshold! The King seemed confounded.

CHAPTER XVI

The Man of the People

The room was crammed with strangers and National Guards, whom curiosity had drawn into it. The Queen was therefore checked in her first impulse, which was to rush to the new arrival, sponge away the blood with her handkerchief, and address to him some of the comforting words which spring from the heart. But she could not help rising a little on her seat, extend her arms towards him, and mutter his Christian name.

Calm and gloomy, he waved his hand to the strangers. In a soft but firm voice, he said: "You will excuse me, but I have business with their Majesties."

The National Guard began to remonstrate that they were there to prevent anybody talking with the prisoners. But Charny pressed his bloodless lips and frowned. Opened his riding coat to show that he carried pistols, he repeated in a voice as gentle as before, but twice as menacing: "Gentlemen, I have already had the honor to tell you that I have private business with the King and the Queen."

At the same time, he waved them to go out. On this voice, and the mastery Charny exercised over others, Damas and the two bodyguards resumed their energy. Temporarily impaired, they cleared the room by driving the gapers and volunteer soldiers before them. The Queen now comprehended what use this man would have been in the royal carriage instead of Lady Tourzel, whom she had let etiquette impose on them.

Charny glanced round to make sure that only the faithful were at hand, and said as he went nearer Marie Antoinette: "I am here, my lady. I have some seventy hussars at the town gate. I believe I can depend on them. What do you order me to do?"

"Tell us first what has happened to you, my poor Charny?" she said in German.

He made a sign towards Malden, whom he knew to understand the speaker's language.

"Alas, not seeing you, we thought you were dead," she went on in French.

"Unhappily, it is not I but my brother who is slain—poor Isidore! But my turn is coming."

"Charny, I ask you what happened, and how you came to keep so long out of the way?" continued the Queen. "You were a defaulter, George, especially to me," she added in German and in a lower voice.

"I thought my brother would account for my temporary absence," he said, bowing.

"Yes, I know. To pursue that wretch of a man, Drouet. And we feared for awhile that you had come to disaster, in that chase."

"A great misfortune did befall me, for despite all my efforts, I could not catch up with him. A post-boy returning let him know that your carriage had taken the Varennes Road, when he was thinking it had gone to Verdun. He turned into the woods, where I pulled my pistols on him, but they were not loaded. I had taken Dandoins' horse, and not the one prepared for me. It was fate, and who could help it? I pursued him none the less through the forest, but I only knew the roads, so that I was thrown by my horse falling into a ditch! In the darkness, I was but hunting a shadow, and he knew it in every hollow. Thus I was left alone in the night, cursing with rage."

She offered her hand to him, and he touched it with his tremulous lips.

"Nobody replied to my calls. All night long I wandered, and only at daybreak came out at a village on the road from Varennes to Dun. As it was possible that you had escaped Drouet as he escaped me, it was then useless for me to go to Varennes. Yet as he might have had you stopped there, and I was but one man and my devotion was useless, I determined to go on to Dun.

"Before I arrived, I met Captain Deslon with a hundred hussars. He was fretting in the absence of news. He had seen Bouille and Raigecourt racing by towards Stenay, but they had said nothing to him, probably from some distrust. But I know Deslon to be a loyal gentleman. I guessed that your Majesty had been detained at Varennes, and that Bouille and his companion had taken flight to get help. I told Deslon all, adjured him to follow me with his cavalry, which he did, but leaving thirty to guard the Meuse Bridge.

"An hour afterward, we were at Varennes—four leagues in an hour. I wanted to charge and upset everything between us and your Majesty, but we found breastworks inside of works; and to try to ride over them was folly. So I tried parleying. A post of the National Guards being there, I asked leave to join my hussars with those inside, but it was refused me. I asked to be allowed to get the King's orders direct, and that was about to be refused likewise. I spurred my steed, jumped two barricades, and guided by the tumult, galloped up to this spot just when my... your Majesty fell back from the balcony. Now, I await your orders," he concluded.

The Queen pressed his hand in both hers.

"Sire," she said to the King, still plunged in torpor; "have you heard what this faithful servitor is saying?"

The King gave no answer, and she went over to him.

"Sire, there is no time to lose, and indeed too much has been lost. Here is Lord Charny with seventy men, sure he says, and he wants your orders."

Louis shook his head, though Charny implored him with a glance, and the Queen by her voice.

"Orders? I have none to give, being a prisoner. Do whatever you like."

"Good, that is all we want," said the Queen. "You have a blank warrant, you see," she added to her follower whom she took aside. "Do as the King says, whatever you see fit." In a lower voice she appended, "Do it swiftly and with vigor, or else we are lost!"

"Very well," returned the Lifeguards officer. "Let me confer a moment with these gentlemen, and we will carry out what we determine immediately."

Choiseul entered, carrying some letters wrapped in a bloodstained handkerchief. He offered this to Charny without a word. The count understood that it came from his brother, and putting out his hand to receive the tragic inheritance, he kissed the wrapper. The Queen could not hold back a sigh. Charny did not turn around to her, but said as he thrust the packet into his breast: "Gentlemen, can you aid me in the last effort I intend?"

"We are ready for anything."

"Do you believe we are a dozen men staunch and able?"

"We are eight or nine, anyway."

"Well, I will return to my hussars. While I attack the barriers in front, you storm them in the rear. By favor of your diversion, I will force through, and with our united forces we will reach this spot where we will extricate the King."

They held out their hands to him by way of answer.

"In an hour," said Charny to the King and Queen, "you shall be free, or I dead."

"Oh, count, do not say that word," said she. "It causes me too much pain."

George bowed in confirmation of his vow, and stepped towards the door without being appalled by the fresh uproar in the street. But as he laid his hand on the knob, it flew open and gave admission to a new character who mingled directly in the already complicated plot of the drama.

This was a man in his fortieth year. His countenance was dark and forbidding, his collar open at the throat, his unbuttoned coat, the dust on his clothes, and his eyes red with fatigue—all indicated that he had ridden far and fast under the goad of fierce feeling. He carried a brace of pistols in his sash girdle and a sabre hung by his side.

Almost breathless as he opened the door, he appeared relieved only when he saw the Royal Family. A smile of vengeance flitted over his face. Without troubling about the other persons around the room, and by the doorway itself, which he almost blocked up with his massive form, he thundered as he stretched out his hand: "In the name of the National Assembly, you are all my prisoners!"

As swift as thought Choiseul sprang forward with a pistol in hand and offered to blow out the brains of this intruder, who seemed to surpass in insolence and resolution all they had met before. But the Queen stopped the menacing hand with a still swifter action and said in an undertone to the count: "Do not hasten our ruin! Prudence, my lord! Let us gain time for Bouille to arrive."

"You are right," said Choiseul, putting up the firearm.

The Queen glanced at Charny, whom she had thought would have been the first to intervene. But, astonishing thing! Charny seemed not to want the new-comer to notice him, and shrank into the darkest corner apparently in that end. She did not doubt him, or that he would step out of the mystery and shadow at the proper time.

The threatening move of the nobleman against the representative of the National Assembly had passed over without the latter appearing to remark his escape from death. Besides, an emotion other than fear seemed to monopolize his heart. There was no mistaking his face's expression. It was the expression of the hunter who has tracked the lion to its den, with the lioness and their cubs, and with their jackals—among whom was devoured his only child!

But the King had winced at the word "Prisoners," which had made Choiseul revolt.

"Prisoners, in the name of the Assembly? What do you mean? I do not understand you."

"It is plain and easy enough," replied the man. "In spite of the oath you took not to go out of France, you have fled in the night, betraying your pledge, the Nation and the people. Hence the nation has cried: 'To arms!' She has risen, and said by the voice of one of your lowest subjects, not less powerful because it comes from below: 'Sire, in the name of the people, the nation and the National Assembly, you are my prisoner!'"

In the adjoining room, a cheer burst at the words.

"My lady," said Choiseul to the Queen in her ear, "do not forget that you stopped me, and that you would not suffer this insult if your pity had not interfered for this bully."

"It will go for nothing if we are revenged," she replied.

"But if not?"

She could only groan hollowly and painfully. But Charny's hand was slowly reached over the duke's shoulder and touched the Queen's arm. She turned quickly.

"Let that man speak and act—I answer for him," said the count.

Meanwhile the monarch, stunned by the fresh blow dealt him, stared with amazement at the gloomy figure which had spoken so energetic a language, and curiosity was mingled with it from his belief that he had seen him before.

"Well, in short, what do you want? Speak," he said.

"Sire, I am here to prevent you and the Royal Family taking another step towards the frontier."

"I suppose you come with thousands of men to oppose my march," went on the King, who became grander during his discussion.

"No, Sire, I am alone, or with only another, General Lafayette's aid-de-camp, sent by him and the Assembly to have the orders of the Nation executed. I am sent by Mayor Bailly, but I come mainly on my own behalf, to watch this envoy, and blow out his brains if he flinches."

All the hearers looked at him with astonishment. They had never seen the commoners, but oppressed or furious, and begging for pardon or murdering all before them. For the first time, they beheld a man of the people upright, with folded arms, feeling his force and speaking in the name of his rights. Louis saw quickly that no quarter was to be hoped for from one of this metal. He said in his eagerness to finish with him: "Where is your companion?"

"Here he is, behind me," said he, stepping forward so as to disclose the doorway. There was seen a young man in staff-officer's uniform, who was leaning against the window. He was also in disorder, but it was out of fatigue, not force. His face looked mournful. He held a paper in his hand.

This was Captain Romeuf: Lafayette's aid, and a sincere patriot. But during Lafayette's dictature, while he was superintending the Tuileries, he had shown so much respectful delicacy that the Queen had thanked him on several occasions.

"Oh, it is you?" she exclaimed, painfully surprised. "I never should have believed it," she added, with the painful groan of a beauty who feels her fancied invincible power failing.

"Good, it looks as if I were quite right to come," muttered the second deputy, smiling.

The impatient King did not give the young officer time to present his warrant. He took a step towards him rapidly and snatched it from his hands.

"There is no longer a King in France," he uttered after having read it.

The companion of Romeuf smiled as much as to say: "I knew that all along." The Queen moved towards the King to question him at these words.

"Listen, madam," he said, "to the decree that the Assembly has presumed to issue." In a voice shaking with indignation, he read the following lines:

> *"It is hereby ordered by the Assembly, that the Home Secretary shall send messengers into every department with the order for all functionaries, National Guards, and troops of the line in the country, to arrest or have arrested, all persons howsoever attempting to leave the country. As well as to prevent all departure of goods, arms, ammunition, gold and silver, horses and vehicles. And in case these messengers overtake the King, or any members of the Royal Family, and those who connive at their absconding, the said functionaries, National Guards and troops of the line are to take, and hereby are bound to take, all measure possible to check the said absconding, prevent the absconders continuing their route, and give an account immediately to the House of Representatives."*

The Queen listened in torpor. But when the King finished, she shook her head to arouse her wits and said: "Impossible—give it to me," and she held out her hand for the fateful message. In the meantime, Romeuf's companion was encouraging the National Guards and patriots of Varennes with a smile. Though they had heard the tenor of the missive, the Queen's expression of "Impossible!" had startled them.

"Read, Madam, if still you doubt," said the King with bitterness. "It is written and signed by the Speaker of the House."

"What man dares write and sign such impudence?"

"A peer of the realm—the Marquis of Beauharnais."

Is it not a strange thing, which proves how events are mysteriously linked together, that the decree stopping Louis in his flight should bear a name, obscure up to then, yet about to be attached in a brilliant manner with the history of the commencement of the 19th Century?

The Queen read the paper, frowning. The King took it to re-peruse it, and then tossed it aside so carelessly that it fell on the sleeping prince and princess's couch. At this, the Queen, incapable of self-restraint any longer, rose quickly with an angry roar. Seizing the paper, she crushed it up in her grip before throwing it afar, with the words: "Be careful, my lord—I would not have such a filthy rag sully my children."

A deafening clamor arose from the next room, and the Guards made a movement to rush in upon the illustrious fugitives. Lafayette's aid let a cry of apprehension escape him. His companion uttered one of wrath.

"Ha," he growled between his teeth, "is it thus you insult the Assembly, the Nation and the people? Very well, we shall see! Come, citizens!" he called out, turning to the men without. They were already excited by the contest, and armed with guns, scythes mounted on poles like spears, and swords. They were taking the second stride to enter the room, and Heaven only knows what would have been the shock of two such enmities, had not Charny sprang forward. He had kept aloof during the scene, and now grasping the National Guards man by the wrist as he was about to draw his sabre, he said: "A word with you, Farmer Billet; I want to speak with you."

Billet, for it was he, emitted a cry of astonishment. He turned pale as death, stood irresolute for an instant, and then said as he sheathed the half-drawn steel: "Have it so. I have to speak with you, Lord Charny." He proceeded to the door and said: "Citizens, make room if you please. I have to confer with this officer. But have no uneasiness," he added in a low voice, "there shall not escape one wolf, he or she, or yet a whelp. I am on the lookout and I answer for them!"

As if this man had the right to give them orders, though he was unknown to them all—save Charny—they backed out and left the inner room free. Besides, each was eager to relate to those without what had happened inside, and enjoin all patriots to keep close watch. In the meantime, Charny whispered to the Queen: "Romeuf is a friend of yours; I leave him with you—get the utmost from him." This was the more easy as Charny closed the door behind him to prevent anybody, even Billet, entering.

CHAPTER XVII

The Feud

The two men, on facing each other, looked without the nobleman making so much as a courtly bow. More than that, it was Billet who spoke first.

"The count does me the honor to say he wants to speak with me. I am waiting for him to be good enough to do so."

"Billet," began Charny, "how comes it that you are here on an errand of vengeance? I thought you were the friend of your superiors the nobles, and besides, a faithful and sound subject of his Majesty."

"I was all that, count. I was your most humble servant—though I cannot say your friend—in as much as such an honor is not vouchsafed to a farmer like me. But you may see that I am nothing of the kind at present."

"I do not follow you, Billet."

"Why need you? Am I asking you the reason for your fidelity to the King, and your standing true to the Queen? No, I presume you have your reasons for doing this, and as you are a good and wise gentleman, I expect your reasons are sound or at least meet for your conscience. I am not in your high position, count, and have not your learning. But you know, or you have heard, I am accounted an honest and sensible man. And you may suppose that, like yourself, I have my reasons—suiting my conscience, if not good."

"Billet, I used to know you as far different from what you are now," said Charny, totally unaware of the farmer's grounds for hatred against royalty and nobility.

"Oh certainly, I am not going to deny that you saw me unlike this," replied Billet with a bitter smile. "I do not mind telling you, count, how this is. I was a true lover of my country, devoted to one thing and two persons: the men were the King and Dr. Gilbert—the thing, my native-land. One day the King's men—I confess that this began to set me against him," said the farmer, shaking his head—"broke into my house and stole away a casket. It was a precious trust left me by Dr. Gilbert.

"As soon as I was free, I started for Paris, where I arrived on the evening of the thirteenth of July. It was right in the thick of the riot over the busts of Necker and the Duke of Orleans. Fellows were carrying them about the street, with cheers for those two, doing no harm to the King, when the royal soldiers charged upon us. I saw poor chaps, who had committed no offense but shouting for persons they had probably never seen, fall around me. Some with their skulls laid open with saber slashes, others with their breasts bored by bullets. I saw Prince Lambesq, a friend of the King, drive women and children inside the Tuileries gardens, who had shouted for nobody, and trample under his horse's hoofs an old man. This set me still more against the King.

"Next day I went to the boarding school where Dr. Gilbert's son Sebastian was kept. I learned from the poor lad that his father was locked up in the Bastille on the King's order, sued for by a lady of the court. So I said to myself, this King, whom they call kind, has moments when he errs, blunders or is ignorant. And I ought to amend one of the faults the King so makes—which I proposed to do by contributing all my power to destroying the Bastile. We managed that—not without its being a tough job, for the soldiers of the King fired on us, and killed some two hundred of us, which gave me a fresh wrinkle on the kindness of the King. But in short, we took the Bastille. In one of its dungeons I found Dr. Gilbert, for whom I had risked death a hundred times, and the joy of finding him made me forget that and a lot more. Besides, he was the first to tell me that the King was kind, ignorant for the most part of the shameful deeds perpetrated in his name, and that one must not bear him a grudge, but cast it on his ministers. Now, as all that Dr. Gilbert said at that time was Gospel, I believed Dr. Gilbert.

"The Bastille being captured, Dr. Gilbert safe and free, and Pitou and myself all well, I forgot the aforesaid atrocities. The charges in the Tuileries garden, the shooting in the street, the two hundred men slain by Marshal Saxe's sackbut, which is or was a gun on the Bastile ramparts, and the imprisonment of my friend on the mere application of a court dame. But pardon me, count," Billet interrupted himself, "all this is no concern of yours, and you cannot have asked to speak with me to hear the babble of a poor uneducated rustic. You who are both a high noble and a learned gentleman."

He made a move to lay hold of the doorknob and re-enter the other room. But Charny stopped him for two reasons, the first that it might be important to learn why Billet acted thus, and again, to gain time.

"No; tell me the whole story, my dear Billet," he said. "You know the interest my poor brothers and I always bore you, and what you say engages me in a high degree."

Billet smiled bitterly at the words "My poor brothers."

"Well, then," he replied, "I will tell you all. With regret that your poor brothers—particularly Lord Isidore, are not here to hear me."

This was spoken with such singular intonation that the count repressed the feeling of grief that the mention of Isidore's name had aroused in his soul. He waved his hand for the farmer to continue, as Billet was evidently ignorant of what had happened to the viscount whose presence he desired.

"Hence," proceeded the yeoman, "when the King returned to Paris from Versailles, I saw in it merely the return home of a father to his children. I walked with Dr. Gilbert beside the royal carriage, making a breastwork for those within it of my body, and shouting 'Long live the King!' to split the ear. This was the first journey of the King, blessings and flowers were all around him. On arriving at the City Hall, it was noticed that he did not wear the white cockade of his fathers, but he had not yet donned the tricolored one. So I plucked mine from my hat and gave it him, as they were roaring that he must sport it. And therefore he thanked me, to the cheering of the crowd. I was wild with glee at the King wearing my own favor, and I shouted Long Life to him louder than anybody.

"I was so enthusiastic about our good King that I wanted to stay in town. My harvest was ripe and cried for me; but pooh, what mattered a harvest? I was rich enough to lose one season, and it was better for me to stay beside this good King to be useful. This Father of the People, this Restorer of French Liberty, as we dunces called him at the time. I lost pretty near all the harvest because I trusted it to Catherine, who had something else to look after than my wheat. Let us say no more on that score.

"Still, it was said that the King had not quite fairly agreed to the change in things, that his movements were forced and constrained. That he might wear the tricolor cockade in his hat, but the white one was in his heart. They were slanderers who said this. It was clearly proved that at the Guards' Banquet, the Queen put on neither the national nor the French cockade, but the black one of her brother, the Austrian Emperor. I own that this made my doubts revive. But as Dr. Gilbert pointed out, 'Billet, it is not the King who did this, but the Queen. And the Queen being a woman, one must be indulgent towards her.' I believed this so deeply that, when the ruffians came from Paris to attack the Versailles Palace —though I did not hold them wholly in the wrong—it was I who ran to rouse General Lafayette. He was in the sleep of the blessed, poor dear man! But I brought him on the field in time to save the Royal Family.

"On that night I saw Lady Elizabeth hug General Lafayette, and the Queen give him her hand to kiss, while the King called him his friend. And I said to myself, says I: 'Upon my faith, I believe Dr. Gilbert is right. Surely, not from fear would such high folks make such a show of gratitude, and they would not play a lie if they did not share this hero's opinions, howsoever useful he may be at this pinch to them all.' Again I pitied the poor Queen, who had only been rash, and the poor King, only feeble. But I let them go back to Paris without me—I had better to do at Versailles. You know what, Count Charny!"

The Lifeguardsman uttered a sigh recalling the death of his brother Valence.

"I heard that this second trip to the town was not as merry as the former," continued Billet. "Instead of blessings, curses were showered down; instead of shouts of 'Long Live!' those of 'Death to the lot!'. Instead of bouquets under the horses hoofs and carriage wheels, dead men's heads carried on spear-points. I don't know, not being there, as I stayed at Versailles. Still, I left the farm without a master—but pshaw!—I was rich enough to lose another harvest after that of '89! However, one fine morning, Pitou arrived to announce that I was on the brink of losing something dearer, which no father is rich enough to lose: his daughter!"

Charny started, but the other only looked at him fixedly as he went on. "I must tell you, lord, that a league off from us, at Boursonne, lives a noble family of mighty lords, terribly rich. Three brothers were the family. When they were boys and used to come over to Villers Cotterets, the two younger of the three were wont to stop on my place. They did me the honor to say that they never drank sweeter milk than my cows gave, or ate finer bread than my wife made. And from time to time they would add—I believing they just said it in payment of my good cheer, ass that I was—that they had never seen a prettier lass than my Catherine. Lord bless you, I thanked them for drinking the milk, and eating the bread, and finding my child so pretty into the bargain! What would you do? As I believed in the King, though he is half a German by the mother's side, I might believe in noblemen who were wholly French.

"So when the youngest of all, Valence, was killed at Versailles, bravely doing his duty as a nobleman on the October Riot night, what a blow that was to me! His brother saw me on my knees before the body, shedding almost as many tears as he shed blood. His eldest brother, I mean, who never came to my house. Not because he was too proud, I will do him that fair play, but because he was sent to foreign parts while young. I think I can still see him in the damp courtyard. There where I carried the poor young fellow in my arms, so that he should not be hacked to pieces like his comrades. They whose blood so dyed me that I was almost as reddened as yourself, Lord Charny. He was a pretty boy, whom I still see riding to school on his little dappled pony, with a basket on his arm. Thinking of him thus, I believe I can mourn him like yourself, my lord. But I think of the other, and I weep no more," said Billet.

"The other? What do you mean." cried the count.

"Wait, we are coming to it," was the reply. "Pitou had come to Paris, and let a couple of words drop to show that it was not my crops so much in danger as my child—not my fortune, but my happiness. So I left the King to fend for himself in the city. Since he meant the right thing, as Dr. Gilbert assured me, all would go for the best, whether I was at hand or not, and I returned on my farm.

"I believed that Catherine had brain fever, or something I would not understand, but was only in danger of death. The condition in which I found her made me uneasy, all the more as the doctor forbade me from the room till she was cured. The poor father in despair, not allowed to go into the sickroom, could not help hanging round the door. Yes, I listened. It was then that I learned that she was at death's point, almost out of her senses with fever, mad because her lover had gone away! Her gallant, not her sweetheart! See? A year before, I had gone away, but she had smiled on my going instead of grieving. My going left her free to meet her gallant!

"Catherine returned to health but not to gladness! A month passed. Then two, three, six months passed without a single beam of joy kissing the face which my eyes never quitted. One morning, I saw her smile, and shuddered. Was not her lover coming back that she should smile? Indeed, a shepherd who had seen him prowling about a year before, told me that he had arrived that morning. I did not doubt that he would come over on my ground that evening, or rather on the land where Catherine was mistress. I loaded up my gun at dark and laid in wait—"

"You did this, Billet?" queried Charny.

"Why not?" retorted the farmer. "I lay in wait right enough for the wild boar coming to make mush of my potatoes, the wolf to tear my lambs' throats, the fox to throttle my fowls. Am I not to lay in wait for the villain who comes to disgrace my daughter?"

"But your heart failed you at the test, Billet, I hope," said the count.

"No, not the heart, but the eye and the hand," said the other. "A track of blood showed me that I had not wholly missed, only you may understand that a defamed maid had not wavered between father and scoundrel. When I entered the house, Catherine had disappeared."

"And you have not seen her since?"

"No. Why should I see her? She knows right well that I should kill her on sight."

Charny shrank back in terror mingled with admiration for the massive character confronting him.

"I retook the work on the farm," proceeded the farmer. "What concern of mine was my misfortune, if France were only happy? Was not the King marching steadily in the road of Revolution? Was he not to take his part in the Federation? Might I not see him again whom I had saved in October, and sheltered with my own cockade? What a pleasure it must be for him to see all France gathered on the parade-ground at Paris, swearing like one man the unity of the country!

"So, for a space, while I saw him, I forgot all. Even to Catherine—no, I lie—no father forgets his child! He also took the oath. It seemed to me that he swore clumsily and evasively, from his seat instead of at the Altar of the Country. But what did that matter? The main thing was that he did swear. An oath is an oath. It is not the place where he takes it that makes it holy, and when an honest man takes an oath, he keeps it. So the King should keep his word. But it is true that when I got home to Villers Cotterets—having no child now, I attended to politics. I heard say that the King was willing to have Marquis Favras carry him off, but the scheme had fallen through. That the King had tried to flee with his aunts, but that had failed. That he wanted to go out to St. Cloud, whence he would have hurried off to Rouen, but that the people prevented him leaving town. I heard all this but I did not believe it. Had I not with my own eyes seen the King hold up his hand to high heaven on the Paris Parade-ground, and swear to maintain the nation? How could I believe that a king, having sworn in the presence of three hundred thousand citizens, would not hold his pledge to be as sacred as that of other men? It was not likely!

"Hence, as I was at Meaux Market yesterday—I may as well say I was sleeping at the postmaster's house, with whom I had made a grain deal. I was astonished to see in a carriage changing horses at my friend's door, the King, the Queen and the Dauphin! There was no mistaking them; I was in the habit of seeing them in a coach. On the sixteenth of July, I accompanied them from Versailles to Paris. I heard one of the party say: 'The Chalons Road!' This man in a buff waistcoat had a voice I knew. I turned and recognized—who but the gentleman who had stolen away my daughter! This noble was doing his duty by playing the flunky before his master's coach."

At this, he looked hard at Charny to see if he understood that his brother Isidore was the subject; but the hearer was silent as he wiped his face with his handkerchief.

"I wanted to fly at him, but he was already at a distance. He was on a good horse and had weapons—I had none. I ground my teeth at the idea that the King was escaping out of France, and this ravisher was escaping me, but suddenly another thought struck me. Why look ye; I took an oath to the Nation too, and while the King breaks his, I shall keep mine. I am only ten leagues from Paris, which I can reach in two hours on a good nag. It is but three in the morning. I will talk this matter over with Mayor Bailly, an honest man who appears to be one of the kind who stick to the promises they make. This point settled, I wasted no time. I begged my friend the posting-house keeper to lend me his national Guards uniform, and his sword and pistols. And I took the best horse in his stables—all without letting him know what was in the wind, of course. Instead of trotting home, I galloped hellity-split to Paris.

"Thank God I got there in time! The flight of the King was known, but not the direction. Lafayette had sent his aid Romeuf on the Valenciennes Road, but mark what a thing chance is! They had stopped him at the bars, and brought him back to the Assembly. There, he walked in at the very nick when Mayor Bailly, informed by me, was furnishing the most precise particulars about the runaways. There was nothing but the proper warrant to write and the road to state. The thing was done in a flash. Romeuf was dispatched on the Chalons Road, and my order was to stick to him, which I am going to do. Now," concluded Billet, with a gloomy air, "I have overtaken the King, who deceived me as a Frenchman, and I am easy about his escaping me! I can go and attend to the man who deceived me as a father; and I swear to you, Lord Charny, that he shall not escape me either."

"You are wrong, my dear Billet—woeful to say," responded the count.

"How so?"

"The unfortunate young man you speak of has escaped."

"Fled?" cried Billet with indescribable rage.

"No, he is dead," replied the other.

"Dead?" exclaimed Billet, shivering in spite of himself, and sponging his forehead on which the sweat had started out.

"Dead," repeated Charny, "for this is his blood which you see on me, and which you were right just now in likening to that from his brother, slain at Versailles. If you doubt, go down into the street, where you will find his body laid out in a little yard, like that of Versailles, struck down for the same cause for which his brother fell."

Billet looked at Charny, who spoke in a gentle voice, but with haggard eyes and a frightened face. Then suddenly he cried: "Of a truth, there is justice in heaven!" He darted out of the room, saying: "I do not doubt your word, lord, but I must assure my sight that justice is done."

Charny stifled a sigh as he watched him go, and dashed away a tear. Aware that there was not an instant to lose, he hurried to the Queen's room. And as soon as he walked directly up to her, he asked how she had got on with Romeuf.

"He is on our side," responded the lady.

"So much the better," said Charny, "for there is nothing to hope in that quarter."

"What are we to do then?"

"Gain time for Bouille to come up."

"But will he come?"

"Yes, for I am going to fetch him."

"But the streets swarm with murderers," cried the Queen. "You are known, you will never pass! You will be hewn to pieces George... George!"

But smiling without replying, Charny opened the window on the back garden, waved his hand to the King and the Queen, and jumped out over fifteen feet. The Queen sent up a shriek of terror and hid her face in her hands. But the man ran to the wind, and by a cheer, allayed her fears. Charny had scaled the garden wall, and was disappearing on the other side. It was high time, for Billet was entering.

CHAPTER XVIII

On the Back Track

Billet's countenance was dark; thoughtfulness lowered the brows over his deeply investigating eyes. He reviewed all the prisoners, and made note of the one missing. Charny's flight was recent; the window was being closed by the Colonel after him. By bending forward, Billet could see the count vaulting over the garden wall. It followed that the agreement made between Captain Romeuf and the Queen was for him to stand down.

Behind Billet, the outer room was filled as before with the scythe-bearers, musketeers and swordsmen. He dismissed them with a gesture. These men seemed to obey this chief, to whom they were attracted by magnetic influence, because they divined in him a plebeian like themselves. He maintained a patriotism, or hatred, equal to their own. His glance meeting theirs told him that he might rely on them, even in case he had to proceed to violence.

"Well, have they decided to go?" he asked Romeuf.

The Queen threw on him one of those side looks, which would have blasted him if they had the power of lightning. Without replying, she clutched the arm of her chair, as though to clamp herself to it.

"The King begs a little more time, as they have not slept in the night, and their Majesties are dying of fatigue?" said Romeuf.

"Captain," returned Billet bluntly, "you know very well that it is not because their Majesties are fatigued that they sue for time, but because they hope in a few instants that Lord Bouille will arrive. But it will be well for their Majesties not to dally," added Billet with emphasis, "for if they refuse to come out willingly, they will be lugged by the heels."

"Scoundrel!" cried Damas, darting at the speaker with his sword up.

Billet turned to face him, but with folded arms. He had in truth no need to defend himself, for eight or ten men sprang into the room, and the colonel was threatened by ten different weapons. The King saw that the least word or move would lead to all his supporters being shot or chopped to rags, and he said,"It is well. Let the horses be put to, we are going."

One of the Queen's women, who traveled in a cab with her companion after the royal coach, screamed and swooned. This awakened the boy prince and his sister, who wept.

"Fie, sir, you cannot have a child that you are so cruel to a mother," said the Queen to the farmer.

"No, madam," replied he with a bitter smile, "I have no child now. There is to be no delay about the horses," he went on to the King. "The horses are harnessed, and the carriage at the door."

Approaching the window, the King saw that all was ready. In the immense din, he had not heard the horses brought up. Seeing him through the window, the mob burst into a threatening shout. He turned pale.

"What does your Majesty order?" inquired Choiseul of the Queen. "We had rather die than witness this outrage."

"Do you believe Lord Charny has got away?" she asked quickly in an undertone.

"I can answer for that."

"Then let us go. But in heaven's name, for your own sake as well as ours, do not quit us."

The King understood her fear.

"I do not see any horses for Lord Choiseul and Damas," observed he.

"They can follow as they like," said Billet. "My orders are to bring the King and the Queen, and do not speak of them."

"But I declare that I will not go without them having their horses," broke forth the monarch with more firmness than was expected from him.

"What do you say to that?" cried Billet to his men swarming into the room. "Here is the King, not going because these gentlemen have no horses!"

The mob roared with laughter.

"I will find them," said Romeuf.

"Do not quit their Majesties," interposed Choiseul. "Your office gives you some power over the people, and it depends on your honor that not a hair of their head should fall."

Romeuf stopped, while Billet snapped his fingers.

"I will attend to this," said he, leading the way. But stopping on the threshold, he frowned and said, "But you will fetch them along, eh lads?"

"Oh, never fear," replied the men with a peal of laughter, evidencing that no pity was to be expected in case of resistance.

At such a point of irritation, they would certainly have used roughness and shot down anyone resisting. Billet had no need to come upstairs again. One of them by the window watched what happened in the street.

"The horses are ready," he said. "Out you go!"

"Out, and be off!" said his companions with a tone admitting no discussion.

The King took the lead. Romeuf was supposed to look particularly after the family, but the fact is, he had need to take care of himself. The rumor had spread that he was not only carrying out the Assembly's orders with mildness, but he actively favored the flight of one of the most devoted upholders of the Royals, who had only quitted them in order to hurry up Marquis Bouille to their rescue. The result was that on the sill, while Billet's conduct was glorified by the gathering, Romeuf heard himself qualified as a traitor and an aristocrat.

The party stepped into the carriage and the cab, with the two Lifeguards on the box. Valory had asked as a favor, that the King would let him and his comrade be considered as domestics, since they were no longer allowed to act as his soldiers.

"As things stand," he pleaded, "princes of the blood royal might be glad to be here. The more honor for simple gentlemen like us."

"Have it so," said the sovereign tearfully, "you shall not quit me ever."

Thus they took in reality the place of couriers. Choiseul closed the door.

"Gentlemen," said the King, "I positively give the order that you shall drive me to Montmedy. Postilions, to Montmedy!"

But with one voice, the united populations of many towns replied: "To Paris!"

In the lull, Billet pointed with his sword and said: "Postboys, take the Clermont Road."

The vehicle whirled round to obey this order.

"I take you all for witness that I am overpowered by violence," said Louis XVI.

Exhausted by the effort he had made, the unfortunate King, who had never shown so much will before, fell back on the rear seat between the Queen and his sister. In five minutes, after going a couple of hundred paces, a great clamor was heard behind. As they were placed, the Queen was the passenger who could first get her head out of the window. She drew in almost instantly, covering her eyes with both hands, and muttering: "Oh, woe to us! They are murdering Choiseul."

The King tried to rise, but the two ladies pulled him down. The carriage turned the road, and they could not see what passed at twenty paces that way. Choiseul and Damas had mounted their horses at Sausse's door, but Romeuf's had been taken away from the post-house. He and two cavalrymen followed on foot, hoping to find a horse or two. Either of the hussars and dragoons, who had been led off by the people, or those abandoned by their masters. But they had not gone fifteen steps before Choiseul perceived that the three were in danger of being smothered, pressed down and scattered in the multitude. He stopped, letting the carriage go on. And judging that Romeuf was of the most value to the Royal Family in this strait, he called to his servant, James Brisack, who was mixed up with the press.

"Give my spare horse to Captain Romeuf."

Scarce had he spoken the words, than the exasperated crowd enveloped him, yelling: "This is the Count of Choiseul, one who wanted to take away the King! Down with the aristocrat—death to the traitor!"

Everyone knows how rapidly the effect follows the threat in these popular commotions. Torn from his saddle, Count Choiseul was hurled back and swallowed up in that horrible gulf of the multitude. In that epoch of deadly passions, one emerged from such a crowd only in fragments. But at the same time as he fell, five persons rushed to his rescue. These were Damas, Romeuf, Brisack and two others—the last having lost the lead horse so that his hands were free for his master's service. Such a conflict arose as when Indians wage around the body of a fallen warrior whom they do not wish scalped.

Contrary to all probability, Choiseul was not hurt, or at least not fatally, despite the ugly weapons used against him. A soldier parried with his musket a scythe thrust aimed at him, and Brisack warded off another with a stick he had snatched from a hand in the medley. This stick was cleft like a reed, but the cut was so turned as to wound only the count's horse.

"This way the dragoons!" called Adjutant Foucq.

Some soldiers rushed up at the call, and cleared a space in their shame at the officer being murdered among them. Romeuf sprang into the open space.

"In the name of the National Assembly, and of General Lafayette, whose deputy I am, lead these gentleman to the town-hall!" he vociferated.

Both names of the Assembly and the general enjoyed full popularity at this period, and exerted their usual effect.

"To the town-hall," roared the concourse.

Willing hands made a united effort, and Choiseul and his companions were dragged towards the council rooms. It took well over an hour to get there. Each minute had its threat and attempt to murder, and every opening the protectors left was used to thrust with a pike or pitchfork or sabre.

However, the municipal building was reached at last, where only one town's officer remained, extremely frightened at the responsibility devolving on him. To relieve him of this charge, he ordered that Choiseul, Damas and Floirac should be put in the cells, and watched by the National Guards.

Romeuf thereupon declared that he would not quit Choiseul, who had shielded him and so brought on himself what happened. So the town official ordered that he should be put in the cell along with him. Choiseul made a sign for his groom Brisack to get away and see to the horses. Not much pulled about, they were in an inn, guarded by the volunteers. Romeuf stayed till the Verdun National Guard came in, when he entrusted the prisoners to them, and went his way with the officers' pledge that they would keep them well.

Isidore Charny's remains were dragged into a weaver's house, where pious but alien hands prepared them for the grave. Isadore was less fortunate than his brother Valence, who at least was mourned over by his brother, Billet and Gilbert. But at that time, Billet was a devoted and respectful friend. We know how these feelings changed into hate—as implacable as the better sentiments had been deep.

CHAPTER XIX

The Dolorous Way

In the meantime, the Royal Family continued on the road to Paris. They advanced slowly, for the carriage could not move but at the gait of the escort, and that was composed mostly of men on foot. Their ranks were filled up with women and children, the women lifting their babes up in their arms to see the King dragged back to the capital. They would probably never have seen him under other circumstances.

The coach and the cab, with the ladies in waiting, seemed like a ship with her tender in a human sea. Incidents stirred up the sea into heaving furiously at times, when the coach disappeared under the billows, then appeared very slow to emerge. Though it was six miles to Clermont, the terrible escort did not lessen in number, as those who dropped off were replaced by new-comers from the countryside who wanted to have a peep at the show.

Of all the captives on and in this ambulatory prison, the worst exposed to the popular wrath and the plainest butt of the menaces were the unhappy Lifeguards on the large box seat. As the order of the National Assembly made the Royal Family inviolable, the way to vent spite on them by proxy was to plague these men. Bayonets were continually held to their breasts. Some scythes gleamed over their heads, or some spear glided like a perfidious serpent in the gaps. It would pierce the flesh with its keen sting, and return to the wielder, who was often disgusted that he had not drawn more blood.

All at once they saw a man without hat or weapon split the crowd, his clothing was smeared with mud and dust. After having addressed a respectful bow to the King and the Queen, he sprang upon the forepart of the carriage, upon the box between the two Lifeguards. The Queen's outcry was of fear, joy and pain. She had recognized Charny.

Fear, for what he did was so bold that it was a miracle he had reached the perch without receiving some wound. Joy, for she was happy to see that he had escaped the unknown dangers he must have run, all the greater as imagination was outstripped by the reality. Pain, for she comprehended that Charny's solitary return implied that nothing was to be expected from Bouille.

In fact, while Charny had reached the royalists at Grange-au-Bois on a horse he picked up on the road, his attempt to guide the army ended in failure. A canal which he had not noted down in his survey, perhaps cut since then, was brimful of water. He nearly lost his life, as he did his horse, in trying to swim across it. All he could do on scrambling out on the other side from his friends, was to wave them a farewell. For he understood that the cavaliers as a mass could not succeed where he had fallen short.

Confounded by the audacity of this recruit to the lost cause, the mob seemed to respect him for this boldness. At the turmoil, Billet, who was riding at the head, turned and recognized the nobleman.

"Ha, I am glad that nothing happened him," he said. "But woe to whomsoever tries this again, for he shall certainly pay for the two."

At two in the afternoon, they arrived at St. Menehould. Loss of sleep and weariness was telling on all the prisoners, but particularly on the Dauphin. He was feverish and wanted to be undressed and put to bed, as he was not well. But St. Menehould was the place most enraged against the Royal Family. So no attention was paid to the King who ordered a stop. A contradictory order from Billet led to the change of horses being hooked on the pole. The Queen could not withstand her child's complaints, and holding the little prince up at the window to show him to the people, shivering and in tears, she said: "Gentlemen, in pity for this boy, stop!"

"Forward, March!" shouted Billet.

"Forward," repeated the people.

Billet passed the carriage window to take his place in the front when the Queen appealed to him, "For shame, sir. It is plain, I repeat, that you never were a father."

"And I repeat, madam, that I was a father once, but am one no longer."

"Do as you will, for you are the stronger. But beware! For no voice cries more loudly to heaven than that of these little ones!"

The procession went on again. It was cruel work passing through the town. If kings could learn anything, the enthusiasm excited by sight of Drouet would have been a dreadful lesson. But both captives saw merely blind fury in the cheers. They saw but rebels in these patriots, who were convinced that they were saving their country.

Perhaps it was the King's impression that Paris alone was perverted, that urged him into the evil course. He had relied on "his dear provinces." But here were the dear rurals, not only escaping him, but turning pitilessly against him. The country folk had frightened Choiseul in Sommevelle, imprisoned Dandoins at St. Menehould, fired on Damas at Clermont, and lately killed Isidore Charny under the royal eyes. All classes rose against him.

It would have cut him worse had he seen what the spreading news did. It roused all the country to come—not to stare and form an escort—but to kill him. The harvest was so bad that this country was called "Blank Champagne," and here came the King who had brought in the thievish hussar and the pillaging pandour to trample the poor fields under their horses' hoofs. But the carriage was guarded by an angel and two cherubs.

Lady Elizabeth was twenty-seven, but her chastity had kept the unfading brilliancy of youth on her brow. The Dauphin was ailing and shivering on his mother's knee. The princess, fair as the blondes can be, was looking out with her firm but astonished gaze. The men saw these—the Queen bent over her boy, and the King downhearted—and their anger abated, or sought another object on which to turn it.

They yelped at the Lifeguardsmen. Insulted them, called those noble and devoted hearts traitors and cowards. Meanwhile, the June sun made a fiery rainbow in the chalky dust flung up by the endless train upon those hotheads, heated by the cheap wine of the taverns.

Half a mile out of the town, an old Knight of St. Louis was seen galloping over the fields. He wore the ribbon of the order at his buttonhole. As it was first thought that he came from sheer curiosity, the crowd made room for him. He went up to the carriage window, hat in hand, saluted the King and the Queen, and hailed them as Majesties. The people had measured true force and real majesty, and were indignant at the title being given away from them to whom it was due. They began to grumble and threaten.

The King had already learned what this growl portended from hearing it around the house at Varennes.

"Sir Knight," he said to the old chevalier, "the Queen and myself are touched by this publicly expressed token of your devotion. But in God's name, get you hence—your life is not safe."

"My life is the King's, and the finest day of it will be when laid down for the King."

Hearing this speech, some growled.

"Retire," said the King. "Make way there, my friends, for Chevalier Dampierre."

Those near who heard the appeal, stood back. But unfortunately, the horseman was squeezed in and used the whip and spur on the animal unable to move freely. Some trodden-on women screamed, a frightened child cried, and on the men shaking their fists, the old noble flourished his whip. Thereupon the growl changed to a roar. The grand popular and leonine fury broke forth.

Dampierre was already on the edge of the forest of men. He drove in both spurs which made the steed leap the ditch where it galloped across the country. He turned, and waving his hat, cried: "God save the King!"—a final homage to his sovereign, but a supreme insult to the people.

Off went a gun. He pulled a pistol from his holsters and returned the fire. Everyone who had firearms, let fly at him. The horse fell, riddled with bullets. Nobody ever knew whether the man was slain outright or not by this dreadful volley. The multitude rushed like an avalanche where rider and steed had dropped, some fifty paces from the royal carriage. One of those tumults arose such as surge upon a dead body in battle. Then, out of the disordered movements, the shapeless chaos, the gulf of yells and cheers... up rose a pike surmounted by the white head of the luckless Chevalier Dampierre. The Queen screamed and threw herself back in the vehicle.

"Monsters, cannibals, assassins!" shouted Charny.

"Hold your tongue, count," said Billet, "or I cannot answer for you."

"What matters? I am tired of life. What can befall me worse than my poor brother?"

"Your brother was guilty and you are not," replied Billet.

Charny started to jump down from the box but the other Lifeguard restrained him, while twenty bayonets bristled to receive him.

"Friends," said the farmer in his strong and imposing voice, as he pointed to Charny, "whatever this man says or does, never heed—I forbid a hair of his head being touched. I am answerable for him to his wife."

"To his wife?" muttered the Queen, shuddering as though one of the steel points menacing her beloved had pricked her heart, "Why does he say to his wife?"

Billet could not have himself told. He had invoked the name of the count's wife, knowing how powerful such a charm is over a mob composed mainly of men with wives. They were late reaching Chalons, where the King, in alighting at the house prepared for the family, heard a bullet whizz by his ear. Was it an accident, where so many were inexperienced in arms, or an attempt at regicide?

"Some clumsy fellow," said he coolly. "Gentlemen, you ought to be careful—an accident soon happens."

Apart from this shot, there was a calmer atmosphere to step into. The uproar ceased at the house door, and murmurs of compassion were heard. The table was laid out with elegance, astonishing the captives. There were servants also. But Charny claimed their role for himself and the other Lifeguards, hiding under the pretended humility the intention to stay close to the King for any event.

Marie Antoinette understood this. But in her heart rumbled Billet's words about Charny's wife, like a storm brewing. Charny, whom she had expected to take away from France, to live abroad with her, was now returning to Paris to see his wife Andrea again! He was ignorant of this ferment in her heart, from not supposing she had heard the words. Besides, he was busy over some freshly conceived hopes. Having been sent in advance to study the route, he had conscientiously fulfilled his errand. He knew the political tone of even each village. Chalons had a royalist bias from it being an old town, without trade, work or activity. It was peopled by nobles, retired businessmen and contented citizens.

Scarcely were the royal party at table than the County Lieutenant, whose house they were in, came to bow to the Queen. She looked at him uneasily, from having ceased to expect anything good. But he said, "May it please your Majesty to let the maids of Chalons offer flowers?"

"Flowers?" repeated she, looking with astonishment from him to Lady Elizabeth. "Pray, let them come."

Shortly after, twelve young ladies, the prettiest they could find in the town, tripped up to the threshold where the Queen held out her arms to them. One of them, who had been taught a formal speech, was so effected by this warm greeting that she forgot it all and stammered the general opinion: "Oh, your Majesty, what a dreadful misfortune!"

The Queen took the bunch of flowers and kissed the girl.

"Sire," whispered Charny to the King, "something good may be done here. If your Majesty will spare me for an hour, I will go out and inquire how the wind turns."

"Do so, but be prudent," was the reply. "I shall never console myself if harm befalls you. Alas, two deaths are enough in one family."

"Sire, my life is as much the King's as my brothers'."

In the presence of the monarch, his stoicism could be worn, but he felt his grief when by himself.

"Poor Isidore," he muttered, while pressing his hand to his breast to see if he still had the papers of the dead in his pocket. They were handed to him by Count Choiseul, and he had promised himself to read them as he would the last will of his loved one.

Behind the girls came their parents, almost all nobles or members of the upper middle class. They came timidly and humbly, to crave permission to offer their respect to their unfortunate sovereigns. They could hardly believe that they had seen the unfortunate Dampierre hewn to pieces under their eyes a while before. Charny came back in half an hour. It was impossible for the keenest eye to read the effect of his reconnoiter on his countenance.

"All is for the best, Sire," replied he to the King's inquiry. "The National Guard offer to conduct your Majesty to-morrow to Montmedy."

"So you have arranged some course?"

"With the principal citizens. It is a church feast to-morrow, so that they cannot refuse your request to go to hear service. At the church door, a carriage will be waiting which will receive your Majesties. Amid the cheering, you will give the order to be driven to Montmedy, and you will be obeyed."

"That is well," said Louis. "Thank you Count, and we will do this if nothing comes between. But you and your companions must take some rest; you must need it more than we."

The reception was not prolonged far into the night, so that the Royal Family retired about nine. A sentinel at their door let them see that they were still regarded as prisoners. But he presented arms to them. By his precise movement, the King recognized an old soldier.

"Where have you served, my friend?" he inquired.

"In the French Guards, Sire," answered the veteran.

"Then I am not surprised to see you here," returned the monarch; for he had not forgotten that the French Guards had gone over to the people on the 13th July, 1789.

This sentinel was posted at their sleeping room door. An hour afterwards, he asked to speak with the leader of the escort, who was Billet, on his being relieved of guard-mounting. The farmer was taking supper with the rustics, who flocked in from all sides. He was endeavoring to persuade them to stay in town all night. But most of them had seen the King, which was mainly what brought them, and they wanted to celebrate the holiday at home. Billet tried to detain them, because the aristocratic tendency of the old town alarmed him. It was in the midst of this discussion that the sentinel came to talk with him. They conversed in a low voice, most lively.

Next, Billet sent for Drouet, and they held a similar conference. After this they went to the postmaster, who was Drouet's friend, and the same line of business made them friendlier still. He saddled two horses, and in ten minutes, Billet was galloping on the road to Rheims, and Drouet to Vitry.

Day dawned. Hardly six hundred men remained of the numerous escort, and they were fagged out. They had passed the night on straw in the street, which they had brought with them. As they shook themselves awake in the dawn, they might have seen a dozen men in uniform enter the Lieutenancy Office and come out hastily shortly after.

Chalons was headquarters for the Villeroy Company of Lifeguards, and ten or twelve of the officers came to take orders from Charny. He told them to don full dress and be on their horses by the church door for the King's exit. These were the uniformed men whom we have seen.

Some of the peasants reckoned their distance from home in the morning, and about two hundred more departed, in spite of their comrades' pleadings. This reduced the faithful to a little over four hundred only. To the same number might be reckoned the National Guards devoted to the King. Besides, as hinted, the town was aristocratic.

When the word was sent to Billet and Drouet to hear what they said about the King and the Queen going to hear mass, they could not be found. Nothing, therefore, opposed their desire. The King was delighted to hear of the absence, but Charny shook his head. He did not know Drouet's character, but he knew Billet's.

Nevertheless, all the augury was favorable. And indeed, the King not only came out of church amid cheers, but the royalist gathering had assumed colossal proportions. Still, it was not without apprehension that Charny encouraged the King to make up his mind.

He put his head out of the carriage window and said, "Gentlemen, yesterday at Varennes, violence was used against me. I gave the order to be driven to Montmedy but I was constrained to go towards a revolted capital. Then I was among rebels, but now I am among honest subjects, to whom I repeat, 'To Montmedy!'"

"To Montmedy!" echoed Charny, and the others shouted the same. And to the chorus of "Long live the King!", the carriage was turned round and retook the road it had yesterday traveled.

In the absence of Billet and Drouet, the rustics seemed commanded by the French Guardsman, who had stood sentry at the royal door. Charny watched the crowd as he made his men move through it, and the scowls showed that they did not approve of it. They let the National Guards pass them, and massed in their rear as a rearguard. In the foremost ranks marched the pike and spear-men. Then fifty who carried muskets and fowling pieces, manœuvring so neatly that Charny was disquieted. But he could not oppose it, and he was unable to understand it. He was soon to have the explanation.

As they approached the town gates, in spite of the cheering, they heard another sound like the dull rolling of a storm. Suddenly Charny turned pale and laid his hand on the Lifeguard next him.

"All is lost," he gasped. "Do you not hear that drum?"

They turned the corner into a square where two streets entered. One came from Rheims, the other from Vitry, and up each was marching a column of National Guards. One numbered eighteen hundred, the other more than two thousand. Each was led by a man on horseback. One was Billet, the other Drouet.

Charny saw why they had disappeared during the night. Fore-warned no doubt, of the counteraction in preparation, they had gone off for reinforcements. They had concerted their movements so as to arrive simultaneously. They halted their men in the square, completely blocking the road. Without any cries, they began to load their firearms. The procession had to stop.

"What is the matter?" asked the King, putting his head out of the window. Charny was pale and gritting his teeth.

"Why, my lord, the enemy has gone for reinforcements. They stand yonder, loading their guns. Meanwhile, behind the Chalons National Guards, the peasants are ready with their guns."

"What do you think of all this?"

"That we are caught between two fires, which will not prevent us passing, but what will happen to your Majesty I cannot tell."

"Very well, let us turn back. Enough blood has been shed for my sake, and I weep bitter tears for it. I do not wish one drop more to flow. Let us return."

"Gentlemen," said Charny, jumping down and taking the leader horse by the bridle, "the King bids us turn back."

At the Paris Gate, the Chalons National Guards, now useless, gave place to those from Rheims and Vitry.

"Do you not think I behaved properly, madam?" inquired Louis of his wife.

"Yes—but I think Count Charny obeyed you very easily," was her comment.

She fell into one of those gloomy reveries which was not entirely due to the terrible situation in which she was hedged in.

CHAPTER XX

Mirabeau's Successor

The royal carriage sadly traveled the Paris Road, watched by the two moody men who had forced it to alter its direction. Between Epernay and Dormans, Charny, from his stature and his high seat, could distinguish a four-in-hand coach approaching from the way of Paris. He guessed that it brought grave news of some important character.

Indeed, it was hailed with cheers from the National Assembly, and contained three officials. One was Hatour Maubourg, Lafayette's right hand man. The others were Petion and Barnave, members of the House.

Of the three, the oldest leaving his own carriage and stepped up to the royal one. Roughly opening the door, he said: "I am Petion, and these are Barnave and Latour, members of the Assembly. We were sent by it to serve you as escort, and see that the wrath of the populace does not anticipate justice with its own hand. Close up there to make room for me."

The Queen darted on all three one of those disdainful glances which the haughty daughter of Maria Theresa deigned to let fall from her pride. Latour was a gentleman of the old school, like Lafayette, and he could not support the glance. He declined to enter the carriage on the grounds that the occupants were too closely packed.

"I will get into the following one," he said.

"Get in where you like," said Petion. "My place is with the King and the Queen, and in I go."

He stepped in at the same time. He looked one after the other at the King, the Queen, and Lady Elizabeth—who occupied the back seat.

"Excuse me, madam," he said to the last, "but the place of honor belongs to me as representative of the Assembly. Be obliging enough to rise and take the front seat."

"Whoever heard of such a thing?" muttered the Queen.

"Sir!" began the King.

"That is the way of it. So rise, madam, and give your place to me."

Lady Elizabeth obeyed, with a sign of resignation to her brother and sister. Latour had gone to the cab to ask the ladies to let him travel with them. Member Barnave stood without, wavering about entering the conveyance where seven persons were.

"Are you not coming, Barnave?" asked Petion.

"Where am I to put myself?" inquired the somewhat embarrassed man.

"Would you like my place?" demanded the Queen tartly.

"I thank you, madam," rejoined Barnave, stung. "A seat in the front will do for me."

A place was made by Lady Elizabeth drawing the Princess Royal to her side, while the Queen took the Dauphin on her knee. Barnave was thus placed opposite the Queen.

"All ready," cried Petion, without asking the King. "On you go!"

The vehicle resumed the journey, to cheers from the National Assembly. It was the people who stepped into the royal carriage with their representatives. There was silence, during which each studied the others except Petion, who seemed in his roughness to be indifferent to everything.

Jerome Petion, alias Villeneuve, was about thirty-two. His features were sharply defined. His merit lay in the exaltation, clearness and straightforwardness of his political opinions. Born at Chartres, he was a lawyer when sent to Paris in 1789, as member of the Assembly. He was fated to be Mayor of Paris, enjoy popularity effacing that of Bailly and Lafayette, and die on the Bordeaux salt meadow wastes, devoured by wolves. His friends called him the Virtuous Petion. He and Camille Desmoulins were republicans when nobody else in France knew the word.

Pierre Joseph Marie Barnave was born at Grenoble; he was hardly thirty. In the Assembly, he had acquired both his reputation and great popularity by struggling with Mirabeau, as the latter's popularity waned. All the great orator's enemies were necessarily friends of Barnave, and had sustained him. He appeared but five-and-twenty, with bright blue eyes, a largish mouth, turned-up nose and sharp voice. But his form was elegant. A duelist and aggressive, he looked like a young military captain in citizen's dress. He was worth more than he seemed. He belonged to the Constitutional Royalist party.

"Gentlemen," said the King as he took his seat, "I declare to you that it never was my intention to quit the kingdom."

"That being so, the words will save France," replied Barnave, looking at him ere he sat down.

Thereupon something strange transpired between this scion of the country middle class and the woman descended from the greatest throne of Europe. Each tried to read the other's heart, not like two political foes, hiding state secrets, but like a man and a woman seeking mysteries of love.

Barnave aimed in all things to be the heir and successor of Mirabeau. In everybody's eyes, Mirabeau passed for having enjoyed the King's confidence and the Queen's affection. We know what the truth was. It was not only the fashion then to spread libels, but to believe in them. Barnave's desire to be Mirabeau in all respects is what led him to be appointed one of the three Commissioners to bring back the Royal Family. He came with the assurance of the man who knows that he has the power to make himself hated, if he cannot make himself loved.

The Queen divined this with her woman's eye, if she did not perceive it. She also observed Barnave's moodiness. Half a dozen times in a quarter of an hour, Barnave turned to look at the three Lifeguards on the box. He examined them with scrupulous attention, and dropped his glance to the Queen more hard and hostile than before.

Barnave knew that one of the trio was Charny, but could not tell which one. Public rumor accredited Charny as the Queen's paramour. Barnave was jealous, though it is hard to explain such a feeling in him; but the Queen guessed that, too. From that moment she was stronger. She knew the flaw in the adversary's breastplate, and she could strike true.

"Did you hear what that man who was conducting the carriage said about the Count of Charny?" she asked of Louis XVI.

Barnave gave a start which did not escape the Queen, whose knees were touching his.

"He declared, did he not, that he was responsible for the count's life?" rejoined the sovereign.

"Exactly, and that he answered for his life to his wife."

Barnave half closed his eyes, but he did not lose a syllable.

"Now the countess is my old friend Andrea Taverney. Do you think, on our return to Paris, that it will be handsome to give him leave to go and cheer his wife? He has run great risks, and his brother has been killed on our behalf. I think that to claim his continued service beside us would be to act cruelly to the happy couple."

Barnave breathed again and opened his eyes fully.

"You are right, though I doubt that the count will accept it," returned the King.

"In that case, we shall both have done our duty—we in proposing it, and the count in refusing."

By magnetic sympathy, she felt that Barnave's irritation was softening. At the same time that his generous heart understood that he had been unfair to her, his shame sprang up. He had borne himself with a high head like a judge, and now she suddenly spoke the very words which determined her innocence of the charge which she could not have foreseen, or her repentance. Why not innocence?

"We would stand in the better position," continued the Queen, "from our not having taken Count Charny with us. And from my thinking, on my part, that he was in Paris when he suddenly appeared by the side of our carriage."

"It is so," proceeded the monarch. "But it only proves that the count has no need of stimulant when his duty is in question."

There was no longer any doubt that she was guiltless. How was Barnave to obtain the Queen's forgiveness for having wronged her as a woman? He did not dare address her, and was he to wait till she spoke the first? She said nothing at all, as she was satisfied with the effect she had produced. He had become gentle, almost humble. He implored her with a look, but she did not appear to pay him any heed.

He was in one of those moods where, to rouse a woman from inattention, he would have undertaken the twelve labors of Hercules—at the risk of the first being too much for him.

He was beseeching "the Supreme Being," which was the fashionable God in 1789, for some chance to bring attention upon him. When all at once—as though the Ruler, under whatever title addressed, had heard the prayer—a poor priest who waited for the King to go by, approached from the roadside to see the august prisoner the nearer. He said as he raised his supplicating hands and tear-wet eyes: "God bless your Majesty!"

It was a long time since the crowd had a chance of flying into anger. Nothing had presented itself since the hapless Knight of St. Louis, whose head was still following on the pike-point. This occasion was eagerly embraced. The mob replied to the reverence with a roar, they threw themselves on the priest in a twinkling. He was flung down and would have been flayed alive, but the frightened Queen appealed to Barnave.

"Oh, sir, do you not see what is going on?"

He raised his head, plunged a rapid look into the ocean which submerged the priest, and rolled in growling and tumultuous waves up to the carriage. He burst the door with such violence that he would have fallen out if the Princess Elizabeth had not caught him by the coat.

"You villains!" he shouted. "Tigers, who cannot be French men! Or France, the home of the brave, has become a den of assassins!"

This apostrophe may appear bombastic to us, but it was in the style of the period. Besides, the denunciator belonged to the National Assembly, and supreme power spoke by his voice. The crowd recoiled and the old man was saved. He rose and said, "You did well to save an old man, young sir—he will ever pray for you."

He made the sign of the cross, and went his way. The throng opened to him, dominated by the voice and attitude of Barnave, who seemed the statue of Command. When the victim was gone from sight, the young deputy simply and naturally retook his seat, as if he were not aware he had saved a human life.

"I thank you, sir," said the Queen.

These few words set him quivering over all his frame. In all the long period during which we have accompanied Marie Antoinette, though she had been more lovely, never had she been more touching.

Barnave was contemplating so much motherly grace, when the prince uttered a cry of pain at the moment when he was inclined to fall at the knees of dying Majesty. The boy had played some roguish trick on the virtuous Petion, who had deemed it proper to pull his ears. The King reddened with anger, the Queen turned pale with shame. She held out her arms and pulled the boy from between Petion's knees, so that Barnave received him between his. She still wished to draw him to her but he resisted, saying: "I am comfortable here."

Through motherly playfulness or womanly seductiveness, she allowed the boy to stay. It is impossible to tell what passed in Barnave's heart: he was both proud and happy. The prince set to playing with the buttons of the member's coat, which bore the motto: "Live Free or Die."

"What does that mean?" he wanted to know.

As Barnave was silent, Petion interpreted.

"My little man, that means that the French have sworn never to know masters again, if you can understand that? Explain it otherwise, Barnave, if you can."

The other was hushed. The motto, which he had thought sublime, seemed almost cruel at present. But he took the boy's hand and respectfully kissed it. The Queen wiped away a tear, risen from her heart. The carriage, a moving theatre of this little episode, continued to roll forward through the hooting of the mob, bearing to death six of the eight passengers.

CHAPTER XXI

Another Dupe

On arriving at Dormans, the party had to get out at an inn, as nothing was prepared for them. Charny got down first to have the Queen's orders, but she gave him a look to imply that he was to keep in the background. He hastened to obey without knowing the cause. It was Petion who entered the hotel, and acted as quartermaster. He did not give himself the trouble to come out again, and it was a waiter who told the Royals that their rooms were ready.

Barnave was embarrassed, as he wanted to offer his arm to the Queen. But he feared that she who had been wont to rail at exaggerated etiquette, would nevertheless invoke it now. So he waited. The King stepped out, followed by the Queen. She held out her arms for her son, but he said as if he knew his part to please his mother: "No, I want to stay with my friend Barnave."

Marie Antoinette submitted with a sweet smile. Barnave let lady Elizabeth pass out with the Princess Royal before he alighted, carrying the boy in his arms. Lady Tourzel closed the march, eager to snatch the royal child from these plebeian arms. But the Queen made her a sign which cooled the ardor of the aristocratic governess. Barnave did not say anything on finding that the Virtuous Petion had taken the best part of the house, as he set down the prince on the second landing.

"Mamma, here is my friend Barnave going away," cried he.

"Very right, too," observed the Queen on seeing the attics reserved for her and her family.

The King was so tired that he wished to lie down. But the bed was so short that he had to get up in a minute, and called for a chair. With a cane-bottomed chair eking out a wooden one, he lengthened the couch.

"Oh, Sire," said Malden, who brought the chair. "Can you pass the night thus?"

"Certainly. Besides, if what the ministers say be true, many of my subjects would be only too glad to have this loft, these chairs and this pallet."

He laid on this wretched bed, a prelude to his miserable nights in the Temple Prison. When he came in to supper, he found the table set for six. Petion had added himself to the Royal Family.

"Why not eight, then, for Messieurs Latour Maubourg and Barnave?" jeered the King.

"M. Barnave excused himself, but M. Petion persisted," replied the waiter.

The grave, austere face of the deputy appeared in the doorway. The King bore himself as if alone, and said to the waiter: "I sit at table with my own family solely, without guests. If not, we do not eat at all."

Petion went away furious, and heard the door bolted after him. The Queen looked for Charny during the meal, wishing that he had disobeyed her. Her husband was rising after finishing supper, when the waiter came to state that the first floor parlors were ready for them. They had been decked out with flowers, by the forethought of Barnave.

The Queen sighed. A few years before, she would have had to thank Charny for such attentions. Moreover, Barnave had the delicacy not to appear to receive his reward; just as the count would have acted. How was it a petty country lawyer should show the same attentions and daintiness as the most eminent courtier? There was certainly much in this to set a woman—even a queen—a-thinking. Hence she pondered over this mystery half the night.

What had become of Count Charny during this interval? With his duty keeping him close to his masters, he was glad to have the Queen's signal for him to take some leisure for lonely reflection. After having been so busy for others lately, he was not sorry to have time for his own distress. He was the old-time nobleman, more a father than a brother to his younger brothers. His grief had been great at Valence's death, but at least he had a comfort in the second brother Isidore, on whom he placed the whole of his affection. Isidore had become more dear still since he was his intermediary with Andrea.

The less Charny saw of Andrea, the more he thought of her. And to think of her was to love her. She was a statue when he saw her, but when he departed she became colored and animated by the distance. It seemed to him that internal fire sprang up in that alabaster mold, and he could see the veins circulate blood and the heart throb.

It was in these times of loneliness and separation that the wife was the real rival of the Queen. In the feverish nights, Charny saw the tapestry cleft or the walls melt, to allow the transparent statue to approach his couch. With open arms, murmuring lips, and kindled eye, the fire of her love beamed from within. He also would hold out his arms, calling the lovely vision, and try to press the phantom to his heart. But, alas! The vision would flee. Embracing vacancy, he would fall from his breathless dream into sad and cold reality.

Therefore, Isidore was dearer to him than Valence, and he had not the chance to mourn over him as he had over the cadet of the family. Both had fallen for the same fatal woman, and into the abyss of the same cause full of pitfalls. For them he would certainly fall.

Alone in an attic, shut up with a table which bore an old-fashioned three-wicked oil lamp, he drew out the bloodstained papers, the last relics of his brother. He sighed, raised his head and opened one letter. It was from poor Catherine Billet. Charny had suspected the connection some months before Billet had at Varennes given him confirmation of it. Only then had he given it the importance it should have taken in his mind. Now he learned that the title of mistress had become holy by its promotion to that of mother. And in the simple language Catherine used, all her woman's life was given in expiation of her fault as a girl. A second and a third, showed the same plans of love, maternal joys, fears of the loving, pains and repentance.

Suddenly, among the letters, he saw one whose writing struck him. To this was attached a note of Isidore's, sealed with his arms in black wax. It was the letter which Andrea had enjoined him to give her husband in case he were mortally hurt, or read to him if unable. The note explained this and concluded: "I league to my brother the Count of Charny poor Catherine Billet, now living with my boy in the village of Villedovray."

This note had totally absorbed him. But finally he turned his attention to that from his wife. After reading the explanation three times, he shook his head and said in an undertone: "I have no right to open this letter; but I will so entreat her that she will let me read it."

Dawn surprised him, devouring with his gaze this letter damp with frequent pressing it with his lips. Suddenly in the midst of the bustle for the departure, he heard his name called, and he hurried out on the stairs. Here he met Barnave, inquiring for the Queen, and charging Valory to get the order for the start. It was easy to see that Barnave had had no more sleep than the count. They bowed to each other, and Charny would surely have remarked the jealous gleam in the member's eye, if he had been able to think of anything but the letter of his wife, which he pressed to his heart under his arm.

On stepping into the coach once more, the royal pair noticed they had only the population of the town to stare at them, and cavalry to escort them. This was an attention of Barnave's. He knew what the Queen had suffered from the squalid and infected peasants pressing round the wheels, the severed head, and the threats to her guards. He pretended to have heard of an invasion by the Austrians to help Marquis Bouille, and he had turned towards the frontier all the irregularly armed men.

The hatred of the French for the foreign invader was such that it made them forget for the moment that the Queen was one of them. She guessed to whom she owed this boon, and thanked him with a look. As she resumed her place in the conveyance, she glanced out to see Charny, who had taken the outer seat beside the Guards. He wanted to be in the danger, in hopes that a wound would give him the right to open his wife's letter. He did not notice her looking for him, and that made her sigh, which Barnave heard. Uneasy about it, he stopped on the carriage step.

"Madam," he said, "I remarked yesterday how accommodated we were in here. If you like, I will find room in the other carriage with M. Latour-Maubourg."

While suggesting this, he would have given half his remaining days—not that many were left him!—to have her refuse the offer.

"No, stay with us," she quickly responded.

At once, the Dauphin held out his little hands to draw him to him, saying: "My friend Barnave! I do not want him to go."

Barnave gladly took his former place. The prince went over to his knee from his mother's. The Queen kissed him on his cheek as he passed, and the member looked at the pink spots caused by the pressure like Tantalus at the fruit hanging over his head. He asked leave to kiss the little fellow, and did it with such ardor that the boy cried out. She lost none of this incident in which Barnave was staking his head.

Perhaps she had no more slept than Charny or the deputy; perhaps the animation inflaming her eyes was caused by fever. At any rate, her purple lips and rosy cheeks all made her that perilous siren who, with one golden tress, would draw her adorers over the whirlpool's edge.

The carriage went faster. At this rate, they would be able to dine at Chateau Thierry. Before they got to Meaux that evening, Lady Elizabeth was overpowered by sleep, and laid down in the middle of the vehicle. Her giving way had caused her to lean against Petion, who deposed in his report that she had tried to tempt him with love, and had rested her head on his virtuous shoulder—that pious creature!

The halt at Meaux was in the bishop's palace. It was a gloomy structure, which still echoed those sinister wails from Bossuet's study that presaged the downfall of monarchy. The Queen looked around for support, and smiled on seeing Barnave.

"Give me your arm," she said, "and be my guide in this old palace. I dare not venture alone, lest the great voice is heard which one day made Christianity shudder with the outcry: 'The Duchess Henriette is dead!'"

Barnave sprang forward to offer his arm, while the lady cast a last glance around, fretted by Charny's obstinate silence.

"Do you seek someone?" he asked.

"Yes; the King."

"Oh, he is chatting with Petion."

Appearing satisfied, the Queen drew Barnave into the pile. She seemed a fugitive, following some phantom and looking neither before her nor behind. She only stopped, breathless, in the great preacher's sleeping chamber, where chance placed her confronting the portrait of a lady. Mechanically looking, she read the label: "Madam Henriette." She started without Barnave understanding why. From the name he guessed.

"Yes," he observed, "not Henrietta Maria of England, not the widow of the unfortunate Charles the First, but the wife of the reckless Philip of Orleans. Not she who died of cold in the Louvre Palace, but she who died of poison at St. Cloud, and sent her ring to Bossuet. Rather would I have it her portrait," he said after a pause "for such a mouth as hers might give advice. But, alas! Such are the very ones death seals up."

"What could Charles the First's widow furnish me in the way of advice?" she inquired.

"By your leave, I will try to say. 'Oh, my sister (Seems to say this mouth) do you not see the resemblance between our fates? I come from England as you from Austria, and was a foreigner to the English as you are to the French. I might have given my husband good counsel, but was silent or gave him bad. Instead of uniting him to his people, I excited him to war against them. I gave him the counsel to march on London with the Irish. Not only did I maintain correspondence with the enemies of England, but twice I went over into France to bring back foreign troops'. But why continue the bloody story which you know?"

"Continue," said the Queen, with dark brow and pleated lip.

"The portrait would continue to say: 'Sister, finally the Scotch delivered up their monarch, so that he was arrested just when he dreamed of escaping into France. A tailor seized him, a butcher led him into prison, a carter packed the jury, and a beer-vendor presided over the assembly. In order that nothing odious should be omitted in the trial and the sentence, it was carried out by a masked deaths-man striking off the victim's head.' This is what the picture of Henrietta Maria would say. God knows that nothing is lacking for the likeness. We have our brewer in Santerre for Cromwell, our butcher in Lengedre, not Harrison, and all the other plebeians who will conduct the trial. Even the conductor of this array is a lowborn peasant. What would you say to the picture?"

"I would say: 'Poor dear princess, you are reading me a page of history not giving me advice.'"

"If you do not refuse to follow it, the advice would be given you by the living," rejoined Barnave.

"Dead or living, those who can advise ought to do so. If good, it should be followed."

"Dead or living, one kind alone is given. Gain the people's love."

"It is so very easy to gain your people's love!"

"Why, madam, they are more your people than mine. And the proof is that they worshiped you when you first came here."

"Oh sir, dwell not on that flimsy thing, popularity."

"Madam," returned Barnave, "if I, springing from my obscure sphere, won this popularity, how much easier for you to keep it than I to conquer it? But no," continued he, warming with the theme, "to whom have you confided this holy cause of monarchy, the loftiest and most splendorous? What voices and what arms do you choose to defend it? Never was seen such ignorance of the times and such forgetfulness of the characteristics of France! Why, you have only to look at me for one instance—who solicited the mission of coming to you with the single end of offering myself, devoting myself—"

"Hush, someone is coming," interrupted the Queen. "We must refer to this, M. Barnave, for I am ready to listen to your counsel and heed you."

It was a servant announcing that dinner was waiting. The two Lifeguards waited at table, but Charny stood in a window recess. Though under the roof of one of the first bishops, the meal was nothing to brag of. Nonetheless, the King ate heartily.

The Dauphin had been asking for strawberries, but was told along the road that there were none, though he had seen the country lads devouring them by the handfuls. So the poor little fellow had envied the rustic urchins, who could seek the fruit in the dewy grass like the birds that revel at nature's bounteous board.

This desire had saddened the Queen, who called Charny in a voice hoarse with emotion. At the third call, he came to the door with a dish of strawberries. When the door opened, he found Barnave already there. In his hand was a platter of the fruit.

"I hope the King and the Queen will excuse my intruding," said Charny, "but I heard the prince ask for strawberries several times during the day. Finding this dish on the bishop's table, I made so bold as to take and bring it."

"Thank you, count," said the Queen to Charny, "but M. Barnave has divined my want, and I have no farther need of you."

Charny bowed without a word and returned to his place. The Dauphin thanked the member, and the King asked him to sit down between the boy and the Queen to partake of the meal, bad as it was. Charny beheld the scene without a spark of jealousy. But he said, on seeing this poor moth singe its wings at the royal light: "Still another going to destruction! A pity, for he is worth more than the others." But returning to his thought, he muttered: "This letter, what can be in this letter?"

CHAPTER XXII

The Center of Catastrophes

After the repast, the King called the three Lifeguards into council with the Queen and Lady Elizabeth.

"Gentlemen," he began, "yesterday, M. Petion proposed that you should flee in disguise, but the Queen and I opposed the plan for fear it was a plot. This day he repeats the offer, pledging his honor as a representative, and I believe you ought to hear the idea."

"Sire, we humbly beg," replied Charny for the others, "that we may be free to take the hint or leave it."

"I pledge myself to put no pressure on you. Your desires be done."

The astonished Queen looked at Charny without understanding the growing indifference in his determination not to swerve from his duty. She said nothing, but let the King conduct the conversation.

"Now that you reserve freedom, here are Petion's own words," he went on. "Sire, there is no safeguard for your attendants in Paris. Neither I, nor Barnave, nor Latour can answer for shielding them, even at peril of our lives. For their blood is claimed by the people.'"

Charny exchanged a look with the other two bodyguards, who smiled with scorn.

"Well?" he said.

"M. Petion suggests that he should provide three National Guards suits, and you might get away in them this night."

Charny consulted his brother officers who replied with the same smile.

"Sire," he replied, "our days are set apart for your Majesty. Having deigned to accept the homage, it is easier for us to die than separate. Do us the favor to treat us as you have been doing. Of all your court and army and Lifeguards, three have stood staunch. Do not rob them of the only glory they yearn for, namely, to be true to the last."

"It is well, gentlemen," said the Queen. "But you understand that you are no longer servants, but brothers." She took her tablets from her pockets. "Let us know the names of your kinsfolk so that, should you fall in the struggle, we can tell your loved ones how it happened, and soothe them as far as in our power lies."

Malden named his old, infirm mother and Valory his young orphan sister. The Queen stopped in her writing to wipe her eyes.

"Count," she said, turning to Charny, "we know that you have no one to mention as you have lost your two brothers—"

"Yes, they had the happiness to perish for your sake," said the nobleman. "But the latter to fall leaves a poor girl, recommended in a kind of will found upon him. He stole her away from her family, who will never forgive her. So long as I live, she and her child shall never want, but as your Majesty says with her admirable courage, we are all in the face of death. If death strikes me down, she and her babe will be penniless. Madam, deign to write the name of this poor country girl, and if I die like the others of the house of Charny, for my august master and noble mistress, lower your generosity to Catherine Billet and her child, in Villedovray."

No doubt the idea of George Charny expiring like his brothers was too dreadful a picture for the hearer, for in swaying back with a faint cry, she let the tablets fall and sank giddily on a chair. The two Guards hastened to her, while Charny caught up the memo-book and inscribed the name and address. The Queen recovered and said: "Gentlemen, do not leave me without kissing my hand."

The Lifeguards obeyed, but when it came Charny's turn, he barely brushed the hand with his lips. It seemed to him sacrilege, when he was carrying Andrea's letter on his heart. The Queen sighed. Never had she so accurately measured the depth of the gulf between her and her lover, widening daily.

The Guards replied the next day to the Committeemen, and confirmed that they would not change their attire from what the King authorized them to wear. Barnave had an extra seat placed in front of them, with two grenadiers to occupy it so as to shield them in some degree. At ten A. M. they quitted Meaux for Paris, from which they had been five days absent. What an unfathomable abyss had deepened in those few days.

At a league beyond Meaux, the accompanying sightseers took an aspect more frightful than before. All the dwellers of the Paris suburbs flocked to the road. Barnave tried to make the postilions go at a trot, but the Claye National Guard blocked the way with their bayonets, and it would be imprudent to try to break that dam. Comprehending the danger, the Queen supplicated the deputies not to vex the mob—it was a formidable storm growling, and felt to be coming. Such was the press, that the horses could hardly move at a walk.

It had never been hotter, the air seemed afire. The insolent curiosity of the people pursued the royal prisoners right up to the carriage interior. Men mounted upon it and clung to the horses. It was a miracle that Charny and his comrades were not killed over and over again. The two grenadiers failed to fend off the attacks, appeals in the name of the Assembly were drowned by the hooting. Two thousand men formed the vanguard, and double that number closed up the rear. On the flanks rolled an incalculable gathering.

The air seemed to fail as they neared Paris, as though that giant inhaled it all. The Queen was suffocating, and when the King begged for a glass of wine, it was proposed that he should have a sponge dipped in gall and vinegar.

At Lavillette, the multitude was beyond the power of sight to estimate; the pavement was so covered that they could not move. Windows, walls, doors... all were crammed. The trees were bending under the novel living fruit. Everybody wore their hats, for the walls had been placarded: "Flogging for whoever salutes the King: hanging for him who insults him."

All this was so appalling that the Commissioners dared not go down St. Martin's Street. It had become a crowded way full of horrors, where Berthier Savigny had been torn to pieces, and other barbarities committed. So they made the circuit, and went by the Champs Elysees. The concourse of spectators was still more great, and broke up the ranks of the soldiery. It was the third time Louis had entered by this dread entrance.

All Paris rushed hither. The King and the Queen saw a vast sea of heads—silent, sombre and threatening, with hats on. Still more alarming was the double row of National Guards, all the way to the Tuileries, their muskets held butt up as if at a funeral. It was a funeral procession indeed, for the monarchy of seven centuries! This slowly toiling carriage was the hearse taking royalty to the grave.

On perceiving this long file of Guards, the soldiers of the escort greeted them with "Long Live the Nation!" and that was the cry bursting out along the line from the barrier to the palace. All the bystanders joined in, a cry of brotherhood uttered by the whole of France, but this one family was excluded.

Behind the cab following the royal carriage came a chaise, open but covered with green boughs on account of the heat. It contained Drouet and two others, who had arrested the King. Fatigue had forced them to ride. Billet alone was indefatigable, as if revenge made him bronze. He kept on horseback, and seemed to lead the whole procession.

Louis noticed that the statue of his ancestor, on Louis XV Square, had the eyes bandaged. Petion explained that it was in token of the blindness of rulers. In spite of all, the mob burst all bars and stormed the carriage. Suddenly the Queen saw at the windows those hideous men with implacable speech, who come to the surface on certain days, like the sea monsters seen only in tempestuous weather. Once she was so terrified that she pulled down the sash, whereupon a dozen furious voices demanded the reason.

"I am stifling," she stammered.

"Pooh! We will stifle you in quite another way, never fear," replied a rough voice while a dirty fist smashed the window.

Nevertheless the cortege reached the grand terrace steps.

"Oh, gentlemen, save the Lifeguards," cried the Queen, particularly to Barnave and Petion.

"Have you any preference?" asked the former.

"No," she answered, looking at him full and square.

The next ten minutes were the cruelest of her life. She was under the impression, not that she would be killed—prompt death would be nothing—but made the sport of the mob, or dragged away into jail. From thence she would issue only after a trial, handing her over to ignominious death.

As she stepped forth, under the ceiling of steel made by the swords and bayonets of the soldiers, Barnave gathered to cover her. Even as a giddiness made her close her eyes, she caught a glimpse down the flashing vista of a face she remembered. This face seemed to be the centre of the multitudinous eyes of the mob. From his glance would come the cue for her immolation. It was the terrible man who had in a mysterious manner at Taverney Manor raised the veil over the future. He whom she had seen at Sevres on returning from Versailles. He who appeared merely to foretell great catastrophes or to witness their fulfillment. And yet if Cagliostro, was he not dead in the dungeons of the Pope?

To be assured that her sight did not deceive her, she darted down the tunnel of steel, strong against realities, but not against this sinister vision. It seemed to her that the earth gave way under her tread. That all whirled around her: palace, gardens, trees, and the countless people. That vigorous arms seized her and carried her away amid deafening yells. She heard the Lifeguards shouting, calling the wrath upon them to turn it aside from its true aim. Opening her eyes an instant, she beheld Charny between the pair hurled from the box. Pale and handsome as ever, he fought with ten men at once, with the nobleman's smile of scorn and the martyr's light in his gaze. From Charny, her eyes went back to the man whose myrmidons ruled the storm and swept her out of the maelstrom. With terror, she undoubtedly recognized the magician of Taverney and Sevres.

"You, it is you!" she gasped, trying to repel him with her rigid hands.

"Yes, it is I," he hissed in her ear. "I still need you to push the throne into its last gulf, and so I save you!"

She could support no more, but screaming, she swooned. Meanwhile the mob, defrauded of the chief morsel, were tearing the Lifeguards to pieces and carrying Billet and Drouet in triumph.

CHAPTER XXIII

The Bitter Cup

When the Queen came to her senses, she was in her sleeping room in the Tuileries. Her favorite bed-chamber women, Lady Misery and Madam Campan were at hand. Though they told her the Dauphin was safe, she rose and went to see him. He was asleep after the great fright.

She looked at him for a long time, haunted by the words of that awful man: "I save you because you are needed to hurl the throne over into the last abyss." Was it true that she would destroy the monarchy? Were her enemies guarding her that she might accomplish the work of destruction better than themselves? Would this gulf close after swallowing the King, the throne, and herself? Would not her two children go down in it also? In religions of the past alone, is innocence safe to disarm the gods? Abraham's sacrifice had not been accepted, but it was not so in Jephthah's case.

These were gloomy thoughts for a Queen, gloomier still for a mother. She shook her head and went slowly back to her rooms. She noticed the disorder she was in, so she took a bath and was attired more fitly. The news awaiting her was not so black as she had feared. All three Lifeguards had been saved from the mob, mainly by Petion, who screened a good heart under his rough bark. Malden and Valory were in the palace: bruised and wounded, but alive. Nobody knew where Charny was in refuge, after having been snatched from the ruffians.

At these words from Madam Campan, such a deadly pallor came over the Queen's countenance that the Lady thought it was from anxiety about the count. She hastened to say, "But there need be no alarm about his coming back to the palace. The countess has a town house, and of course he will hasten there."

This was just what she feared, and what made her lose color. She was about to dress, as if she would be allowed to go out of the palace prison to inquire about his fate, when he was announced as present in the other room.

"Oh, he is keeping his word," muttered the Queen, which her attendants did not understand.

Her toilet hastily completed, she ordered the count to be introduced into her sitting room, where she joined him. He had also dressed for the reception, for he wore the naval uniform in which she had first seen him. Never had he been calmer, handsomer and more elegant, and she could not believe that this beau was the man whom she had seen the mob fall upon a while before.

"Oh, my lord, I hope you were told how distressed I was on your behalf, and that I was sending out for tidings?"

"Madam, you may be sure that I did not go away till I learned that you were safe and sound," was his rejoinder. "And now that I am assured by sight, and hearing of the health of your children and the King, I think it proper to ask leave to give personal news to my lady the countess."

The Queen pressed her hand to her heart as if to ascertain if this blow had not deadened it. Then she said in a voice almost strangled by the dryness of her throat: "It is only fair, my lord. And I wonder how it is that you did not ask before this."

"The Queen forgets my promise not to see the countess without her permission."

"I suppose though, in your ardor to see the lady again, you could do without it?"

"I think the Queen unjust to me," he replied. "When I left Paris, I believed it was to part from her forever. During the journey, I did all that was humanly possible to make the journey a success. It is not my fault that I did not lose my life like my brother, or was not cut to pieces on the road or in the Tuileries Gardens. Had I the honor to conduct your Majesty across the frontier, I should have lived in exile with you. Or if I were fated to die, I should have died without seeing the countess. But I repeat, I cannot, being again in town, give the lady this mark of indifference. Not to show her I am alive, particularly as I no longer have my brother Isidore as my substitute. At all events, either M. Barnave is wrong, or your Majesty was of the same opinion only yesterday."

The Queen glided her arm along the chair-arm, and following the movement with her body said, "You must love this woman fondly to give me this pain so coldly?"

"Madam... There was a time when I did not think of such a thing, as there was but one woman in the world for me. This woman was placed too high above me for me to hope for her, as well as under an indissoluble bond. You gave me as wife Mdlle. Andrea Taverney—imposed her on me! In these six years, my hand has not twice touched hers. Without necessity, I have not spoken a word to her, and our glances have not met a dozen times. My life has been occupied by another love: the thousand tasks, cares and combats agitating man's existence in camp and court. I have coursed the King's highways, entangling the thread the master gave me in the intrigues of fate. I have not counted the days, or months, or years... for time has passed most rapidly from my being enwrapped in these tasks.

"But not so has the Countess of Charny fared. Since she has had the affliction of quitting your Majesty, after having displeased you I suppose, she has lived lonely in the Paris summerhouse. Accepting the neglect and isolation without complaining, she has not the same affections as other women from her heart being devoid of love. But she may not accept without complaint my forgetting the simplest duty and the most commonplace attentions."

The Queen demurred, "Good gracious, my lord, you are mightily busy about what the countess thinks of you according to whether you see her or not! Before worrying yourself, it would be well to know whether she does think of you in the hour of your departure, or in that of your return."

"I do not know about the hour of my return," said Charny, "but I do know that she thought about me when I departed."

"So you saw her before you went?"

"I had the honor of stating that I had not seen the countess since I promised the Queen not to see her."

"Then she wrote to you? confess it!" cried Marie Antoinette.

"She confided a letter for me to my brother Isidore."

"A letter which you read? What does she say? She promised me—but let us hear quickly. What does she say in this letter? Speak, see you not that I am on thorns?"

"I cannot repeat what it says, as I have not read it."

"You destroyed it unread?" exclaimed she delightedly. "You threw it in the fire? Oh Charny, if you did that, you are the most true of lovers, and I was wrong to scold—for I have lost nothing." She held out her arms to lure him to his former place, but he stood firm.

"I have not torn it or burnt it," he replied.

"But then, how came you not to read it?" questioned she, sinking back on the chair.

"The letter was to be given me if I were mortally wounded. But alas! It was the bearer who fell. He being dead, his papers were brought to me, and among them was this, the countess's letter."

She took the letter with a trembling hand and rang for lights. During the brief silence in the dusk, her breathing could be heard along with the hurried throbbing of her heart. As soon as the candlesticks were placed on the mantle shelf, before the servant left the room, she ran to the light. She looked on the paper twice without ability to read it.

"It is flame," she said. "Oh, God!" she ejaculated, smoothing her forehead to bring back her sight, and stamping her foot to calm her hand by force of will. In a husky voice utterly like her own, she read: "This letter is intended not for me, but for my brother Count Charny, or to be returned to the countess. It is from her I had it with the following recommendation. If in the enterprise undertaken by the count, he succeeds without mishap, return the letter to the countess."

The reader's voice became more panting as she proceeded.

"If he is grievously hurt, but without mortal danger, his wife prays to be let join him."

"That is clear," said the Queen falteringly. And in a scarcely intelligible voice she added, "'Lastly, if he be wounded to the death, give him the letter or read it to him if he cannot, in order that he should know the secret contained before he dies.'

"Do you deny it now, that she loves you?" demanded the Queen, covering the count with a flaming look.

"The countess love me? What are you saying?" cried Charny.

"The truth, unhappy woman that I am!"

"Love me? Impossible!"

"Why, for I love you?"

"But in six years, the countess has never let me see it, never said a word!"

The time had come for Marie Antoinette to suffer so keenly, that she felt the need to bury her grief like a dagger in the depth of his heart.

"Of course," she sneered. "She would not breathe a word, she would not let a token show, and the reason is because she was well aware that she was not worthy to be your wife."

"Not worthy?" reiterated Charny.

"She cherished a secret which would slay your love," continued the other, more and more maddened by her pain.

"A secret to kill our love?"

"She knew you would despise her after she told it."

"I, despise the countess? Tut, tut!"

"Unless one is not to despise the girl who is a mother without being a wife."

It was the man's turn to become paler than death, and lean on the back of the nearest chair.

"Madam, you have said too much or too little, and I have the right for an explanation."

"Do you ask a queen for explanations?"

"I do," replied Charny.

The door opened, and the Queen turned to demand impatiently, "What is wanted?"

It was a valet who announced Dr. Gilbert, come by appointment. She eagerly bade him send him in.

"You call for an explanation about the countess," she continued to the count. "Well, ask it of this gentleman, who can give it better than anybody else."

Gilbert had come in so as to hear the final words, and he remained on the threshold, mute and standing. The Queen tossed the letter to Charny, and took a few steps to gain her dressing room. The count barred her passage and grasped her wrist.

"My lord, methinks that you forget I am your Queen," said Marie Antoinette, with clenched teeth and en-fevered eye.

"You are an ungrateful woman who slanders her friend. A jealous woman who defames another, and that woman the wife of a man who has for three days risked his life a score of times for you. The wife of George Count of Charny. Justice must be rendered in face of her you have calumniated and insulted! Sit down and wait."

"Well, have it so," railed the Queen. "Dr. Gilbert," she pursued, forcing a shallow laugh, "you see what this nobleman desires."

"Dr. Gilbert, you hear what the Queen orders," rebuked Charny with a tone full of courtesy and dignity.

"Oh madam," said Gilbert, sadly regarding the Queen as he came forward. "My Lord Count," he went on to the gentleman, "I have to tell you of the shame of a man and the glory of a woman. A wretched earthworm fell in love with his lord's daughter, the Lady of Taverney. One day, he found her in a mesmeric trance, and without respect for her youth, beauty and innocence, this villain abused her. Thus the maid became a woman, the mother before marriage. Mdlle. Taverney was an angel—Lady Charny is a martyr!"

"I thank Dr. Gilbert," said the count, wiping his brow. "Madam," he proceeded to the Queen, "I was ignorant that Mdlle. Taverney was so unfortunate—that Lady Charny was so worthy of respect. Otherwise, believe me, six years would not have elapsed before I fell at her feet and adored her as she deserves."

Bowing to the stupefied Queen, he stalked forth without the baffled one making a move to detain him. But he heard her shriek of pain when the door closed between them. She comprehended that over those portals, the hand of the demon of jealousy was writing the dread doom: "Leave hope behind who enter here."

CHAPTER XXIV

At Last They Are Happy!

It is easy for us who know the state of Andrea's heart to imagine what she suffered from the time of Isidore's leaving. She trembled for the grand plot failing or succeeding. If succeeding, she knew the count's devotion to his masters too well not to be sure that he would never quit them in exile. If failure, she knew his courage too well not to be sure that he would struggle till the last moment, so long as hope remained, and beyond that. So she had her eye open to every light, and her ear to every sound.

On the following day, she learned with the rest of the population that the King had fled from the capital in the night, without any mischance. She had suspected the flight, and as Charny would participate, she was losing him by his going far from her. Sighing deeply, she knelt in prayer for the journey to be happy.

For two days, Paris was dumb and without news. Then the rumor broke forth that the King had been stopped at Varennes. No details, just the word. Andrea hunted up on the map the little obscure point on which attention was centred. There she lived on hopes, fears and thought. Gradually came the details precious to her, particularly when news came that a Charny, one of the royal bodyguard, had been killed. Isidore or George? For two days, while this was undecided, Andrea's heart oscillated in anguish indescribable. Finally, the return of the august prisoners were heralded. They slept at Meaux.

At eleven in the morning, veiled and dressed most plainly, she went and waited till three o'clock at the east end. For it was supposed that the party would enter by St. Martin's suburb. At that hour, the mob began to move away, hearing that the King was going round to enter through the Champs Elysees. It was half the city to cross afoot, as no vehicles could move in the throng, unexampled since the Taking of the Bastille. Andrea did not hesitate, and was one of the first on the spot where she had still three mortal hours to wait.

At last the procession appeared, we know in what order. She hailed the royal coach with a cry of joy, for she saw Charny on the box. A scream which seemed an echo of her own, though different in tone, arose. She saw a girl in convulsions in the crowd. She would have gone to her help, though three or four kind persons flew to her side, but she heard the men around her pour imprecations on the three on the box seat. On them would fall the popular rage as the scapegoats of the royal treachery. When the coach stopped, they would be torn to pieces. And Charny was one!

She resolved to do her utmost to get within the Tuileries gardens. This she managed by going round about, but the crush was so dense that she could not get into the front. She retired to the waterside terrace, where she saw and heard badly. But that was better than not seeing at all. She saw Charny, indeed, on the same level, little suspecting that the heart beating for him alone was so near. He probably had no thought for her, only for the Queen—forgetting his own safety to watch over hers.

Oh, had she known that he was pressing her letter on his heart, and offering her the last sigh which he thought he must soon yield! At last the coach stopped amid the howling, groaning and clamor. Almost instantly, around it rose an immense turbulence. Weapons were swaying like a steel wheat-field shaken by the breeze. Precipitated from the box, the three Lifeguards disappeared as if dropped into a gulf. Then there was such a back-wave of the crowd that the retiring rear ranks broke against the terrace front.

Andrea was shrouded in anguish, she could hear and see nothing. Breathless and with outstretched arms, she screamed inarticulate sounds into the midst of the dreadful concert of maledictions, blasphemy, and death cries. She could no longer understand what went on. The earth turned, the sky grew red, and a roar as of the sea rang in her ears. She fell half dead, knowing that she lived only by her feelings of suffering.

A sensation of coolness brought her around. A woman was putting to her forehead a handkerchief dipped in river water. She remembered her as having fainted when the royal coach came into sight, without guessing what sympathy attached her to this mistress of her husband's brother—for this was Catherine Billet.

"Are they dead?" was her first question.

Compassion is intelligent. Those around her understood that she asked after the three Lifeguardsmen.

"No, all three are saved."

"The Lord be praised! Where are they?"

"I believe in the palace."

Rising and shaking her head to see where she was, she went around to the Princes' Court and sprang into the janitor's room. This man knew the countess as having been in attendance when the court first came back from Versailles. He had also seen her go away, with Sebastian in her carriage. He related that the Guardsmen were safe. Count Charny had gone out for a little while, when he returned dressed in naval uniform to appear in the Queen's rooms, where he probably was at that period.

Andrea thanked the good fellow and hastened home, now that George was safe. She knelt on her praying stand, to thank heaven, with all her soul going up to her Maker. She was plunged in ecstasy when she heard the door open. She wondered what this earthly sound could be, disturbing her in her deepest reverie.

The shadow in the doorway was dim, but her instinct told her who it was without the girl announcing: "My lord the Count of Charny." Andrea tried to rise, but her strength failed her. Half turning, she slid down the slope of the stand, leaning her arm on the guard.

"The count?" she murmured, disbelieving her eyes.

The servant closed the door on her master and mistress.

"I was told you had recently returned home? Am I rude in following you indoors so closely?" he asked.

"No, you are welcome my lord," she replied, trembling. "I was so uneasy that I left the house to learn what had happened."

"Were you long out?"

"Since morning. I was first out to St. Martin's Bars, and then went to the Champs Elysees. There I saw..." she hesitated. "I saw the Royal Family, and you. Momentarily I was set at ease, though I feared for you when the carriage should set you down. Then I went into the Tuileries Gardens, where I thought I should have died."

"Yes, the crowd was great. You were crushed, and I understand—"

"No," said Andrea, shaking her head, "that was not it. I inquired and learned that you were unhurt, so that I hastened home to thank God on my knees."

"Since you are so praying, say a word for my poor brother."

"Isidore, Poor youth! Was it he, then?" exclaimed Andrea.

She let her head sink on her hands. Charny stepped forward a few steps to regard the chaste creature at her devotions. In his look was immense commiseration, together with a longing restrained. Had not the Queen said—or rather revealed—that Andrea loved him?

"And he is no more?" queried the lady, turning round after finishing her prayer.

"He died, madam, like Valence. And for the same cause, fulfilling the same duty."

"And in the great grief which you must have felt, you still thought of me?" asked Andrea in so weak a voice that her words were barely audible.

Luckily Charny was listening with the heart as well as ear.

"Did you not charge my brother with a message for me?" he inquired. "A letter to my address?"

She rose on one knee and looked with anxiety upon him.

"After poor Isidore's death, his papers were handed to me, and among them was this letter."

"And you have read it—ah!" she cried, hiding her face in her hands.

"I ought to know the contents only if I were mortally wounded, and you see I have returned safe. Consequently, as you see, it is intact, as when you gave it to Isidore."

"Oh, what you have done is very lofty—or very unkind," muttered the countess, taking the letter.

Charny stretched out his hand and caught her hand in spite of an effort to retain it. As Charny persisted, she uttered a reproachful "Oh!" and sighed almost with fright. But she gave way, leaving it quivering in his clasp. Embarrassed, she didn't know where to turn her eyes to avoid his glance, which she felt was fastened on her. Unable to retreat, as her back was against the wall, she said: "I understand—you came to restore the letter."

"For that, and another matter. I have to beg your pardon heartily, Andrea."

She shuddered to the bottom of her soul, for this was the first time he had addressed her so informally. The whole sentence had been spoken with indescribable softness.

"Pardon of me, my lord? On what grounds?"

"For my behavior towards you these six years."

"Have I ever complained?" she asked, eyeing him in profound astonishment.

"No, because you are an angel."

Despite herself, her eyes were veiled, and tears welled out.

"You weep, Andrea," exclaimed Charny.

"Excuse me, my lord," she sobbed, "but I am not used to being thus spoken to. Oh, heavens!" She sank into an easy chair, hiding her face in her hands for a time. Then withdrawing them, she said, "Really, I must be going mad."

She stopped. While she had her eyes hid, Charny had fallen on his knees to her.

"Oh! On your knees to me?" she said.

"Did I not say I must ask your forgiveness?"

"What can this mean?" she muttered.

"Andrea, it means that I love you," he answered in his sweetest voice.

Laying her hand on her heart, she uttered a cry. Springing upright as though impelled by a spring under her feet, she pressed her temples between her hands and cried, "He loves me? This cannot be."

"Say that it is impossible you should love me, but not that I should love you."

She lowered her gaze on the speaker to see if he spoke truly, and his eyes said more than his tongue. Though she might doubt the words, she could not the glance.

"Oh God, in all the world is there a being more unfortunate than me?" she cried.

"Andrea, tell me that you love me," continued Charny, "or at least that you do not hate me?"

"I? Hate you?" she said with a double flash from the calm eyes, usually so limpid and serene. "Oh, my lord, it would be very wrong to take for hate the feeling you inspire."

"But if not hate or love, what is it?"

"It is not love, because I am not allowed to love you. But did you not hear me call myself the unhappiest of God's creatures?"

"Why are you not allowed to love me, when I love you with all the strength of my soul?"

"Oh, that I cannot, dare not, must not tell you," replied she, wringing her hands.

"But if another should tell me what you cannot, dare not, must not tell?" he demanded.

"Heaven!" she gasped, leaning her hands on his shoulder.

"Suppose I know? And that, considering you the more worthy because of the noble way you have borne that woe, it was that terrible secret which determined me upon telling you that I loved you?"

"If you did this, you would be the noblest and most generous of men."

"Andrea, I love you," cried he, three times.

"Oh God, I knew not that there could be such bliss in this world," she said, lifting her arms heavenward.

"Now, in your turn, tell me that you love me."

"Oh no, that I dare not. But you may read that letter," said Andrea.

While she covered her face with her hands, he sharply broke the letter seal and read the first lines. Parting her hands, and with the same movement drawing her upon his heart, he said, "How shall I love you enough, saintly creature, to make you forget what you have undergone in these six years!"

"Oh God, if this be a dream, let me never awake, or die on awakening," prayed Andrea. Her knees bending like a reed beneath the weight of so much happiness.

And now, let us forget these who are happy to return to those who hate, suffer or are struggling. And perhaps their evil fate will forget them, too.

CHAPTER XXV

Correcting the Petition

On the Field of Mars, the Altar of the Country still stood. It was set up for the anniversary of the Bastille Capture, a skeleton of the past. On this sixteenth of July, it was used as a table on which was spread a petition to the Assembly, which considered that the King had practically abdicated by his flight, and that he ought to be replaced by "Constitutional methods." This was a cunning way to propose the Duke of Orleans as Regent. Politics is a fine veil, but the people see through it if they are given time.

There was some discussion by the persons called on to sign over these very words. They might have been glossed over by the man in charge of the paper, the pen and the ink. But a man of the people, judging by his manners and dress, with a frankness next to roughness, stopped the secretary abruptly.

"Halt, this is cheating the people," said he.

"What do you mean?"

"This stuff about replacing the abdicated King by 'constitutional means.' You want to give us King Stock instead of King Log. You want to rig up royalty again, and that is just what we don't want any more of."

"No more Kings! Enough of royalty!" shouted most of the lookers on.

The secretary was Brissot, a Jacobin. And strange thing, here were the arch-revolutionists, the Jacobins, defending royalty!

"Have a care, gentlemen," cried he and his supporters. "With no royalty and no king, the Republic would come, and we are not ripe for anything of that kind."

"Not ripe?" jeered the Commoner. "A few such suns as shone on Varennes when we nabbed the skulking King, will ripen us."

"Let's vote on this petition."

"Vote," shouted those who had clamored for no more royalty.

"Let those who do not want Louis XVI, or any other king, put up their hand," cried the plebeian in a lusty voice.

Such a powerful number held up their hands that the Ayes had it beyond a necessity of farther trial.

"Good," said the stranger. "To-morrow is Sunday, the seventeenth. Let all the boys come out here to sign the petition as amended to our liking. I, Billet, will get the right sort ready."

At this name, everybody recognized Farmer Billet. The Taker of the Bastille, the hero of the people, the volunteer envoy who had accompanied Lafayette's dandy aid to Varennes, where he arrested the King, whom he had brought back to Paris. Thus, at the first start, the boldest of the politicians had been surpassed by—a man of the people, the embodied instincts of the masses! The other leaders said that a storm would be raised, and that they had best get permission of the Mayor to hold this meeting on the morrow.

"Very well," said Billet. "Obtain leave. And if refused you, I will wrest it from them."

Mayor Bailly was absent when Brissot and Desmoulins called for the leave. His deputy verbally granted it, but sent word to the House what he had done. The House was caught napping, for it had done nothing in fixing the status of the King after his flight. As if from an enemy of the rulers, the decree was passed that "The suspension of the executive power will last until the King shall have accepted and signed the Constitutional Act." Thus he was as much of a king as before; the popular petition became useless.

Whoever claimed the dethronement of a monarch who was constitutionally maintained by the House, so long as the King agreed to accomplish this condition, was a rebel, of course. The decree was to be posted throughout the town next morning at eight. Prudent politicians went out of the town. The Jacobins retired, and their vulgar member, Santerre, the great brewer of the working quarter, was chosen to go and withdraw the petition from the Altar of the Country.

But some meant to attend, in spite of governmental warning. They were like the wolves and vultures who flock to the battlefields. Marat was confined to his cellar by his monomania, but he yelled for the Assembly to be butchered, and cried for a general massacre out of which he would wade a universal dictator. Verriere, the abominable hunchback, careened about on a horse like the spectre of the Apocalypse, and stopped at every crossroad to invite the masses to meet on the Field of Mars. So the thousands went to the rendezvous, to sign the paper. And to sing and dance and shout "The Nation Forever!"

The sun rose magnificently. All the petty trades-folk who cater to the multitude swarmed on the parade-ground, where the Altar of the Country stood up in the middle like a grand catafalque[12]. By half past four, a hundred and fifty thousand souls were present. Those who rise early are usually bad sleepers, and who has not slept well is commonly in a bad humor.

In the midst of the chatter, a woman's scream was heard. On the crowd flocking round her, she complained of having been stabbed in the ankle while leaning against the altar. Indeed the point of a gimlet was seen sticking through the boards. In a twinkling, the planks were torn down and two men were unearthed in the hollow. They were old cronies, sots who had taken a keg of liquor with them and eatables, and stolen a march on the crowd by hiding here overnight.

Unfortunately for them, the mob thought they made peepholes for a mean purpose, and cried that the keg contained powder to blow up the signers of the petition. They forgot that these new Guido Fawkes hardly looked the sort to blow themselves up with their victims.

Be this as it may, they were taken to the police court, where the magistrates laughingly released them. But the washer-women, great sticklers for women not to be probed in the ankle by gimlets, gave them a beating with the paddles used in thumping linen. This was not all. At the cry that powder was found getting spread, they were taken from the women and slain. A few minutes after, their heads were cut off and the ready pikes were there to receive them on their points.

The news was perverted on its way to the Assembly, where the heads were stated to be of two friends of order, who had lost them while preaching respect to the law. The Assembly at once voted the City to be under martial law.

Santerre, sent by the Jacobin Club to withdraw their petition before Billet transformed it, found that worthy the centre

---

12 A decorated platform or framework on which a coffin rests in state during a funeral

of the immense gathering. He did not know how to write, but he had let someone guide his hand when he "put his fist" to it.

The brewer went up the steps of the altar, announced that the Assembly proclaimed anyone a rebel who dared demand the dethronement of the King, and said he was sent to call in the petition. Billet went down three steps to face the brewer. The two members of the lower orders looked at each other, examining the symbols of the two forces ruling France, the town and the country. They had fought together to take the Bastille, and acknowledged that they were brothers.

"All right," said Billet, "we do not want your petition. Take yours back to the Jacobins, we will start another."

"And fetch it along to my brewery in the St. Antoine Suburb, where I will sign it and get my men and friends to do the same."

He held out his broad hand in which Billet clapped his. At sight of this powerful alliance, the mob cheered. They began to know the worth of the brewer, too. He went away with one of those gestures expressive of meeting again, which the lower classes understood.

"Now look here," said Billet, "the Jacobins are afraid. They have a right to back out with their petition, but we are not afraid, and we have the right to draw up another."

"Hurrah for another petition! All be on hand to-morrow."

"But why not to-day?" cried Billet. "Who knows what may happen to-morrow?"

"He's right," called out many. "To-day—at once!"

A group of enlightened men flocked round Billet. They were members of the Invisibles like him, and besides, strength has the loadstone's power to attract.

Roland and his celebrated wife, with Dr. Gilbert, wrote the petition. It was read in silence, while all bared their head to this document dictated by the people. It declared that the King had abdicated the throne by his flight, and called for a fresh House to "proceed in a truly national manner to try the guilty ruler and organize a new executive power."

It answered to everybody's wish, so that it was applauded at the last phrase. Numbered sheets were served out all over the place, for the signatures to be written on them by the many who sought to sign. During this work, which was so quietly done that women were strolling about the groups with their children, Lafayette arrived with his special guard, who were paid troops. But he could not see any cause to intervene, and marched away.

On the road, he had to overtake one barricade, which was set up by the gang who had slaughtered the two Peeping Toms of the Altar of the Country. One of his aids had been fired at in this scuffle, and the report ran to the House that in a severe action, Lafayette had been shot and his officers wounded. The house sent a deputation to inquire. This party of three found the multitude still signing, and signing a document so harmless that they personally said they would put their own names to it if they were not in an official position.

In the conflict of no importance between the mob and the National Guards, two prisoners had been made by the latter. As usual in such cases, they had nothing to do with the riot. The principal petitioners asked their release.

"We can do nothing in the matter," replied the deputation. "But send a committee to the City Hall, and the liberation will be given."

Billet was unanimously chosen chairman of a party of twelve. They were kept waiting an hour before the Mayor Bailly came to receive them. Bailly was pale but determined. He knew he was unjust, but he had the Assembly's order at his back, and he would carry it out to the end. Billet walked straight up to him, saying in his firm tone, "Mayor, we have been kept waiting an hour."

"Who are you and what have you to say to me?"

"I am surprised you should ask who I am, Mayor Bailly. But those who turn off the right road do not always get back on the track. I am Farmer Billet."

Bailly was reminded of one of the Takers of the Bastille, who had tried to save the objects of public wrath from the slaughterers. The man who had given the King the tricolor cockade; who had aroused Lafayette on the night when the Royal Family were nearly murdered; the leader who had not shrank from making the King and the Queen prisoners.

"As for what I have to say," continued he, "we are the messengers of the people assembled on the parade-ground. We demand the fulfillment of the promise of your three envoys—that the two citizens unjustly accused, and whose innocence we guarantee, shall be set free straightway."

"Nonsense! Whoever heard of promises being kept that were made to rioters?" returned Bailly, trying to go by.

The committee looked astonished at one another, and Billet frowned.

"Rioters? So we are rioters now, eh?"

"Yes. Factious folk, among whom I will restore peace by going to the place."

Billet laughed roughly, in that way which is a menace on some lips.

"Restore peace? Your friend Lafayette has been there, and your three delegates, and they will say it is calmer than the City Hall Square."

At this juncture, a captain of militia came running up in fright to tell the Mayor that there was fighting on the Field of Mars. "Fifty thousand ragamuffins are making ready to march on the Assembly."

Scarce had he got the words out before he felt Billet's heavy hand on his shoulder.

"Who says this?" demanded the farmer.

"The Assembly."

"Then the Assembly lies." The captain drew his sword on him, which he seized by the hilt and the point, and wrenched from his grasp.

"Enough, gentlemen," said Bailly. "We will ourselves see into this. Farmer Billet, return the sword. And if you have any influence over those you come from, hasten back to make them disperse."

Billet threw the sabre at the officer's feet.

"Disperse be hanged! The right to petition is recognized by decree, and till another revokes it, nobody can prevent citizens expressing their wishes. Mayor, or National Guards commander, or others. Come to the place—we will be there before you."

Those around expected Bailly to give orders for the arrest of this bold speaker, but he knew that this was the voice of the people, so loud and lofty. He made a sign, and Billet and his friends walked out. When they arrived on the parade-ground, the crowd was a third larger. Say, sixty thousand old women and men. There was a rush for the news.

"The two citizens are not released. The mayor will not answer, except that we are all rioters."

The "rioters" laughed at this title, and went on signing the petition, which had some five thousand names down. By night it would be fifty thousand, and the Assembly would be forced to bow to such unanimity. Suddenly the arrival of the military was shouted. Bailly and the city officials were leading the National Guards hither. When the bayonets were seen, many proposed retiring.

"Brothers, what are you talking of?" said Billet, on the Altar of the Country. "Why this fear? Either martial law is aimed at us, or not. If not, why should we run? If it is, the riot act must be read, and that will give time to get away."

"Yes, yes," said many voices, "we are lawfully here. Wait for the summons to disperse. Stand your ground."

The drums were heard and the soldiers appeared at three entrances into the ground. The crowd fell back towards the Altar, which resembled a pyramid of human bodies. One corps was composed of four thousand men from the working quarter. Lafayette, who did not trust them, had added a battalion of his paid Guards to them. They were old soldiers, Fayettists, who had heard of their god being fired on and were burning to avenge the insult.

While Bailly was received by the "booing" of the boys, one shot was fired from the mob in that part, which sent a bullet to slightly wound a dragoon. The Mayor ordered a volley, but of blank cartridge from those soldiers around him. But the Fayettists also obeyed the command, and fired on the mass at the Altar, a most inoffensive crowd. A dreadful scream arose there, and the fugitives were seen leaving corpses behind them, with the wounded dragging themselves in trails of blood! Amid the smoke and dust, the cavalry rushed in chase of the running figures.

The broad expanse presented a lamentable aspect, for it was mostly women and children who had been shot and cut down. An aid galloped up to the East-end battalions and ordered them to march on their side and sweep the mob away till they had formed a junction with the other corps. But these workingmen pointed their guns at him and the cavalry running down the fugitives, and made them recoil before the patriotic bayonets. All who ran in this direction found protection.

Who gave the order to fire? None will ever know. It remains one of those historical mysteries, inexplicable despite the most conscientious investigations. Neither the chivalric Lafayette nor the honest Bailly liked bloodshed, and this stain clung to them to the end. In vain were they congratulated by the Assembly. In vain did their press organs call this slaughter a constitutional victory. This triumph was branded like all those days when the slain were given no chance to fight. The people who always fit the cap to the right head call it "The Massacre of the Champ de Mars."

CHAPTER XXVI

Cagliostro's Counsel

Paris had heard the fusillade and quivered, feeling that she had been wounded and the blood was flowing. The Queen had sent her confidential valet Weber to the spot to get the latest news. To be just to her and comprehend the hatred she felt for the French, she had suffered so much during the flight to Varennes that her hair had turned white.

It was a popular idea, shared by her own retinue, that she was a witch. A Medea able to go out of the window in a flying car. She kept her jailers on the alert, but they also frightened her. She had dreams of scenes of violence.

She waited with anxiety for her envoy's return. The mobs might have overturned this old, decrepit, trimming Assembly of which Barnave had promised the help, and which might now want help itself. The door opened. She turned her eyes swiftly thither, but instead of her foster-brother, it was Dr. Gilbert with his stern face. She did not like this royalist, whose constitutional ideas made him almost a republican, but she felt respect for him. She submitted to his influence when he was near.

"You, doctor?" she said with a shiver.

"It is I, madam. I bring you more precise news than what you expected by Weber. He was on the side of the Seine, where no blood was spilled, while I was where the slaughter was committed. A great misfortune has taken place—the court party has triumphed."

"Oh, you would call this a misfortune, doctor!"

"Because the triumph is one of those which exhaust the victor, and lay him beside the dead. Lafayette and Bailly have shot down the people, so that they will never be able to serve you again. They have lost their popularity."

"What were the people doing when shot down?"

"Signing a petition demanding the removal of the King."

"And you think they were wrong to fire on men doing that?" returned the sovereign, with a kindling eye.

"I believe it better to argue with them than shoot them."

"Argue about what?"

"The King's sincerity."

"But the King is sincere!"

"Excuse me, madam. Three days ago, I spent the evening trying to convince the King that his worst enemies were his brothers and the fugitive nobles abroad. On my knees I entreated him to break off dealings with them, and frankly adopt the Constitution, with a revision to the impracticable articles. I thought the King was persuaded, for he kindly promised that all was ended between him and the nobles who fled. But behind my back he signed, and induced you to sign, a letter which charged his brother to get the aid of Prussia and Austria."

The Queen blushed like a schoolboy caught in fault. But a boy would have hung his head—she only held hers the stiffer and higher.

"Have our enemies spied in our private rooms?" she asked.

"Yes, madam," tranquilly replied the doctor, "which is what makes such double-dealing on the King's part so dangerous."

"But sir, this letter was written wholly by the royal hand. After I signed it too, the King sealed it up and handed it to the messenger."

"It has been read none the less."

"Are we surrounded by traitors?"

"All men are not Charnys."

"What do you mean?"

"Alas, Madam! One of the fatal tokens foretelling the doom of Kings is their driving away from them those very men whom they ought to 'grapple to them by hooks of steel.'"

"I have not driven Count Charny away," said the Queen bitterly. "He went of his own free will. When monarchs become unfortunate, their friends fall off."

"Do not slander Count Charny," said Gilbert mildly, "or the blood of his brothers will cry from their graves that the Queen of France is an ingrate. Oh, you know I speak the truth, madam. That on the day when unmistakable danger impends, the Count of Charny will be at his post, and that the most perilous."

"But I suppose you have not come to talk about Count Charny," she said testily, though she lowered her head.

"No, madam. But ideas are like events, they are attached by invisible links, and thus are drawn forth from darkness. No, I come to speak to the Queen. I beg pardon if I addressed the woman, but I am ready to repair the error. I wish to say that you are staking the woe or good of the world on one game. You lost the first round on the sixth of October; you won the second, in the courtiers' eyes, on this sad day; and to-morrow, you will begin what is called the rub. If you lose, with it goes the throne, liberty and life."

"Do you believe that this prospect makes us recede?" queried the proud one, quickly rising.

"I know that the King is brave, and the Queen heroic, so I never try to do anything with them but reason. Unfortunately, I can never pass my belief into their minds."

"Why trouble about what you believe useless?"

"Because it is my duty. It is sweet in such times to feel—though the result is unfruitful—that one has done his duty."

She looked him in the face and asked, "Do you think it possible to save the King and the throne?"

"I believe for him, and hope for the other."

"Then you are happier than I," she responded with a sad sigh. "I believe both are lost, and I fight merely to salve my conscience."

"Yes. I understand that you want a despotic monarchy, and the King an absolute one. Like the miser who will not cast away a portion of his gold in a shipwreck, so that he may swim to shore with the rest, you will go down with it all. Why not cut loose of all burdens, and swim towards the future?"

"To throw the past into a gulf is to break with all the crowned heads of Europe."

"Yes, but it is to join hands with the French people."

"Our enemies," returned Marie Antoinette.

"Because you taught them to doubt you."

"They cannot struggle against a European Coalition."

"Believe in a Constitutional King at their head, and they will make a conquest of Europe."

"They would need a million armed men for that."

"Armed men do not conquer Europe, but an idea will. Europe will be conquered when flags advance over the Alps and across the Rhine bearing the mottoes: 'Death to tyranny!' and 'Freedom to all!'"

"Really, sir, there are times when I am inclined to think the wise are madmen."

"Ah, you know not that France is the Madonna of Liberty, whose coming the people await at her borders. She is not merely a nation, as she advances with her hands full of freedom—but immutable Justice and eternal Reason. If you do not profit by all not yet committed to violence, if you dally too long, these hands will be turned to rend herself.

"Besides, none of these kings whose help you seek is able to make war. Two empires, or rather an empress and a minister, deeply hate us—but they are powerless! Catherine of Russia and William Pitt. Your envoy to Pitt, the Princess Lamballe, can get him to do much to prevent France becoming a republic. But he hates the King, and will not promise to save him. Is not Louis the Constitutional King? The crowned philosopher who disputed the East Indies with him, and helped America to wrest herself from Briton's grasp? He desires only that the French will have a sequel to his Charles the Beheaded."

"Oh, who can reveal such things to you?" gasped the Queen.

"The same who tell me what is in the letters you secretly write."

"Have we not even a thought that is our own?"

"I tell you that the Kings of Europe are enmeshed in an unseen net, where they write in vain. Do not resist madam, but put yourself at the head of ideas which will otherwise spurn you if you take the lead. This net will be your defense when you are outside of it, and the daggers threatening you will be turned towards the other monarchs."

"But you forget that the kings are our brothers, not enemies as you style them."

"But Madam, if the French are called your sons, you will see how little account are your brothers, according to politics and diplomacy. Besides, do you not perceive that all these monarchs are tottering towards the gulf? To suicide? While you, if you liked, might be marching towards the universal monarchy, the empire of the world!"

"Why do you not talk thus to the King?" said the Queen, shaken.

"I have. But like yourself, he has evil geniuses who undo what I have done. You have ruined Mirabeau and Barnave, and will treat me the same—whereupon the last word will be spoken."

"Dr. Gilbert, await me here!" said she. "I will see the King for a while, and will return."

He had been waiting a quarter of an hour when a different door opened than that she had left by, and a servant in the royal livery entered. The servant looked around warily, then approached Gilbert. He made a masonic sign of caution, then handed him a letter and glided away.

Opening the letter, Gilbert read: "Gilbert, you waste your time. At this moment, the King and the Queen are listening to Lord Breteuil fresh from Vienna, who brings this plan of policy: 'Treat Barnave as you did Mirabeau. Gain time, swear to the Constitution, and execute it to the letter to prove that it is unworkable. France will cool and be bored, as the French have a fanciful head and will want novelty, so that the mania for liberty will pass. If it does not, we shall gain a year, and by that time we shall be ready for war.'

"Leave these two condemned beings, still called King and Queen in mockery, and hasten to the Groscaillou Hospital. There, an injured man is in a dying state, but not so hopeless as they. He may be saved, while they are not only lost, but will drag you down to perdition with them!"

The note had no signature, but the reader knew the hand of Cagliostro. Madam Campan entered from the Queen's apartments. She brought a note to the effect that the King would be glad to have Dr. Gilbert's proposition in writing, while the Queen could not return from being called away on important business.

"Lunatics," he said after musing. "Here, take them this as my answer."

And he gave the lady Cagliostro's warning as he went out.

CHAPTER XXVII

The Squeezed Lemon

On the day after the Constitutional Assembly dissolved, the second of October, Barnave was ushered into the Grand Study at his usual hour for seeing the Queen. On the day of the King taking the oath to the Constitution, Lafayette's aids and soldiers had been withdrawn from the palace, and the King had become less hampered, if not more powerful.

It was slender satisfaction for the humiliations they had lately undergone. In the street one day, when out for carriage exercise, some voices shouted "Long live the King!" Immediately, a roughly dressed man walking beside the coach laid his unwashed hand on the window ledge, and mocked in a loud voice: "Do not believe them! The only cry is, 'The Nation Forever!'"

The Queen had been applauded at the Opera, where the "house was packed." But the same precaution could not be adopted at the Italians, where the pit was taken in advance. When the hirelings in the gallery hailed the Queen, they were hushed by the pit. Looking into the pit to see who these were who so detested her, the Queen saw that the leader was the Arch-Revolutionist, Cagliostro, the man who had pursued her from her youth. Once her eyes were fastened on his, she could not turn hers aloof, for he exercised the fascination of the serpent on the bird.

The play commenced and she managed to tear her gaze aloof for a time. But ever and anon it had to go back again, from the potent magnetism. It was fatal possession, as by a nightmare. Besides, the house was full of electricity. Two surcharged clouds were floating about, restless to thunder at each other. A spark would send forth the double flame.

Madam Dugazon had a song to sing with the tenor in this opera of Gretry, "Unforeseen Events." She had the line to sing: "Oh, how I love my mistress!"

The Queen divined that the storm was to burst, and involuntarily she glanced towards the man controlling her. It seemed to her that he gave a signal to the audience, and from all sides was hurled the cry: "No more mistresses! No more masters! Away with kings and queens!"

She screamed and hid her eyes, unable to look any longer on this demon of destruction who ruled the disorder. Pursued by the roar: "No more masters, no more kings and queens!" she was borne fainting to her carriage. She received Barnave standing, though she knew the respect he cherished for her, and saw that he was paler and sadder than ever.

"Well," she said, "I suppose you are satisfied, since the King has followed your advice and sworn to the Constitution?"

"You are very kind to say my advice has been followed," returned Barnave, bowing, "but if it had not been the same as that from Emperor Leopold and Prince von Kaunitz, perhaps his Majesty would have put greater hesitation in doing the act. The only one to save the King, if the King—"

"Can be saved, do you imply?" questioned she, taking the dilemma by the horns with the courage, or rashness peculiar to her.

"Lord preserve me from being the prophet of such miseries! And yet I do not want to dispirit your Majesty too much, or leave too many deceptions as I depart from Paris to dwell afar from the throne."

"Going away from town, and me?"

"The work of the Assembly of which I am a member has terminated, and I have no motive to stay here."

"Not even to be useful to us?"

"Not even that." He smiled sadly. "For indeed, I cannot be useful to you in any way now. My strength lay in my influence over the House and at the Jacobin club. In my painfully acquired popularity, in short. But the House is dissolved, the Jacobins are broken up, and my popularity is lost."

He smiled more mournfully than before. She looked at him with a strange glare which resembled the glow of triumph.

"You see, sir, that popularity may be lost," she said.

By his sigh, she felt that she had perpetrated one of those pieces of petty cruelty which were habitual to her. Indeed, if he had lost it in a month, was it not for her? The angel of death, like Mary Stuart, to those who tried to serve her?

"But you will not go?" she said.

"If ordered to remain by the Queen, I will stay, like a soldier who has his furlough but remains for the battle. But if I do so, I become more than weak – I become a traitor."

"Explain. I do not understand," she said, slightly hurt.

"Perhaps the Queen takes the dissolved Assembly as her enemy?"

"Let us define matters. Although there were friends of mine in that body, you will not deny that the majority were hostile."

"It never passed but one bill that could be considered an act of hostility to your Majesty and the King. That was the decree that none of its members could belong to the Legislature. That snatched the buckler from your friends' arms."

"But also the sword from our foemen's hand, methinks."

"Alas, you are wrong. The blow comes from Robespierre, and is dreadful like everything from that man. As things were, we knew whom we had to meet. With all uncertainty, we strike in the fog. Robespierre wishes to force France to take the rulers from the class above us or beneath. Above us there is nothing, the aristocracy having fled. But the electors would not seek representatives among the noble. The people will choose deputies from below us, and the next House will be democratic, with slight variations."

The Queen began to be alarmed from following this statement.

"I have studied the new-comers: particularly those from the South," went on Barnave. "They are nameless men, eager to acquire fame, the more as they are all young. They are to be feared, as their orders are to make war on the priests and nobles. Nothing is said as to the King. But if he will be merely the executive, he may be forgiven the past."

"How? They will forgive him? I thought it lay in the King to pardon?" exclaimed her insulted majesty.

"There it is—we shall never agree. These new-comers, as you will unhappily have the proof, will not handle the matter in gloves. For them, the King is an enemy. The nucleus, willingly or otherwise, of all the external and internal foes. They think they have made a discovery though, alas! They are only saying aloud what your ardent adversaries have whispered the entire time."

"But the King, the enemy of the people?" repeated the lady. "Oh, M. Barnave, this is something you will never induce me to admit, for I cannot understand it."

"Still it is the fact. Did not the King accept the Constitution the other day? Well, he flew into a passion when he returned within the palace, and wrote that night to the Emperor."

"How can you expect us to bear such humiliations?"

"Ah, you see, madam! He is the born enemy by his character. He was brought up by the chief of the Jesuits, and his heart is always in the hands of the priests. They are the opponents of free government, involuntarily but inevitably counter to a Revolution. Without his quitting Paris, he is with the princes at Coblentz, with the clergy in Lavendee, and with his allies in Vienna and Prussia. I admit that the King does nothing, but his name is cloaked in plots. In the cabin, pulpit and castle, the poor, good, saintly King is prated about—so that the revolution of pity is opposed to that of Freedom."

"Is it really you who cast this up, M. Barnave, when you were the first to be sorry for us."

"I am sorry for you still, lady. But there is this difference: that I was sorry in order to save you, while these others want to ruin you."

"But, in short, have these new-comers, who have vowed a war of extermination on us, any settled plan?"

"Not that I am aware madam, but I can catch a few vague ideas. They want to suppress the title of Majesty in the opening address, and set a plain arm-chair beside the Speaker's instead of a throne-chair. The dreadful thing is that Bailly and Lafayette will be done away with."

"I shall not regret that," quickly said the Queen.

"You are wrong, madam, for they are your friends—"

She smiled bitterly.

"Your last friends, perhaps. Cherish them, and use what power they have. Their popularity will fly, like mine."

"This amounts to your leading me to the brink of the crater and making me measure the depth without telling me I may avoid the eruption."

"Oh, that you had not been stopped on the road to Montmedy!" sighed Barnave, after being mute for a spell.

"Here we have M. Barnave approving of the flight to Varennes!"

"I do not approve of it. But the present state is its natural consequence, and so I deplore its not having succeeded. Not as a member of the House, but as Barnave your humble servant. Ready to give his life, which is all he possesses."

"Thank you," replied the Queen. "Your tone proves you are the man to hold to your word. But I hope no such sacrifice will be required of you."

"So much the worse for me. For if I must fall, I would wish it were in a death-struggle. The end will overtake me in my retreat, but your friends are sure to be hunted out. I will be taken, imprisoned and condemned, yet perhaps my obscure death will be unheard of by you. But should the news reach you, I shall have been so little a support to you, that you will have forgotten the few hours of my use."

"M. Barnave," said Marie Antoinette with dignity, "I am completely ignorant what fate the future reserves to the King and myself, but I do know that the names of those to whom we are beholden are written on our memory, and nothing ill or good that may befall them will cease to interest us. Meanwhile, is there anything we can do for you?"

"Only give me your hand to kiss."

A tear stood in her dry eyes, as she extended to the young man the cold white hand which had at a year's interval been kissed by the two leaders, Mirabeau and Barnave.

"Madam," said he, rising, "I cannot say I will save the monarchy. But if lost, I can say I went down with it."

She sighed as he went forth. But her words were: "Poor squeezed lemon, they did not take much time to leave nothing of you but the peel!"

CHAPTER XXVIII

The Field of Blood

Lugubrious was the scene which met the eye of a young man who trod the Champ de Mars, after the tragedy of which Bailly and Lafayette were the principal actors. It was illumined by the moon two-thirds full, rolling among huge black clouds, in which it was lost now and then. It had the semblance of a battle field, covered with maimed and dead. Amid which, some men wandered like shades. They were charged to throw the lifeless into the River Seine and load up the wounded to be transported to the Groscaillou Hospital.

The young man was dressed like a captain of the National Guards. He paused on the way over the Field, and muttered as he clasped his hands with unaffected terror: "Lord help us. The matter is worse than they gave me to understand."

After looking for a while on the weird work in operation, he approached two men who were carrying a corpse towards the water, and asked: "Citizens, do you mind telling me what you are going to do with that man?"

"Follow us, and you will know all about it," replied one.

He followed them. On reaching the wooden bridge, they swung the body between them as they counted: "One, two, three, and it's off!" and slung it into the tide.

The young officer uttered a cry of terror.

"Why, what are you about, citizens?" he demanded.

"Can't you see, officer?" replied one. "We are clearing up the ground."

"And you have orders to act thus?"

"It looks so, does it not?"

"From whom?"

"From the Municipality."

"Oh," ejaculated the young man, stupefied. "Have you cast many bodies into the stream?" he inquired, after a little pause during which they had returned upon the place.

"Half a dozen or so," was the man's answer.

"I beg your pardon, citizens," went on the captain, "but I have a great interest in the question I am about to put. Among those bodies did you notice one of a man of forty-five or so, six feet high but looking less from his being strongly built? He would have the appearance of a countryman."

"Faith, we have only one thing to notice," said the man. "It is whether the men are alive or dead. If dead, we just fling them overboard; if alive, we send them on to the hospital."

"Ah," said the captain. "The fact is that one of my friends, not having come home, and having gone out here, I am greatly afraid that he may be among the hurt or killed."

"If he came here," said one of the undertakers, shaking a body while his mate held up a lantern, "he is likely to be here still. If he has not gone home, the chances are he has gone to his last long one." Redoubling the shaking to the body lying at his feet, he shouted: "Hey, you! Are you dead or alive? If you are not dead, make haste to tell us."

"Oh, he is stiff enough," rejoined his associate; "he has a bullet clean through him."

"In that case, into the river with him."

They lifted the body and retook the way to the bridge.

"Citizens," said the young officer, "you don't need your lamp to throw the man into the water; so be kind enough to lend it me for a minute. While you are on your errand, I will seek my friend."

The carriers of the dead consented to this request, and the lantern passed into the young man's hands. Thereupon, he commenced his search with care. An expression denoted that he had not spoke of his lost friend merely from the lips, but out of his heart.

Ten or more persons, supplied like him with lights, were engaged likewise in the ghastly scrutiny. From time to time, in the midst of stillness—for the awful solemnity of the picture seemed to hush the voices of the living amid the dead—a name spoken in a loud tone would cross the space. Sometimes a cry, a moan, or a groan would reply to the call. But most often, the answer was gruesome silence.

After having hesitated for a time as though his voice was chained by awe, the young officer imitated the example set him, and three times called out: "Farmer Billet!" No voice responded.

"For sure he is dead," groaned he, wiping with his sleeve the tears flowing from his eyes. "Poor Farmer Billet!"

At this moment, two men came along, bearing a corpse towards the river.

"Mild, I fancy our stiff one gave a sigh," said the one who held the upper part of the body, and was consequently nearer the head.

"Pooh," laughed the other. "If we were to listen to all these fellows, there would not be one dead!"

"Citizens, for mercy's sake," interrupted the young officer, "let me see the man you are carrying."

"Oh, willingly, officer," said the men.

They placed the dead in a sitting posture for him to examine it. Bringing the lantern to it, he uttered a cry. In spite of the terrible wound disfiguring the face, he believed it was the man he was seeking. But was he alive or dead?

This wretch who had gone half way to the watery grave, had his skull cloven by a sword stroke. The wound was dreadful as stated. It had severed the left whisker, and left the cheekbone bare. The temporal artery had been cut, so that the skull and body were flooded with gore. On the wounded side, the unfortunate man was unrecognizable. The lantern-bearer swung the light round to the other side.

"Oh citizens," he cried, "it is he, the man I seek. Farmer Billet."

"The deuce it is—he seems to have his billet for the other world—ha, ha, ha!" said one of the men. "He is pretty badly hammered."

"Did you not say he heaved a sigh?"

"I think so, anyhow."

"Then do me a kindness," and he fumbled in his pocket for a silver coin.

"What is it?" asked the porter, full of willingness on seeing the money.

"Run to the river and bring me some water."

"In a jiffy."

While the fellow ran to the river, the officer took his place and held up the wounded man. In five minutes he had returned.

"Throw the water in his face," said the captain.

The man obeyed by dipping his hand in his hat, which was his pitcher, and sprinkling the slashed face.

"He shivered," exclaimed the young man holding the dying one. "He is not dead. Oh, dear M. Billet, what a blessing I came here."

"In faith, it is a blessing," said the two men; "another twenty paces and your friend would have come to his senses in the nets at St. Cloud."

"Throw some more on him."

Renewing the operation, the wounded man shuddered and uttered a sigh.

"Come, come, he certainly ain't dead," said the man.

"Well, what shall we do with him?" inquired his companion.

"Help me to carry him to St. Honore Street, to Dr. Gilbert's house, if you would like a good reward," said the young captain.

"We cannot do that. Our orders are to heave the dead over, or to hand the hurt to the carriers for the hospital. Since this chap makes out he is not dead, why, he must be taken to the hospital."

"Well, carry him there," said the young man, "and as soon as possible. Where is the hospital?" he asked, looking round.

"Close to the Military Academy, about three hundred paces."

"Then it is over yonder?"

"You have it right."

"The whole of the place to cross?"

"And the long way too."

"Have you not a hand-barrow?"

"Well, if it comes to that, such a thing can be found. Like the water, if a crownpiece or two—"

"Quite right," said the captain. "You shall not lose by your kindness. Here is more money—only, get the litter."

Ten minutes later the litter was found, and the wounded man was laid on a pallet. The two fellows took up the shafts, and the mournful party proceeded towards the military hospital. They were escorted by the young officer, with lantern in hand by the disfigured head. It was a dreadful thing to march over the bloodstained ground this night. They stumbled against the stiffened and motionless remains at every step. Wounded wretches arose, only to fall anew and call for succor. In a quarter of an hour, they crossed the hospital threshold.

CHAPTER XXIX

In the Hospital

Gilbert had obeyed Cagliostro's injunction to go to the Groscaillou Hospital to attend to a patient. At this period, hospitals were far from being organized as at present. Particularly military hospitals like this one, which was receiving those injured in the massacre. Meanwhile, the dead were bundled into the river to save burial expenses, and hide the extent of the crime of Lafayette and Bailly.

Gilbert was welcomed by the overworked surgeons amid the disorder, which opposed their desires being fulfilled. Suddenly in the maze, he heard a voice which he knew, but had not expected there.

"Ange Pitou," he exclaimed, seeing the peasant in a National Guard's uniform by a bed. "What about Billet?"

"He is here," was the answer, as he showed a motionless body. "His head is split to the jaw."

"It is a serious wound," said Gilbert, examining the hurt. "You must find me a private room; this is a friend of mine," he added to the male nurses.

There were no private rooms, but they gave up the laundry room to Dr. Gilbert's special patient. Billet groaned as they carried him thither.

"Ah," said the doctor, "never did an exclamation of pleasure give me such joy as that wrung by pain. He lives—that is the main point."

It was not till he had finished the dressing that he asked the news of Pitou. The matter was simple. Isidore Charny had had Catherine transported to Paris with her babe. Since her disappearance, and the departure of Billet to town also, Mother Billet fell into an increasing state of idiocy. Dr. Raynal said that nothing would rouse her from this torpor but the sight of her daughter. Without waiting for the cue, Pitou started to Paris. He seemed predestined to arrive there at great events.

The first time, he was in time to take a hand in the storming of the Bastille; the next, to help the Federation of 1790; and now he arrived for the Massacre of the Champ de Mars. He heard that it had all come about over a petition drawn up by Dr.

Gilbert, and presented by Billet to the signers. Pitou leared at the doctor's house that he had come home, but there were no tidings of the farmer.

On going to the scene of blood, Pitou happened on the nearly lifeless body, which would have been hurled in the river but for his interposition. It was thus that Pitou hailed the doctor in the hospital, and the wounded man had his chances improved by being in such skillful hands as his friend Gilbert's.

As Billet could not be taken to his wife's bedside, Catherine was more than ever to be desired there. Where was she? The only way to reach her would be through the Charny family. Happily, Ange had been so warmly greeted by her when he took Sebastian to her house, that he did not hesitate to call again. He went there with the doctor in the latter's carriage; but the house was dark and dismal. The count and countess had gone to their country seat at Boursonnes.

"Excuse me, my friend," said the doctor to the janitor who had received the National Guards captain with no friendliness. "Can you not give me a piece of information in your master's absence?"

"I beg pardon, sir," said the porter, recognizing the tone of a superior in this blandness and politeness. He opened the door, and in his nightcap and undress, came to take the orders of the carriage-gentleman.

"My friend, do you know anything about a young woman from the country, in whom the count and countess are taking interest?"

"Miss Catherine?" asked the porter.

"The same," replied Gilbert.

"Yes, sir. My lord and my lady sent me twice to see her and learn if she stood in need of anything. But the poor girl, whom I do not believe to be well off any more than her dear little child, said she wanted for nothing."

Pitou sighed heavily at the mention of the dear little child.

"Well, my friend," continued the doctor, "poor Catherine's father was wounded on the Field of Mars. And her mother, Mrs. Billet, is dying out at Villers Cotterets, which sad news we want to break to her. Will you kindly give us her address?"

"Oh, poor girl, may heaven assist her. She was unhappy enough before. She is living at Villedavray, your honor, in the main street. I cannot give you the number, but it is in front of the public well."

"That is straight enough," said Pitou. "I can find it."

"Thanks, my friend," said Gilbert, slipping a silver piece into the man's hand.

"There was no need of that, sir. For Christians ought to do a good turn amongst themselves," said the janitor, doffing his nightcap and returning indoors.

"I am off for Villedavray," said Pitou.

He was always ready to go anywhere on a kind errand.

"Do you know the way?"

"No, but somebody will tell me."

"You have a golden heart and muscles of steel," said the doctor laughing. "But you want rest, and had better start to-morrow."

"But it is a pressing matter—"

"On neither side is there urgency," corrected the doctor. "Billet's state is serious but not mortal, unless by mischance. Mother Billet may linger ten days yet."

"She don't look it, but of course, you know best."

"We may as well leave poor Catherine another night of repose and ignorance. A night's rest is of importance to the unfortunate, Pitou."

"Then, where are we going, doctor?" asked the peasant, yielding to the argument.

"I shall give you a room you have slept in before. And tomorrow at six, my horses shall be put to the carriage to take you to Villedavray."

"Lord, is it fifty leagues off?"

"Nay, it is only two or three."

"Then I can cover it in an hour or two—I can lick it up like an egg."

"Yes, but Catherine can lick up like an egg the distance from Villedavray to Paris, and the eighteen leagues from Paris to Villers Cotterets?"

"True. Excuse me doctor, for being a fool. Talking of fools —no, I mean the other way about—how is Sebastian?"

"Wonderfully well, you shall see him to-morrow."

"Still at college? I shall be downright glad."

"And so shall he, for he loves you with all his heart."

At six he started in the carriage, and by seven was at Catherine's door. She opened it and shrieked on seeing Pitou: "I know—my mother is dead!" She turned pale and leaned against the wall.

"No; but you will have to hasten to see her before she goes," replied the messenger.

This brief exchange of words said so much in so little time, that Catherine was at once placed face to face with her affliction.

"That is not all," added the peasant.

"What's the other misfortune?" queried Catherine, in the sharp tone of one who has exhausted the measure of human ails, and has no fear of an overflow.

"Master Billet was dangerously wounded on the parade-grounds."

"Ah," said she, much less affected by this news than the other.

"So I says to myself, and Dr. Gilbert bears me out: 'Miss Catherine will pay a visit to her father at the hospital on the way down to her mother's.'"

"But you, Pitou?" queried the girl.

"While you go by stage-coach to help Mother Billet to make her long journey, I will stay by the farmer. You understand that I must stick to him who has never a soul to look after him, see?"

Pitou spoke the words with that angelic simplicity of his, with no idea that he was painting his whole devoted nature.

"You have a kind heart, Ange," said she, giving him her hand. "Come and kiss my little Isidore."

She walked into the house, prettier than ever. She was clad in black, which drew another sigh from Pitou. She had one little room overlooking the garden. Its furniture was merely a bed for the mother and a cradle for the infant. The babe was sleeping, but Catherine pulled a muslin curtain aside for him to see it.

"Oh, the sweet little angel!" exclaimed Pitou.

He knelt as it were to an angel, and kissed the tiny hand. He was speedily rewarded for his devotion, for he felt Catherine's tresses on his head, and her lips on his forehead. The mother was returning the caress given her son.

"Thank you, good Pitou," she said. "Since the last kiss he had from his father, I alone have caressed the child."

"Oh, Miss Catherine!" muttered Pitou, dazzled and thrilled by the kiss as by an electrical shock.

And yet it was purely what a mother's caress may contain of the holy and grateful. Ten minutes afterwards, Catherine, little Isidore and Pitou were rolling in the doctor's carriage towards the hospital. Once there, she handed the child to the peasant with as much or more trust as she would have had in a brother, and walked in at the door.

Dr. Gilbert was by his patient's side, little change had taken place. Despite the beginning of fever, the face was still deadly pale from the great loss of blood, and one eye and the left cheek were swelling.

Catherine dropped on her knees by the bedside, and said as she raised her hands to heaven, "O my God, Thou knowest that my utmost wish has been for my father's life to be spared."

This was as much as could be expected from the girl whose lover's life had been attempted by her father. The patient shuddered at this voice, and his breathing was more hurried. He opened his eyes and his glance, wandering for a space over the room, was fixed on the woman. His hand made a move to repulse this figure, which he doubtless took to be a vision. Their glances met, and Gilbert was horrified to see the hatred which shot towards each, rather than affection.

Catherine rose and went to find Pitou by the door. He was on all fours, playing with the babe. She caught up her boy with a roughness more like a lioness than a woman, and pressed it to her bosom, crying, "My child, oh my child!"

In the outburst were all the mother's anguish, the widow's wails, and the woman's pangs. Pitou proposed seeing her to the stage, but she repulsed him, saying: "Your place is here." Pitou knew nothing but to obey when Catherine commanded.

CHAPTER XXX

The Mother's Blessing

It was six o'clock in the afternoon, broad day, when Catherine arrived home. Had Isidore been alive and she were coming to visit her mother in health, she would have got down from the stage at the end of the village and slipped round upon her father's farm, without going through. But being a widow and a mother, she did not give a thought to rustic jests. She alighted without fear. It seemed to her that scorn and insult ought to be warded off from her by her child and her sorrow, the dark and the bright angel.

At the first she was not recognized. She was so pale and so changed, that she did not seem the same woman. And what set her apart from her class was the lofty air which she had already caught from community with an elegant man. One person knew her again, but not till she had passed by. This was Pitou's aunt Angelique. She was gossiping at the townhouse door with some cronies about the oath required of the clergy, declaring that she had heard Father Fortier say that he would never vow allegiance to the Revolution. He preferred to submit to martyrdom than bend his head to the democratic yoke.

"Bless us and save us!" she broke forth in the midst of her speech. "If here ain't Billet's daughter, and her fondling a-stepping down off the coach."

"Catherine?" cried several voices.

"Yes, but look at her running away down the lane."

Aunt Angelique was making a mistake. Catherine was not running away, and she took the side way simply because she was in haste to see her mother. At the cry, the children scampered after her. As she was fond of them always, and more than ever at present, she gave them some small change with which they returned.

"What is that?" asked the gossips.

"It is Miss Catherine. She asked how her mother was, and when we said the doctor says she is good for a week yet, she thanked us and gave us some money."

"Hem! Then she seems to have taken her pigs to a good market in Paris," sneered Angelique, "to be able to give silver to the urchins who run at her heels."

She did not like Catherine because the latter was young and sweet, and Angelique was old and sour. Catherine was tall and well made, while the other was short and limped. Besides, when Angelique turned her nephew Ange out of doors, it was on Billet's farm that he took refuge. Also, it was Billet who had lugged Father Fortier out of his rectory to say the mass for the country on the day of the Declaration of the Rights of Man.

All these were ample reasons for Angelique to hate Catherine. They were joined to her natural asperity in particular, and the Billet's in general. And when Angelique hated, it was thorough, as becomes a prude and a devotee. She ran to the priest's, to tell him and his sister the fresh scandal of Billet's daughter returning home with her child.

"Indeed," said Fortier. "I should have thought she would drop it into the box at the Foundling Hospital."

"The proper thing to do, for then the thing would not have to blush for his mother."

"That is a new point from which to regard that institution! But what has she come after here?"

"It looks as if to see her mother, who might not have been living still."

"Stay, a woman who does not come to confess?" said the abbé with a wicked smile.

"Oh, that is not her fault!" said the old maid, "but she has had softening of the brain lately. Up to the time when her daughter threw this grief upon her, she was a pious soul who feared God and paid for two chairs when she came to church: one to sit in, the other to put her feet upon."

"But how many chairs did her husband pay for? Billet, the Hero of the Mobs, the Conqueror of the Bastille?" cried the priest, his little eyes sparkling with spite.

"I do not know," returned Angelique simply, "for he never comes to church, while his good wife—"

"Very well, we will settle accounts with him on the day of his good wife's funeral."

In the meantime, Catherine continued her way. One long series of memories of him who was no more, unless his arms were around the little boy whom she carried on her bosom. What would the neighbors say of her shame and dishonor? So handsome a boy would be a shame and disgrace to a peasant! But she entered the farm without fear.

A huge dog barked as she came up. But suddenly recognizing his young mistress, he neared her to the stretch of his chain, and stood up with his fore-paws in the air to utter little joyous yelps. At the dog's barking, a man ran out to see the cause.

"Miss Catherine," he exclaimed.

"Father Clovis," she said.

"Welcome, dear young mistress—the house much needs you, by heaven!"

"And my poor mother?"

"Sorry to say she is just the same, neither worse nor bette. She is dying out like an oil-less lamp, poor dear!"

"Where is she?"

"In her own room."

"Alone?"

"No, no! I would not have allowed that. You must excuse me, Miss Catherine, coming out as the master here. But your having stopped at my house before you went to town made me one of the family, I thought, in a manner of speaking. And I was very fond of you and poor Master Isidore."

"So you know?" said Catherine, wiping away her tears.

"Yes, yes. Killed for the Queen's sake, like his brother. But he has left something behind him, a lovely boy. So while we mourn for the father, we must smile for the son."

"Thank you, Clovis," said she, giving her hand. "But my mother?"

"I had Mother Clement the nurse to sit with her, the same who attended to you—"

"Has my mother her senses yet?" asked the girl hesitating.

"Sometimes I think so, when your name is spoken. That was the great means of stirring her. But since yesterday, she has not showed any signs even when you are spoken of."

He opened the bedroom door and she could glance in. Mother Clement was dozing in a large armchair, while her patient seemed to be asleep. She was not much changed, but her complexion was like ivory in pallor.

"Mother, my dear mother," exclaimed Catherine, rushing into the room.

The dying one opened her eyes and tried to turn her head, as a gleam of intelligence sparkled in her look. But babbling, her movement was abortive, and her arm sank inert on the head of the girl who was kneeling by her side. From the lethargy of the father and the mother had shot two opposite feelings: hate from the former, love from the latter.

The girl's arrival caused excitement on the farm, where Billet was expected, not his daughter. She related the accident to the farmer, and how he was as near death's door as his wife at home. Only he was moving from it on the right side.

She went into her own room, where there were many tears evoked by memories. She had left in the bright dreams of childhood, and a girl's burning passions, and returned with a widow's broken heart. At once she resumed sway over that house in disorder, which her father had delegated to her, to the detriment of her mother.

Father Clovis, thanked and rewarded, retook the road to his "earth," as his hut was called. When Dr. Raynal came next day on his tri-weekly visit, he was glad to see the girl. He broached the great question which he had not dared debate with Billet, whether the poor woman should receive the Last Sacrament. Billet was a rabid Voltairian, while the doctor was a scientist. But he believed it his duty in such cases to warn the family of the dying, and let them settle it.

Catherine was pious and attached little importance to the wrangles between her father and the priest. But the abbé was one of the sombre school, who would have been an inquisitor in Spain. When he found the sufferer unconscious, he said that he could not give absolution to those unable to confess, and went out again. There was no use applying elsewhere, as he was monarch over this parish. Catherine accepted the refusal as still another grief, and went on with her cares as daughter and mother for eight or nine days and nights.

As she was watching by her mother, the door opened, and Pitou appeared on the sill. He came from Paris that morning. Catherine shuddered to see him, fearing that her father was dead. But his countenance, without being what you would call gay, was not that of the bearer of bad news. Indeed, Billet was mending. The doctor had taken care of him since the first day. That morning, he had been moved from the hospital to the doctor's house.

Pitou feared for Catherine, now. His opinion was that, the moment Billet learned what he was sure to ask, how his wife was, he would start for home. What would it be if he found Catherine there? It was Gilbert who had therefore sent Pitou down into the country. But when Pitou expressed their fears about the meeting, Catherine declared that she would not leave her mother's pillow, even if her father slew her there. Pitou groaned at such a determination, but he did not combat it. So he stayed there to intervene, if he might.

During two days and nights, Mother Billet's life seemed to be slipping, breath by breath. It was a wonder how a body lived with so little breath, and how slightly it lived! During the night, when all animation seemed extinct, the patient awoke as it were, and she stared at Catherine, who ran to bring her boy. The eyes were bright when she returned. A sound was heard, and the arms were held out. Catherine fell on her knees beside the bed.

A strange phenomenon then took place. Mother Billet rose on her pillow, slowly held out her arms over the girl's head with the boy, and with a mighty effort, said: "Bless you, my children!" Then she fell back, dead. Her eyes remained open, as though she longed to see her daughter from beyond the grave, from not having seen enough of her before.

CHAPTER XXXI

Fortier Executes His Threat

Catherine piously closed her mother's eyes, with her hand and then with her lips, while Mother Clement lit the candles and arranged other paraphernalia. Pitou took charge of the other details. Reluctant to visit Father Fortier, with whom he stood on delicate ground, he ordered the mortuary mass of the sacristan, and engaged the gravedigger and the coffin-bearers.

Then he went over to Haramont to have his company of militia notified that the wife of the Hero of the People would be buried at eleven on the morrow. It was not an official order, but an invitation. However, it was too well known what Billet had done for this Revolution, which was turning all heads and enflaming all hearts. What danger Billet was even then running for the sake of the masses—for this invitation not to be regarded as an order. All the volunteer soldiers promised their captain that they would be punctual.

Pitou brought the joiner with him, who carried the coffin. He had all the heartfelt delicacy rare in the lowborn, and hid the man and his bier in the outhouse so Catherine should not see it. He hoped to spare her from hearing the sound of the hammering of the nails, and entered the dwelling alone.

Catherine was still praying by the dead, which had been shrouded by two neighbors. Pitou suggested that she should go out for a change of air. Then for the child's sake, upon which she proposed he should take the little one. She must have had great confidence in Pitou, to trust her boy to him for a time.

"He won't come," reported Pitou, presently. "He is crying."

She kissed her mother, took her child by the hand, and walked away with Pitou. The joiner carried in the coffin when she was gone. He took her out on the road to Boursonnes, where she went half a league without saying a word to Pitou. She was listening to the voices of the woodland, which talked to her heart. When she got home, the work was done, and she understood why Ange had insisted on her going out. She thanked him with an eloquent look. She prayed for a long while by the coffin, understanding now that she had but one of the two friends left when Isidore died: her mother and Pitou.

"You must come away," said the peasant, "or I must go and hire a nurse for Master Isidore."

"You are right, Pitou," she said. "My God, how good Thou art to me—and how I love you, Pitou!"

He reeled and nearly fell over backwards. He leaned up against the wall, choking, for Catherine had said that she loved him! He did not deceive himself about the kind of love, but any kind was a great deal for him.

Finishing her prayer, she rose and went with a slow step to lean on his shoulder. He put his arm round her to sustain her; and she allowed it. Turning at the door, she breathed: "Farewell, mother!" and went forth.

Pitou stopped her at her own door, and she began to understand him.

"Why, Miss Catherine," he stammered, "do you not think it is a good time to leave the farm?"

"I shall only leave when my mother shall no longer be here," she replied.

She spoke with such firmness that he saw it was an irrevocable resolve.

"When you do go, you know you have two homes: Father Clovis' and my house."

Pitou's "house" was his sitting room and bedroom.

"I thank you," she replied. Her smile and nod meaning that she accepted both offers. She went into her room without troubling about the young man, who had the knack of finding some burrow.

At ten the next day, all the farmers for miles around flocked to the farm. The Mayor came, too. At half after ten, up marched the Haramont National Guards, with colors tied up in black—not a man was missing. Catherine, dressed in black, with her boy in mourning, welcomed all comers. And it must be said that there was no feeling for her but of respect.

At eleven, some three hundred persons were gathered at the farm. The priest and his attendants alone were absent. Pitou knew Father Fortier, and he guessed that he who had refused the sacraments to the dying woman, would withhold the funeral service under the pretext that she had died unconscious. These reflections, confided to Mayor Longpre, produced a doleful impression. While they were looking at each other in silence, Maniquet, whose opinions were anti-religious, called out: "If Abbé Fortier does not like to say mass, we will get on without it."

But it was evidently a bold act, although Voltaire and Rousseau were in the ascendancy.

"Gentlemen," suggested the mayor, "let us proceed to Villers Cotterets, where we will have an explanation."

The procession moved slowly past Catherine and her little boy, and was going down the road, when the rear guards heard a voice behind them. It was a call, and they turned. A man on a horse was riding from Paris, and part of the rider's face was covered with black bandages. He waved his hat in his hand, and signaled that he wanted the party to stop. Pitou had turned like the others.

"Why, it is Billet," he said. "Good! I should not like to be in Father Fortier's skin."

At that name, everybody halted. He advanced rapidly, and as he neared, all were able to recognize him as Pitou had done. On reaching the head of the line, Billet jumped off his horse, threw the bridle on its neck, and said a lusty: "Good day and thank ye, citizens!" Then he took his proper place leading the mourners, which Pitou had held in his stead. A stable boy took away the horse.

Everybody looked curiously at the farmer. He had grown thinner and much paler. Part of his face and around his left eye had retained the black and blue tint of healing bruises. His clenched teeth and frowning brows indicated sullen rage, which waited the time for a vent.

"Do you know what has happened?" inquired Pitou.

"I know all," was the reply.

As soon as Gilbert had told his patient of the state of his wife, he had taken a cabriolet as far as Nanteuil. As the horse could go no farther, though Billet was weak, he had mounted a post horse. With a change at Levignan, he reached his farm as we know. In two words Mother Clement had told the story. He remounted the horse and stopped the procession, which he descried on turning a wall.

Silent and moody before, the party became more so since this figure of hate led the way. At Villers Cotterets, a waiting party fell into the line. As the cortege went up the street, men, women and children flowed out of the dwellings, saluted Billet, who nodded, and incorporated themselves in the ranks. It numbered five hundred when it reached the church. It was shut, as Pitou had anticipated, so they halted at the door.

Billet had become livid; his expression had grown more and more threatening. The church and the town hall adjoined. The player of the bassoon in the holy building was also janitor at the mayor's, so that he belonged under the secular and the clerical arm. Questioned by Mayor Longpre, he answered that Father Fortier had forbidden any retainer of the church to lend his aid to the funeral. The mayor asked where the keys were, and was told the beadle had them.

"Go and get the keys," said Billet to Pitou, who opened out his long compass-like legs. After five minutes, he returned to say: "Abbé Fortier had the keys taken to his house to be sure the church should not be opened."

"We must go straight to the priest for them," suggested Maniquet, the promoter of extreme measures.

"Let us go to the abbé's," cried the crowd.

"It would take too long," remarked Billet. "And when death knocks at a door, it does not like to wait."

He looked round him. Opposite the church, a house was being built. Some carpenters had been squaring a joist. Billet walked up and ran his arm round the beam, which rested on trestles. With one effort he raised it. But he had reckoned on absent strength. Under the great burden, the giant reeled, and it was thought for an instant that he would fall. It was but a flash. He recovered his balance and smiled terribly. Forward he walked, with the beam under his arm and a slow, firm step.

He seemed one of those antique battering-rams, with which the Caesars overthrow walls. He planted himself before the door, with legs set apart, and the formidable machine began to work. The door was oak, with iron fastenings, but at the third shove, bolts, bars and lock had flown off. The oaken panels yawned, too. Billet let the beam drop. It took four men to carry it back to its place, and not easily.

"Now mayor, have my poor wife's coffin carried to the midst of the choir—she never did harm to anybody, And you, Pitou; collect the beadle, the choirboys and the chanters, while I bring the priest."

Several wished to follow Billet to Father Fortier's house.

"Let me go alone," said he. "Maybe what I do is serious, and I should bear my own burden."

This was the second time in a year's interval that the revolutionist had come into conflict with the son of the church. Remembering what had happened before, a similar scene was anticipated. The rectory door was sealed up like that of the church. Billet looked round for some beam to be used like the other, but there was nothing of the sort. The only thing available was a stone post. A boundary mark, with which the children had played so long at "over-ing" that it was loose in the socket like an old tooth.

The farmer stepped up to it, shook it violently to enlarge its orbit, and tore it clean out. Then raising it like a Highlander "putting the stone," he hurled it at the door, which flew into shivers. At the same time as this breach was made, the upper window opened and Father Fortier appeared, calling on his parishioners with all the power of his lungs. But the voice of the pastor fell lost, as the flock did not care to interfere between him and the wolf.

It took Billet some time to break all the doors down between him and his prey, but in ten minutes, more or less, that was done. At the end of that time, loud shrieks were heard. And by the abbé's most expressive gestures, it was to be surmised that the danger was drawing nearer and nearer him.

In fact, Billet's pale face was suddenly seen to rise behind the priest, as his hand launched out and grabbed him by the shoulder. The priest clutched the window sill. He was of proverbial strength, and it would not be easy for Hercules to make him relax his grip. Billet passed his arm around the priest as a girdle, straightened himself on both legs, and with a pull which would uproot an oak, he tore him away with the snapped wood between his hands. Farmer and priest disappeared within the room,

In the depths, the wailing of the priest was heard dying away like the bellowing of a bull carried off by a lion.

In the meantime, Pitou had gathered up the trembling church staff, who hastened to don the vestments, light the candles and incense, and prepare all things for the death mass. Billet was seen dragging the priest with him as if he were alone, though the abbé still made resistance. This was not a man, but one of the forces of nature: something like a torrent or an avalanche. Nothing human could withstand him, and it took an element to combat with him.

About a hundred steps from the church, the poor abbé ceased to kick, completely overpowered. All stood aside to let the pair go by. The abbé cast a frightened glance on the door, and shivered like a pane of glass. Seeing all his men at their stands, whom he had forbidden to enter the place, he shook his head like one who acknowledges that some resistless power weighed on the church's ministers, if not on itself. He entered the sacristy and came forth in his robes, with the sacrament in his hand. But as he was mounting the altar, Billet stretched out his hand.

"Enough, you faulty servant of God," he thundered. "I only attempted to check your pride, that is all. But I want it known that a sainted woman like my wife can dispense with the prayers of a hateful and fanatical priest like you."

As a loud murmur rose under the vaulted ceiling of the fane, he said: "If this be sacrilege, let it fall on my head."

Turning to the crowd he added: "Citizens, to the cemetery!"

"To the cemetery," cried the concourse which filled not the church alone but the square in front. The four bearers passed their muskets under the bier lifting the body, and as they had come without ecclesiastical pomp, they went forth. Billet conducted the mourners, with six hundred persons following the remains to the burial-ground. It was situated at the end of a lane near Aunt Angelique's house.

The cemetery-gates were closed, but Billet respected the dead. He sent for the gravedigger who had the key, and Pitou brought it with two spades. Fortier had proscribed the dead as unfit for consecrated ground, which the gravedigger had been ordered not to break for her. At this last evidence of the priest's hatred for the farmer, a shiver of menace ran through the gathering. Billet had but a word to say, and Abbé Fortier would have had that satisfaction of martyrdom for which he had howled on the day when he refused to say mass on the Altar of the Country.

But Billet's wrath was that of the people and the lion; he did not retrace his steps to tear. He thanked Pitou with a nod, took the key, opened the gates, passed the coffin in, and followed it. He was followed by the procession. They arrived where the grave had been marked out before the sexton had the order not to open the earth. Billet held out his hand to Pitou for one of the spades.

There, with uncovered heads, Pitou and Billet dug the resting-place for this poor creature under the devouring July sun. Pious and resigned throughout life, she would have been greatly astonished in her lifetime if told what a sensation her death would cause.

The task lasted an hour, without either worker thinking of being relieved. Meanwhile, rope was sought for and was ready. It was still Billet and Pitou who lowered the coffin into the pit. They did all so naturally, that nobody thought of offering help. It would have been a sacrilege to have stayed them from carrying out all to the end. Only at the first clods falling on the coffin, Billet ran his hand over his eyes, and Pitou his sleeve. Then they resolutely shoveled the earth in. When they had finished, Billet flung the spade far from him and gripped Pitou by the hand.

"God is my witness," said he, "that I hold in hand all the simple and grandest virtues on earth: charity, devotion, abnegation, brotherhood—and that I dedicate my life to these virtues." He held out his hand over the grave, saying: "God be again my witness, that I swear eternal war against the King who tried to have me murdered; to the nobles who defamed my daughter; and to the priests who refused sepulcher to my wife!"

Turning towards the spectators full of sympathy with this adjuration, he said: "Brothers, a new assembly is to be convoked in place of the traitors now in session. Select me to represent you in this new parliament, and you will see how I keep my oath."

A shout of universal adhesion hailed this suggestion. And at once over his wife's grave, a terrible altar worthy of the dread vow, the candidature of Billet was proposed, seconded and carried. After this, he thanked his fellow citizens for their sympathy in his affliction, his friendship and his hatred. And each citizen, countryman, peasant and forester, went home carrying in heart the spirit of revolutionary propaganda. In their blindness, the most deadly weapons were afforded by those who were to be destroyed by them—priests, nobles and King!

How Billet kept his oath, with other circumstances which are linked with his return to Paris in the new Legislative Assembly, will be recorded in the sequel entitled "The Countess of Charny."

Made in the USA
Las Vegas, NV
24 April 2025

c1f93056-aff2-49e0-9767-b4f0a39aebe2R02